"Don't even think about it," Tom warned him.

"Look at yourself. You're losing blood fast. No way you're getting past the two of us."

The kid nervously licked his lips. His trembling arm started to dip.

"You just tried to incinerate a federal agent," Diana reminded him. "Not even Jordan Collier can get you out of that."

Wild, bloodshot eyes reminded Tom of a cornered animal. "I'll never betray the Movement," the teen vowed. "You can't make me talk."

"That's what you think," Tom said darkly.

"No, no . . ." The kid's gaze darted toward the cremator. He took a deep breath. An eerie sense of calm came over him. "I won't give you a chance to break me."

Too late Tom realized what the besieged embalmer had in mind. "No!" he shouted, lunging forward, but Braces had already thrown himself facedown onto the trolley. The conveyor belt sped the suicidal youth straight into the open mouth of the cremator. A fresh burst of heat spilled from the oven as flames engulfed the teenager's flailing body. Flesh and clothing blackened and burned. Skin sizzled and popped. His dying screams were mercifully brief.

"Oh my God!" Diana exclaimed. She placed her hand over her mouth in horror. "What kind of fanaticism inspires a sacrifice like that?"

OTHER *THE 4400* BOOKS

The Vesuvius Prophecy
Greg Cox

Wet Work
Dayton Ward & Kevin Dilmore

Coming in October
Promises Broken
David Mack

THE 4400®

WELCOME TO PROMISE CITY

GREG COX

Based upon *THE 4400* created by
Scott Peters and René Echevarria

Pocket Star Books
New York London Toronto Sydney

Pocket Star Books
A Division of Simon & Schuster, Inc.
1230 Avenue of the Americas
New York, NY 10020

First Pocket Star Books paperback edition August 2009

Cover design by Alan Dingman

Manufactured in the United States of America

10 9 8 7 6 5 4 3 2 1

ISBN 978-1-4516-2814-2
ISBN 978-1-4165-6550-5 (ebook)

Court/Judge SDSC
Case Docket No. M242482
Court Hearing Date: 2-13-18 (19)
Offense: HS11350(A)

Dedicated to the city of Seattle and
the entire Pacific Northwest.

The Court has ordered you to enroll in the following Program;

* PC-1000 Deferred Entry of Judgment

You must immediately contact the Provider checked below ↓

page 1

3/8/18

The future enters into us, in order to transform itself in us, long before it happens.

—Rilke

X Deffered Entry of Judgement is set for a period of 12 months Same term 1 year 1 day a week 2 hours a day

✓ Attend self help meetings as directed by the program provider

THE 4400®

WELCOME TO PROMISE CITY

✓ Submit to a drug test at anytime during the DEOJ period, as directed by the court or provider. Said drug test will be at a facility designated by the Court and at your own expense

✓ Remain law abiding in all respects. You

that any new offense may cause reinstatement of Criminal proceeding

✓ attend and successfully complete the following program

✓ County of San Diego PC 1000 program –

ONE

"IT'S TIME, DAD," Kyle said.

He handed his father a syringe of luminous amber fluid. Tom Baldwin turned the syringe over and over as he contemplated the promicin shot in his hands. For most people, the illegal injection offered fifty-fifty odds of gaining a remarkable preternatural ability—or dying a horrible death. But Tom was destined to survive the shot, or so he had been told. According to his son, the future meant for him to gain an ability of his own.

Maybe today . . . ?

"Your ID, sir?"

The voice snapped Tom out of his memory, bringing him back to the present. Knuckles rapped against the driver's-side window of his blue Chrysler sedan. He rolled down the window and handed over his ID to one of the border guards posted at the barricade. A damp January breeze invaded the car, as well as the gassy odor of auto exhaust. Dozens of vehicles were backed up on I-5 while they waited to be allowed to exit Seattle. Judging from the

see referral form attached

boxes and suitcases strapped to the roofs of many of the cars, as well as the ubiquitous U-Haul trailers, many of them were leaving for good.

Less than two months had passed since an outbreak of airborne promicin had ravaged Seattle, killing over nine thousand people, and the city had yet to fully recover from the disaster. The fact that another nine thousand–plus people had been endowed with unnatural abilities against their will had only added to the instability. Not surprisingly, thousands of survivors, especially ordinary people with no special abilities, had chosen to seek safer pastures elsewhere. Over four million people had once lived in the Seattle metro area; nearly a third of that number had now pulled up stakes.

Tom couldn't blame them. Seattle was a dangerous place these days.

And getting more so all the time, he thought.

The guard examined Tom's credentials. A high-collared, pine-colored uniform with silver trim identified her as one of Jordan Collier's self-appointed Peace Officers. "NTAC, huh?" The woman's face hardened; the National Threat Assessment Command was not exactly popular with the followers of Jordan Collier, the undisputed leader of the Promicin-Positive Movement, which had largely taken over Seattle, now known in some circles as "Promise City." During the disaster, his people, who were immune to the plague, having already been exposed to promicin, had stepped forward to maintain order—and had yet to surrender Seattle back to the authorities. Although Collier had yet to officially declare the city's independence, and had refrained from taking any formal title or position, he and his acolytes were pretty much in control of the city's government and infrastructure. As far as the Movement was concerned, NTAC, a division of Homeland Security, was part of the oppressive old order they had usurped—and best relegated to the dustbin of history.

"That's right," Tom said. He couldn't help wondering what kind of a special ability the guard possessed; all of Collier's people had been changed by promicin in one way or another, and believed they had a sacred destiny to change the world. Even the name of the disaster was controversial. Collier and his followers referred to it as "The Great Leap Forward." Most everyone else called it "fifty/fifty."

He kept his voice neutral, not wanting to provoke her. The guard did not appear to be armed, but that hardly mattered where p-positives were concerned. For all Tom knew, this woman could kill him with a thought. "I think you'll find my papers are in order."

The guard squinted at his ID. "I suppose," she conceded grudgingly. "If I were you, though, I'd keep going and never come back." She thrust the papers back at him. "Your kind doesn't belong here anymore."

Tom was tempted to point out that he'd been born and raised in Seattle and had as much right to live there as anyone else, but held his tongue. He had more important matters to deal with today, assuming he ever got out of the city. "See you later," he said curtly. "On my way home."

The guard scowled, but waved him on. An automated aluminum gate arm lifted to let him through. A pair of orange metal pylons flanked the roadway. Although dormant now, the pylons were capable of generating waves of intense pain when activated. They were Promise City's first line of defense.

Tom didn't bother to roll up his window before driving north as he only got about fifty feet before running into a *second* set of checkpoints. This one was manned by grim-faced soldiers toting automatic weapons. Their uniforms and insignia identified them as members of the U.S. Army. A guard approached the driver's side of the car.

Here we go again, Tom thought.

An uneasy stalemate existed between the federal government and Promise City. Needless to say, the Powers That Be were hardly happy to surrender a major American city to a messianic drug dealer with a cultlike following, but the extraordinary abilities of Collier and his people, as well as the futuristic technology at his command, made taking back Seattle a risky endeavor. Even before the plague, Collier's community of p-positive revolutionaries had managed to repel any government attempts to take them into custody. Now, with his army swollen with literally thousands of new recruits, Collier was a force to be reckoned with—and not only in Seattle. It was well-known that he had sleeper agents, capable of generating tornadoes and hurricanes and God knew what else, positioned throughout the entire country, ready to create havoc if the Feds tried to send in the troops to reclaim Seattle.

Which they're bound to try eventually, Tom thought. Everyone figured a major confrontation was inevitable, but nobody wanted a city-sized version of Waco just yet, so forces on both sides were biding their time and holding their breaths. *Just like the rest of us.*

He showed his ID to the soldier, a fresh-faced young man who looked to be about Kyle's age. The guard relaxed only a little when he saw Tom's NTAC credentials. His armed comrades stood by warily, tightly gripping their M16 assault rifles. He didn't blame the soldiers for being edgy; they were on the front lines of an evolutionary civil war. "Please exit your vehicle," the young guard requested. He stepped away from the car door.

Tom sighed impatiently, but didn't raise a fuss. He climbed out of the car. A tan nylon jacket, open-collar polo shirt, and dark trousers protected his muscular frame from the elements. Sandy blond hair crowned his rugged features. Haunted blue eyes hinted at the strain he'd been under for the last four years. He unzipped the Windbreaker to reveal the sidearm holstered at his hip. The guard looked askance at the gun but let it go. Tom stood by while the young soldier entered Tom's name and Social Security number into a handheld PDA, checking it against an ever-growing list of known p-positive "terrorists." Drug-sniffing German shepherds checked out the Chrysler to make sure Tom wasn't smuggling promicin out of the city.

Although openly distributed in certain neighborhoods of Seattle, the artificial neurotransmitter remained strictly illegal throughout the rest of the world. Mere possession of promicin brought a mandatory prison sentence, which hadn't stopped Collier and his disciples from trying to make the drug available to anyone who wanted it, free of charge. And judging from some of the reports Tom had seen, Collier was succeeding in his aims, despite the sort of stringent containment measures Tom was currently experiencing.

After giving his car a clean bill of health, the dogs came over and sniffed Tom as well, just in case he was carrying any promicin on his person. He tried not to flinch as the suspicious canines invaded his personal space.

Good thing I left that syringe back home . . .

Tom sat on his living room couch, cradling the hypo in his palm. The eerie yellow glow of the promicin sent a chill down his spine. He had witnessed firsthand the fatal effect of the drug on those unlucky enough to lose their fifty-fifty shot at making history, watched bright arterial blood stream from their eyes and noses as violent convulsions consumed the last moments of their lives. Taking the shot was like playing Russian roulette, but with worse odds. His own sister had been killed by promicin less than a week ago, along with thousands of other innocent victims . . .

I can't believe I'm seriously considering this, he thought.

"Go ahead, Dad," Kyle urged him. His son, a lanky young man with short brown hair, sat beside him on the couch. He was dressed casually, in a striped white shirt and jeans. A book bag, containing a volume of mystic prophecies, was strapped across his chest. Kyle had already taken the shot, against Tom's wishes, several months ago and dropped out of college to become Jordan Collier's right-hand man. Tom didn't entirely understand how his son's ability worked, but he knew that Kyle had acquired some kind of precognitive gift that had led him to a mysterious book that seemed to prophesy the rise of Collier and the eventual coming of "Heaven on Earth." The cryptic volume had also listed several individuals who were destined to play instrumental roles in the salvation of the world.

Tom's name was on that list.

A few years ago, he would not have taken any of this talk about prophecies and destiny seriously. He had been a hard-nosed federal agent with little patience for sci-fi gobbledygook. But that was before 4400 missing people suddenly appeared outside Seattle with strange new abilities and no memory of where they had been. The 4400 had turned Tom's world upside down, even before he'd discovered that their return had been engineered by time travelers from the future as part of an elaborate plan to avert a mysterious future catastrophe. At first, only those original 4400 returnees had possessed unnatural abilities, but once the neurotransmitter responsible for their gifts had been isolated and replicated—by a secret government-sponsored initiative, ironically enough—the promicin genie had been let out of the bottle. Now, Tom didn't know what to believe. In this brave new world of time travel, telepathy, astral projection, and every other kind of weirdness, why couldn't a musty old book foretell his destiny? Especially if it had been planted in the past by the agents from the future.

But for what purpose?

"It will be okay," Kyle insisted. Certainty, and a near-religious fervor, shone in his gentle brown eyes. Unlike his father, he had total faith in Collier and his vision for the future. "The book says you'll survive."

"I don't know," Tom replied, shaking his head. "I'm not sure I'm ready for this. Not after everything we've been through lately."

His hand went to his left ear, where his fingers found an X-shaped mole hidden behind his earlobe. The telltale stigma was a reminder that, less than a week ago, Tom had been Marked by conspirators from the future, who had taken over the minds and bodies of prominent men and women in an insidious attempt to prevent Collier and his followers from changing the future. The Marked, who belonged to a rival faction opposed to the time travelers who had first returned the 4400 to the present, had injected Tom with microscopic machines—nanites—that had replaced his personality with that of a ruthless imposter who had stopped at nothing, including murder, to carry out the Marked's sinister agenda. In time, Tom's friends and allies at NTAC had seen through the imposter's act and rid Tom of the invading personality—but not before "Tom" had killed at least two men on behalf of the Marked.

The murders still haunted Tom's memory, like a bad dream he couldn't quite shake. He glanced down at the coffee table in front of the couch. The files on the killings, including the victims' photos and obituaries, were spread out across the tabletop. The faces of Curtis Peck and Warren Trask stared up at him. He remembered killing both of them.

Guilt stabbed him. Although he knew intellectually that he wasn't responsible for the men's deaths, that he had been literally possessed by another mind when he had committed those murders, he still wasn't sure he could live with the memories.

Kyle thought that taking the shot would make everything better. That it would justify all the pain and suffering Tom had endured and open the doorway to a better future for the entire human race. Tom wasn't so sure.

"I just got myself back, Kyle. I just got those . . . *things* out of my brain." He placed the syringe down on the table, next to the accusing photos. He looked at his son, hoping Kyle would understand. "I'm not ready to inject another potion from the future into my body. Even if it doesn't kill me, I don't want to change anymore. I want to be just plain, ordinary Tom Baldwin again."

"But . . ." Disappointment was written all over Kyle's long face. He had been pushing the shot on his dad for months. "The prophecy, heaven on Earth . . . you have to take the shot. The future depends on it."

"Maybe," Tom said. He hated to let Kyle down like this. His son's newfound commitment to Collier's cause had too often come between them. Still, he placed the syringe in a padded carrying-case and closed the lid. "But not today."

"Okay," the guard informed him. "You're clear."

Tom got back in his car and drove past the checkpoint. Putting Promise City behind him, at least for the time being, he drove north on I-5. Traffic was brutal for a Sunday afternoon, but eased up once he turned west onto 526. A short ferry ride carried him from the docks at Mukilteo to the southeast corner of Whidbey Island. From there it was a quick drive across the island to his destination: Fort Casey State Park.

Located atop the steep cliffs overlooking the Strait of Juan de Fuca, Fort Casey had been erected in the 1890s to guard the entrance to Puget Sound from naval attacks. Although it had been rendered obsolete by the advent of airpower after World War I, the fort's imposing gun emplacements had been preserved as an historical monument. The massive concrete batteries faced the surging waves below. Antique artillery was mounted on disappearing carriages atop the weathered gray walls. Lookout towers peered out over the batteries. Dilapidated stairwells and catwalks had once served the troops stationed here. A tall white lighthouse had been erected a little farther up the shore, only a short hike from the abandoned fort. Its cozy, whitewashed appearance stood in sharp contrast to the forbidding military ruins.

Tom remembered bringing Kyle here years ago. A nostalgic pang pierced his heart as he recalled how much the boy had enjoyed exploring the old fort. Together, they had manned the ancient guns and pretended to fire upon imaginary battleships. Life had seemed much simpler then. Now Kyle was a grown man, caught up in Jordan Collier's dangerous ambitions, and the real invaders came from across time, not from the sea. Fort Casey was more obsolete than ever.

A grassy field separated the parking lot from the batteries. On sunnier days, the field often attracted kite enthusiasts who filled the sky above the fort with elaborate airborne constructions, but the dismal winter weather had kept visitors away today. A clammy mist hung over the grounds. A steady drizzle fell from an overcast gray sky. There was only one other car parked nearby: a black Lincoln Town Car with Washington plates.

Looks like we've got the place to ourselves, Tom thought. Probably just as well; whatever today's covert meeting was about, it surely wasn't for public consumption. Why else choose such an unorthodox rendezvous point?

Curiosity, as well as the incessant rain, drove him across the field. He grimaced as icy water trickled down the back of his neck; like most native Seattlites, he wouldn't be caught dead carrying an umbrella. A quick dash brought him to an arched concrete doorway at the base of the nearest battery. A riveted iron door flanked the open threshold. He darted into the murky confines of an abandoned shot and powder room. The unlit chamber was as stark and barren as a prison cell. Greenish algae streaked the rough concrete walls. An empty elevator shaft connected the powder room with the guns mounted on upper levels. Rainwater sluiced past the doorway, pooling on the hard stone floor.

Tom shook the rain from his hair and glanced around the shadowy bunker. At first he didn't see anyone and wondered if maybe he had ducked into the wrong storeroom. The old fort was full of secluded nooks and crannies, which no doubt contributed to the location being chosen for this rendezvous. The dense concrete walls discouraged electronic surveillance.

Not taking any chances, I see.

He was about to venture out into the rain again when he heard a rustle of motion behind him. His hand went instinctively to his sidearm as he turned around to see a pair of figures emerge from one of the adjoining storerooms. One was male, the other female. The former was nobody he'd been in any hurry to see again.

"About time you got here," Dennis Ryland said. "You're late."

TWO

Tom's former boss was a lean, dark-haired man about two decades older than Tom. A gray wool overcoat was draped over his gaunt frame. Shrewd brown eyes peered from his vulpine countenance. After being forced out of NTAC in the wake of a major scandal three years ago, Ryland had ended up at the Haspel Corporation, a private security firm that often worked hand in hand with the Feds when it came to cracking down on the 4400 and the other p-positives. If anything, Ryland had even more power now than before—and considerably less oversight. That made him a dangerous man. Too dangerous, as far as Tom was concerned.

"Hello, Dennis," he said coldly. His hand came away from his gun.

Ryland glanced at an expensive Rolex wristwatch. Life in the private sector clearly had its perks. "I was starting to think you'd stood me up."

"I thought about it," Tom confessed. He and Dennis had once been friends, but there was little love lost between them these days. Tom still regarded p-positives as people; Ryland saw them only as threats to be neutralized, and preferably eliminated. Their friendship had not survived that clash of viewpoints. "This had better be worth the trip."

A smirk greeted Tom's hostile tone. "Sorry to drag you all the way out here today," Ryland said, "but, as you know, I'm not exactly welcome in Seattle anymore."

"Imagine that," Tom said. Among other things, Ryland had been behind a plot to poison the original 4400 with an experimental drug that had nearly killed all of the returnees, including Tom's own nephew. Although Ryland had received only a slap on the wrist for his role in the infamous Inhibitor Scandal, Collier and his followers still regarded him as a "war criminal." Banishing Haspelcorp from Seattle had been one of the first items on Collier's agenda. Last Tom had heard, the company was based out of Tacoma now, which was still too close for comfort.

Ryland overlooked Tom's sarcastic tone. He gestured toward his companion: a young Asian woman wearing a belted white trenchcoat. A pixie cut flattered her lustrous black hair. Despite the gloom, a stylish pair of dark glasses concealed her eyes. "You may remember my associate, Ms. Simone Tanaka."

"How could I forget?" Tom said wryly. He and his partner had personally arrested Tanaka over a year and a half ago, after exposing her as part of a now defunct 4400 terrorist cell known as "The Nova Group." He had lost track of her after the NSA took her into custody, and was a bit surprised to find her working with Ryland. Philosophically, the Nova Group and Haspelcorp were on opposite sides of the fence; the Nova Group had even tried to assassinate Ryland a while back. "Keeping kind of odd company, aren't you. For a former radical, I mean."

She shrugged. "Times change. Given the choice between spending the rest of my life locked up in solitary, doped to the gills on the inhibitor, or lending my special talents to the authorities in exchange for certain privileges . . . well, you'd be surprised how flexible one's convictions can turn out to be."

Maybe for some people, Tom thought. Still, he was reluctant to judge Tanaka too harshly. Who knew what sort of pressures Ryland and his cronies had exerted to secure her cooperation? Not to mention the fact that the lines between the good guys and bad guys were getting extremely blurry nowadays. Tanaka wasn't the only person whose alliances had shifted over time. Sometimes not even Tom knew whose side he was on.

"So much for the pleasantries," Ryland said. "Shall we get down to the business?"

Tom shook his head. "Not yet." He eyed the pair suspiciously. "Let me check behind your ears."

"You think I'm Marked?" Ryland snorted at the idea. "You're getting paranoid, Tom."

"I have reason to be." Tom wasn't surprised that Ryland knew about the Marked; no doubt his contacts in the intelligence community had briefed him on the body-snatching conspirators. He circled behind Ryland and Tanaka. "If you don't mind."

Ryland sighed wearily. "If it will put your mind at rest." He let Tom peek behind the ear. To the agent's relief, the skin under the lobe did not bear an X-shaped mole. "You do realize that this is a waste of time, don't you?" Ryland objected. "I hardly need to be possessed by a sinister entity from the future to want to save this country from the 4400 and Collier's seditious Movement."

He's got a point there, Tom conceded. Marking Ryland would be redundant; the man was already obsessed with destroying the 4400. "I guess you and the Marked are on the same page."

"You know what they say," Ryland answered. "The enemy of my enemy, et cetera."

Tom didn't like the sound of that. Was Ryland just pulling his chain, or was he actually in cahoots with the Marked? Lord knows they had similar agendas, and swam in the same lofty military-industrial circles. *That could be serious trouble.*

Convinced that Ryland's prejudices were his own, and not something imposed on him by the Marked, Tom moved on to Tanaka. Was there more to her defection to Ryland's camp than simple expedience? "Excuse me," he said as he came up behind her. "Your glasses."

"Go ahead," Ryland instructed her.

Her back to Tom, she removed her glasses. Slender fingers brushed her hair away from her ear. A whiff of perfume tickled Tom's nostrils. "You do this with every girl you meet?"

I would if I was single, Tom thought. He had been involved with his boss, Meghan Doyle, for months now. And, truth be told, he sometimes checked behind her ear when they were making love or in the shower. He tried to be subtle about it, but he suspected that Meghan knew what he was up to, even if she never said anything. Meghan understood what the Marked had done to him. She had been one of the first people to see through the false Tom's deceptions.

"That's none of your business," he replied. The woman's skin proved equally unblemished and he stepped away from her. She replaced her glasses.

"Satisfied?" Ryland asked him.

"On that score." Tom circled back to face the pair. "Although part of me kind of wishes I had found a Mark on you. It would have explained what happened to the man I used to know."

"I never changed," Ryland insisted. "You're the one who let your sentimental attachment to these menaces blind you to what needs to be done. Speaking of which, I hear that you and Regional Director Doyle are enjoying an unusually close working relationship." He shook his head disapprovingly. "First the Mareva woman, now another p-positive freak?"

Along with several other NTAC staffers, Meghan had been involuntarily infected with promicin during fifty/fifty. And like the other survivors, she had developed a 4400 ability. This had posed a dilemma for NTAC, which was still tasked with carrying out the war on promicin. As a result, the agency had adopted a "don't ask, don't tell" policy regarding all the NTAC employees who had gained abilities against their will. Everyone knew what had happened to them, but they were expected to be discreet about it . . . or face immediate termination.

"Watch it," Tom warned him. He was tempted to pop Ryland in the nose, but chose not to take the bait. After all, he still didn't know why the other man had requested this meeting. "What do you want, Dennis?"

"The same thing as always," Ryland declared, getting down to business. "To stop the 4400 and the other positives from wrecking our way of life and endangering our national security. Today, that means bringing down Collier and his Movement."

He extracted a plastic vial and shook a couple of circular brown tablets into his palm before popping the pills into his mouth. Tom recognized the tablets as ubiquinone, a common nutritional supplement that, in sufficient doses, could provide temporary immunity to promicin. The Feds had been madly stockpiling "U-Pills" for months now, despite Collier's frequent efforts to sabotage the initiative via suspiciously surgical earthquakes and tornadoes. All p-negative NTAC agents now routinely carried emergency doses when in the field. Tom's own supply was tucked in his back pocket.

"Unfortunately," Ryland continued, "as I mentioned before, my people are persona non grata in Seattle, which means it's up to you and your colleagues to dethrone Collier, even if it means taking advantage of your son's connection to Collier."

"Kyle?" Tom bristled at the suggestion. "You want me to exploit my own son?"

Ryland didn't deny it. "As Collier's confidant and right-hand man, he's a unique asset which we'd be fools not to utilize. I realize this puts you in an awkward position, but your duty to this country trumps your familial obligations." His stern tone reminded Tom of how Ryland had once run NTAC's northwest office. "You're still a federal agent, Tom. Don't tell me you approve of Collier turning Seattle into his own private fiefdom?"

"Of course not." Tom didn't trust Collier one bit, even though they had been forced to work together on occasion. In fact, NTAC was already doing its best to keep a close eye on Collier and his organization, given the constraints of the current situation. But he didn't like getting bossed around by the likes of Ryland. "Leave Kyle out of this."

"I wish I could," Ryland said. "I used to attend his birthday parties, remember? As I recall, he really liked that chemistry set I got him when he was eleven." His voice took on a rueful tone. "But Kyle made himself fair game when he hitched his star to Jordan Collier's wagon." He couldn't resist twisting the knife a bit. "You ever think you set a bad example by literally sleeping with the enemy?"

Tom's fists clenched at his sides. "You're not exactly winning me over here, Dennis. Why should I help you?"

"The names Curtis Peck and Warren Trask ring a bell?" Ryland's lean face hardened. Tom flinched at the mention of the men he had murdered while Marked. "I'd hate to see you charged with crimes you committed while not in your right mind, but I can't help thinking that your recent extracurricular activities give me a degree of leverage."

Simone Tanaka cracked a bitter smile. "Gee, this sounds familiar."

"Don't try playing hardball with me." Tom wasn't sure if the other man was bluffing or not, but, once he got over the initial jolt, he gave as good as he got. "I'm not the only one with dirty laundry. You want the world to know that the promicin Collier used to launch his Movement was created by Haspelcorp at your direction? The way I see it, that makes you indirectly responsible for everything that's happened since. Including fifty/fifty."

Ryland scowled, unable to refute Tom's charges. Collier had hijacked Haspelcorp's homemade promicin right under Ryland's nose two years ago. The drug had been intended to create an army of enhanced soldiers to combat the 4400, but Collier had found another use for it, namely offering the drug to the entire world.

"Touché," Ryland said, backing off. He tried another tack. "Suppose I told you that Collier is trying to weaponize promicin? To re-create the airborne version Danny Farrell unleashed on Seattle a few months ago?"

Tom winced at the mention of his nephew's name. Danny hadn't meant to hurt anyone when he'd injected himself with promicin. He had only wanted to gain an ability like his older brother, Shawn, one of the original 4400. But, to his infinite horror, and the world's lasting regret, he'd acquired the ghastly ability to infect everyone around him with a highly contagious form of promicin. Like a modern-day Typhoid Mary, he had spread the plague throughout Seattle before he even realized what was happening. Danny's own mother—Tom's sister—had been the first to die . . .

"I've seen those reports," Tom said skeptically. "Lots of doctored evidence cooked up by the Marked and their friends in high places. They're just trying to provoke the Feds into launching a preemptive strike against Collier."

"Are you willing to take that chance?" Ryland challenged him. "Besides, I have my own sources of information."

"Such as?"

Ryland glanced at Tanaka. The woman removed her glasses to reveal a pair of striking brown eyes. Her dark bronze irises had a thin golden halo around them, giving the eyes an eerie preternatural quality. Tom recalled that Tanaka was capable of seeing vast distances, and through solid objects, with her so-called "spy-eyes." The Nova Group had used her to spy on NTAC during the "Vesuvius Affair." Ryland and his buddies had surely put her ocular gifts to use as well.

"I can also read lips," she reminded him.

Am I buying this? Tom thought. Tanaka's ability was a matter of record, but he wasn't about to take her or Ryland at their word. She had a vested interest in telling Tom whatever her new bosses wanted her to, and Ryland had lied to Tom before.

“If you don’t believe me,” Ryland said, “check it out for yourself.”

Tom broke down and extracted a notepad from his pocket. “How?”

Ryland smiled slyly. “Here’s a question for you. Whatever happened to Danny Farrell’s remains?”

THREE

The prisoner groans upon the floor of the cell. Blood drips from a swollen lip. He clutches the side of his head. A hefty guard stands over the prisoner. He sneers at the man on the floor, then kicks him savagely in the ribs. "You like that, you stupid freak?" he roars. Another guard cackles from outside the cell. No one notices the pale-faced young girl watching from the corner. Her eyes widen in horror.

The prisoner, a tall black man in an orange jumpsuit, tries to climb to his feet, but the beefy guard punches him in the face. He clubs him in the back with a metal truncheon, knocking him facedown onto the rough concrete floor.

"Wait!" the girl screams, but no one hears her. She's only an observer here. Like a ghost.

The guard draws a gun from a holster. He aims it at the helpless prisoner.

"Time to say good-bye, Tyler."

"Stop it!" the girl screams. "You're going to kill him!"

Maia Skouris awoke with a start. Disoriented by the nightmare, it took the teenager a moment to realize that she was safe in her own bed. Her wide brown eyes absorbed the familiar setting. Her straight blond hair was parted down the middle. A poster of Frank Sinatra was pinned to one wall. Dirty laundry littered the floor. Textbooks and homework were piled atop a desk, beside a globe of the world. Her journal rested on an end table next to her bed. Moonlight filtered through the window curtains. A digital alarm clock informed her that it was 3:20 in the morning.

Oh my God, she thought. *That felt so real.*

"Maia? Are you all right?" The bedroom door swung open and her mother rushed into the room. Diana Skouris flicked on the lights as she entered. Her auburn hair was mussed from the bed. A blue cotton nightgown clung to her trim, athletic figure. "I heard you cry out."

"It's okay, Mom," Maia replied, embarrassed by the fuss. "Just a bad dream."

Diana sat down at the edge of the bed. Concerned brown eyes examined her daughter's face. "Just an ordinary dream—or a vision?"

Maia knew what her mother meant. Ever since Maia had returned with the rest of the 4400 five years ago, she had been blessed—or cursed—with occasional glimpses of the future. Sometimes these visions struck her when she was wide awake; other times they came to her in the form of astonishingly vivid dreams. But they *always* came true.

"It's Richard," she blurted. "Richard Tyler." Like her, Tyler was one of the original 4400. Last she'd heard, he had been arrested by the government. "I saw him in prison. One of the guards was trying to kill him!"

"Oh no," Diana murmured. She didn't question Maia's vision. Past experience had taught them both to take the girl's predictions very seriously. "Could you tell when this was happening?"

"I'm not sure," Maia admitted. "Sometime soon, maybe." She hoped they weren't already too late. "We have to save him!"

Her mother frowned. "That could be harder than it sounds. I'll notify NTAC right away, but Homeland Security has him locked up tight in a high-security prison in Virginia. That's way out of my jurisdiction. To be honest, we haven't been allowed access to Richard for months."

Maia was frustrated by her mother's response. What was the good of having an NTAC agent for a mother if she couldn't use her badge to save a man's life? Maia didn't know Richard well, despite the fact that his psycho daughter had once tried to kill her, but the 4400 had to look out for each other. That's what Jordan always said, and Maia found she agreed with him more and more as she got older. Even if her mother still had her doubts about Jordan.

"But, Mom, you *have* to get him out of that jail. He's not safe there!"

"I wish it was that easy, honey." She tugged her robe shut. "But, like it or not, Richard has attacked U.S. soldiers and NTAC agents in the past, so the government regards him as a dangerous terrorist. I'll pass along your warning to the relevant agencies, but otherwise I'm afraid it's out of my hands."

Diana tried to give her daughter a comforting hug, but

Maia pulled away from her. "Jordan wouldn't write Richard off like this," she said sullenly.

"I'm *not* writing him off," her mother protested. A note of exasperation crept into her voice. "And don't you even think of telling Jordan Collier about your vision. We've talked about this before. I don't want you having anything to do with Collier and his cult. It's too dangerous."

Maia pouted and crossed her arms atop her chest. Why didn't her mother understand that Jordan Collier was right about the 4400 and the other positives? *We're* supposed *to change the world for the better. That's why we're here.*

"I'm not a little girl anymore," she said defiantly. "I can make my own decisions."

Diana shook her head. "Not about this. This is serious grown-up business."

"Actually, I'm older than you are," Maia pointed out. "If you look at the calendar."

Born in 1938, Maia had been abducted by the future when she was only eight years old, then returned along with the rest of the 4400 in 2004. Technically, that made her old enough for Social Security, even though she hadn't aged a day while she was missing.

"Don't get cute with me," Diana said. She had adopted the orphaned girl shortly after her return. "Emotionally and physically, you're still only thirteen. And that's way too young to be getting involved with stuff like this."

"But I'm already involved," Maia argued. "I'm one of the 4400. And I can't ignore what I see."

"I know," her mother said sadly. Her voice and expression softened. "Look, I don't want to fight about Jordan

Collier again." She stood up and rubbed her eyes. "I promise I'll do what I can about Richard, but we should try to get back to sleep. Tomorrow is a school day." Leaning over, she tucked Maia back and kissed her on the top of the head. "I'll see you in the morning. Pleasant dreams."

She flicked off the lights on her way out.

Maia waited until she heard her mom head back to her own room, then counted to a hundred just to be safe. Assuming that her mom was safely asleep, she crept out of bed and retrieved her BlackBerry from the top of her dresser. She felt a twinge of guilt for sneaking around like this—the bright pink smartphone was a birthday gift from her mom—but Richard Tyler's life was at stake.

The glow from the BlackBerry's screen lit up her worried face as she hastily texted her best friend, Lindsey Howard. Also a 4400, Lindsey had been involved with the Movement from the beginning. Maia knew she could count on her to get a message to Jordan Collier.

Somebody had to do something to help Richard!

The 4400 Center had been established by Jordan Collier before he turned into a self-styled revolutionary and messiah. The Center was now run by Tom's nephew, Shawn Farrell. One of the original 4400, he had been missing for three years before he was returned.

"Hello, Diana, Uncle Tommy," Shawn greeted the agents as they entered his luxurious king-sized office, which made Tom's own digs back at headquarters look like a closet by comparison. An attractive young man in his mid-twenties, Shawn wore a tailored Armani suit that looked good on his well-built frame. His short blond hair was neatly trimmed. Tom was proud of what a poised and confident individual his nephew had become. He couldn't help wishing that Kyle had turned out more like his cousin. Although Shawn had briefly fallen under Collier's spell as well, he was his own man now.

"Good to see you," Tom said. Even though they were here on business, he gave his nephew a friendly hug. Shawn had lost both his mom and brother to the plague, so Tom wanted to make sure that the young man knew that he was not alone, that he still had a family that cared about him. "Thanks for squeezing us into your schedule."

Shawn chuckled wryly. "Trust me, that's not as hard as it used to be. Now that my political career is defunct, I've got a lot more time on my hands."

I'll bet, Tom thought. Fifty/fifty had pretty much killed Shawn's run for city council. The city was too polarized between positives and negatives to support a candidate who tried to bring both sides together, let alone the brother of the man who had unleashed the plague in the first place. "At least you still have the Center," Tom said.

"I guess." Shawn pointed at an empty in-box. "Although Jordan's Movement is where the real action is. We provide support and services for positives who are uncomfortable with Jordan's radical agenda, mostly folks who got infected during the outbreak, but, to be honest, there doesn't seem to be much of an audience for a middle path anymore. I'm not sure how relevant the Center is these days."

"Don't sell yourself short," Diana said. Her auburn hair was bound up in a ponytail. She wore a black leather jacket over an orange turtleneck sweater. "You represent the mainstream face of the 4400, and a sane alternative to Jordan Collier. That's more important now than ever."

"Maybe." Shawn sounded unconvinced. "Mostly, I've been focusing on my healing practice, which Jordan tolerates because it's good PR for the 4400."

"Well, that's important, too," Tom reminded him. His nephew's remarkable ability to heal all sorts of injuries and illnesses had saved a lot of people, including Tom himself. Shawn had played a crucial role in freeing Tom from the Marked. And had roused Kyle from a seemingly endless coma. "Never forget that."

Shawn's smile returned. "Thanks for the vote of confidence. I appreciate it." He sat down behind his tidy black desk. An oil painting mounted on the wall behind him depicted the glowing ball of white light that had brought the 4400 back from the future. Fresh orchids sprouted from a vase below the painting. "So, how can I help you today?"

Tom hesitated. This was going to be awkward. "It's about Danny," he said finally.

"Danny?" A pained expression washed over Shawn's face. He had been forced to euthanize his own brother to keep the plague from spreading. Tom could only imagine how hard that must have been for him. "What about him?"

Diana spared Tom from having to spell things out. "We'd like your permission to exhume Danny's body."

"What?" Shawn was visibly shocked by the request. "Why?"

"We have reason to be concerned that someone might

try to replicate the airborne version of promicin that Danny exuded after he took the shot," Tom explained. He didn't mention that Ryland was the source of this rumor; Shawn had no reason to trust a man who wanted him dead. "It might be nothing, but we have to be certain."

Shawn slumped against the back of his chair. "I don't know," he said. Hurt eyes gleamed moistly. His voice grew hoarse with emotion. "Can't we just let him rest in peace, next to Mom?"

Danny was buried in Emerald Harbors Cemetery, alongside Tom's sister.

"I wish we could," Tom said. He felt terrible for putting Shawn through this, so soon after he lost his family. "I really do." If necessary, they could try to get a court order to exhume the body, but he'd rather get Shawn's blessing instead. Besides, any legal proceedings would surely alert Collier to their intentions; many of Seattle's judges and lawyers now reported directly to him. Tom extracted a document from beneath his jacket and slid it across the polished desktop toward Shawn. "But we can't take that chance. Nobody wants another fifty/fifty."

Shawn nodded, reluctantly accepting the truth. He reached for a pen.

Diana slipped out of the office to let Tom console his nephew in private. She knew how difficult the discussion had been for both men, but was relieved that they had managed to get Shawn's consent for the exhumation. Before joining NTAC, she had previously worked for the Centers for Disease Control in Atlanta; if it had been up to her, Danny's remains would have been cremated immediately after his death, but, in the chaos following the disaster, this hadn't happened.

I hope that wasn't a serious mistake, she thought.

While her partner was busy with Shawn, she pursued a related errand. A brisk walk led her to the Center's infirmary, where she found Dr. Kevin Burkhoff hard at work in an attached laboratory. The renegade scientist was crouched over a high-powered electron microscope as she entered the lab. Intent on his labors, he didn't hear her approach as she came up behind him. An open bag of sunflower seeds rested on the counter beside the microscope. Brain scans glowed upon a mounted light board. A centrifuge whirred in the background. A medicinal odor permeated the air.

"Dr. Burkhoff? Kevin?"

Startled, he whirled about in surprise. In doing so, he sliced his finger on the edge of a test tube slide. A thin red line appeared briefly on the injured digit, then retracted as his accelerated healing ability kicked in. His alarmed expression relaxed as he recognized his visitor. "Oh, Diana!" He clutched his chest, which must have been beating rapidly. He wiped his bloody finger on the counter. "I didn't hear you come in. You gave me quite a start."

When Diana had first met Kevin Burkhoff three years ago, he had been confined to a mental hospital. Although he had regained his sanity with the help of the 4400, he remained twitchy and full of nervous energy. His lank black hair was in need of combing. Stringy bangs fell across his furrowed brow. Acid burns marred his white lab jacket. Chemical reagents stained his fingertips.

"Sorry about that." She nodded at the microscope. "Anything interesting?"

He glanced around furtively, as though afraid of being overheard. "Don't tell anyone," he whispered, "but I'm still trying to perfect my promicin compatibility test."

"Right." Diana remembered that Shawn had been subsidizing Burkhoff's efforts to make taking the shot less of a life-or-death gamble, the idea being to develop a test that would determine in advance whether promicin would kill you or give you an ability. Back before fifty/fifty, Shawn had urged the public to refrain from taking the shot until the test was ready, but Diana hadn't heard anything about the project since. "How is that going?"

Burkhoff rescued his sunflower seeds from the counter; the unsalted snacks were his sole vice. "It's coming along, but I could have made much more progress by now if I had more support from the authorities. Neither Collier nor the government wants me to continue my work, for their own reasons, and I know they've been putting a lot of pressure on Shawn to shut me down." He poured a handful of seeds into his palm. "I practically have to skulk around like a thief in the night to get any work done!"

"That's too bad," Diana said, sympathizing with the scientist's frustration. She wasn't surprised to hear that his work was unpopular in certain quarters. Certainly, the government wouldn't be happy with any test that took the risk out of taking promicin; that would just lead to more positives in the long run. Collier, though, pretty much wanted the entire world to take the shot; he was more than willing to sacrifice half of humanity on the altar of his brave new world. "But I wonder if the test would really make the decision any easier for people? Even if you knew you were going to survive, you still wouldn't know what kind of ability you were getting. And, frankly, some of them aren't very pretty."

Diana had been dealing with positives for years now, and had seen firsthand how gaining an ability could screw up a person's life. For every individual who acquired an enviable new talent, such as the ability to heal the sick, there was somebody like Danny Farrell who wound up cursed with a ghastly affliction beyond their control. Or Jean DeLynn Baker, who had become the unwilling carrier of a lethal, Ebola-like virus. As it happened, Diana had a unique immunity to promicin, but she wasn't sure she would take the shot even if that was an option. *What if I ended up like Danny or some of the others?*

"You have a point there," Burkhoff conceded. "But plenty of people are taking that risk every day. And half of them are dying because my work is being suppressed!"

"Kevin?" a voice called from the infirmary. "Is everything all right?"

A waiflike young woman entered the lab. Haunting brown eyes graced her delicate features. Wavy light brown hair fell past her shoulders. A cashmere sweater and midlength skirt gave her a timeless appearance. It took her a moment to notice that Burkhoff wasn't alone. A worried look came over her elfin face. "Diana?"

"Hello, Tess," Diana said tightly. She tried to conceal

her discomfort with the other woman's presence. One of the original 4400, Tess Doerner had the unsettling ability to make people do whatever she asked them. Diana had personally come under Tess's control before. It wasn't an experience she was in any hurry to relive. "Kevin and I were just talking."

Her words didn't seem to reassure Tess, who stepped protectively between Diana and Burkhoff. The middle-aged scientist and the much younger woman were an odd couple, who had met when they were both patients at Abendson Psychiatric Hospital, but they were unquestionably devoted to each other. Diana didn't doubt that Tess would do most anything to defend Kevin from NTAC or anyone else who wanted to take advantage of his genius. "What are you doing here, Diana?"

The female agent cut to the chase. "You treated Danny Farrell during his final hours. I want to know what happened to any blood and tissue samples you took from him."

Burkhoff averted his gaze from hers. He fidgeted nervously with his bag of seeds. "Shawn ordered me to destroy all the samples after Danny died."

Diana knew the scientist too well to believe this. Burkhoff never let anything get in the way of his scientific curiosity. "Yes, but what did you *really* do with them?"

"I don't know what you mean," he hedged. Turning away from her, he fumbled with the microscope once more. "Didn't I already answer your question?"

"Come on, Kevin," she pressed him. "You *discovered* promicin. You seriously expect me to believe that you weren't intrigued by a specimen who exuded the stuff from his pores?"

Burkhoff sighed and turned away from the counter. "Well, I may have kept a *few* samples for research purposes, but they're perfectly safe and secure. I followed every applicable containment protocol."

Now we're getting somewhere, Diana thought. "I need to see that for myself."

"All right," he conceded. "Follow me."

Tess tagged along as he led Diana toward a sealed metal door that resembled an airlock. A biohazard decal was prominently affixed to the door. A digital keypad was mounted above the door handle. Burkhoff shielded the keypad with his body as he keyed in a fifteen-digit sequence. "I'm the only person who knows this combination," he insisted, "or could probably remember it. Not even Tess knows the sequence."

Unless she asks for it, Diana thought. The mind-controlling waif hovered nearby as Burkhoff opened the door. A gust of chilled air whooshed from the refrigerated chamber beyond as the airtight seal was broken. Peering past the threshold, Diana spotted a Class Three biological safety cabinet lodged against the far end of the cramped containment closet. A fan hummed atop the stainless-steel silver cabinet. HEPA filters trapped any harmful bacteria or viruses inside. Rubber gloves attached to ports in the cabinet allowed for manipulation of the enclosed materials. A thin layer of frost covered the transparent view window.

"You see," Burkhoff said defensively. "I've taken every reasonable precaution."

So far, so good, Diana admitted, reassured by the sight of the equipment. Burkhoff seemed to have spared no expense to protect his samples. *We should probably confiscate them anyway.* The samples needed to be in the hands of responsible authorities, not somebody as erratic as Kevin Burkhoff, who meant well but often let his scientific zeal overwhelm his judgment, as when he had experimented on Diana against her will.

She was already trying to figure out how she was going to get the samples away from Kevin, despite Tess's worrisome ability, as he stepped forward to wipe the frost from the window. *Maybe we need to come back later when Tess isn't around?*

A startled yelp escaped Burkhoff's lips. "No!" he gasped, practically pressing his nose against the clear Plexiglas barrier. "It's not possible!"

Diana tensed, alarmed by the anxious sound of his voice. "What is it?"

He spun around to face her. The stricken expression on his face was the last thing she wanted to see. He looked pale as a ghost.

"The samples," he blurted. "They're missing!"

FOUR

RICHARD TYLER COULDN'T SLEEP.

Lying on his bunk, the prisoner stared at the ceiling of his lonely cell. Muted fluorescent light spilled through vertical steel bars from the empty corridor outside. A rangy black man in his mid-thirties, he had worn nothing but an orange prison jumpsuit for months now. His shaved head rested against a lumpy pillow. His dark mustache and goatee were neatly trimmed. Although lights-out had been hours ago, he lay awake listening to the nocturnal sounds of the cell block. Muffled snores and sobs came from the adjacent cages; it seemed like more and more positives were taking up residence in the maximum-security prison every day. Rumor had it that both Collier and The 4400 Center had been lobbying aggressively for the release of Richard and his fellow "political prisoners," but without much results. Richard hadn't even laid eyes on a lawyer since he was apprehended in Seattle months ago. Chances were, he was going to rot in this cell for the rest of his life.

That's what I get for taking on the entire U.S. government, he thought. *Even if they didn't give me much choice.*

Not for the first time, he wondered what his life would have been like if he hadn't been abducted by the future back in fifty-one. When he'd shipped out to Korea, he had certainly never intended to end up behind bars in the twenty-first century. A good part of him wished that those meddlesome time travelers had left him alone. Then again, if he hadn't gone AWOL from his own era, he would have never met Lily . . .

His gaze was drawn to a solitary snapshot taped to the wall. The color photo depicted a beautiful blond woman cradling a grinning toddler on her lap. The little girl's dark skin matched her father's. Both mother and daughter beamed happily.

Lily. Isabelle.

Richard's throat tightened as he recalled taking the photo up at the cabin, back before Lily died and everything went to hell. It had been a beautiful summer day in the mountains. Blue skies. Birds singing in the trees. The snapshot was his sole worldly possession and also his most prized. The precious photo was a reminder that once he had been more than just another inmate, that he had been a loving husband and father. For a brief time, they had been happy.

The dim lighting made it hard to make out his loved ones' faces. Feeling a sudden need to see his family close up, he raised his hand and extended his fingers toward the photo. His mind instinctively reached out for it . . .

Nothing happened. The snapshot stayed taped to the wall several feet away. It didn't even flutter.

Oh yeah. He smiled ruefully. Funny how quickly you could get used to moving things with your mind. And how much you missed the convenience of it once it went away. Daily doses of the inhibitor had done a number on his telekinesis. Where once he could hurl heavy objects just by thinking about it, now he couldn't lift a feather unless he did it the old-fashioned way . . . with his fingers.

Sighing wearily, he got out of bed and started across the cell. The concrete floor felt cold beneath his bare feet. Apparently, the warden wasn't inclined to blow his budget on heating. Judging from the recent quality of the meals, there had been some cost-cutting in the kitchen as well. He didn't want to know what kind of meat was in last night's stew.

He was only halfway to the wall when heavy footsteps echoed in the corridor. They came to a halt right outside his cell. "Whoa there!" a gruff voice challenged him. "What you doing up and about, Tyler? Don't you know it's past your bedtime?"

Richard groaned inwardly as he recognized the voice. Turning toward the door, he saw a pair of uniformed guards, standing on the other side of the bars. And not his favorite guards, either. *Just my luck,* he thought. *Grogan and Keech.*

He had nothing against most of the guards stationed here. They were just doing their jobs. But Grogan and his sidekick were different. They got a sadistic charge out of throwing their weight around and making life harder for the inmates. Petty dictators with a grudge against the 4400. They were the last thing Richard needed tonight.

"Just stretching my legs." He retreated back to his bunk. Hopefully, that would be enough to placate the guards.

It wasn't.

"Is that so?" Grogan taunted him. He was a bull-necked bruiser with a florid complexion and a prodigious beer belly. A handlebar mustache carpeted his upper lip. A crew cut barely covered his scalp. A Colt pistol was holstered against one hip. A billy club rested against the other. He looked Richard over suspiciously. "How do I know that you weren't up to no good, Tyler. Plotting a late-night escape maybe?"

I wish, Richard thought. "I'm not going anywhere."

"Damn right you're not!" He chuckled at his own wit, then glanced at his partner. "You believe the nerve of this guy? Thinking he can put one over on us?"

A scrawny, sallow-faced rodent with greasy black hair, Keech was the Laurel to Grogan's Hardy, except that neither of them was particularly funny. "Lotta nerve," he agreed sourly.

"Hey!" Grogan feigned alarm. "You feel that?"

"Feel what?" Keech asked.

"That pull!" Grogan extracted an electronic keycard from his breast pocket. It wobbled between his meaty fingers as he pretended to have trouble holding on to it. "He's tugging on the key with his brain. Trying to pull us closer."

Very funny, Richard thought, not at all amused by the guard's antics. Of course he was doing nothing of the kind.

"Oh yeah," Keech agreed, playing along. "I feel it now."

He limped toward the door, as though pulled by an invisible force. A sneer twisted his lips. "Cocky sonovabitch."

Grogan unhooked his club from his belt. "Guess we'd better teach him a lesson." Smirking, he ran the keycard through a scanner by the door. An electronic lock clicked open and the barred door slid to one side. Grogan swaggered into the cell, brandishing the billy club. He smacked the truncheon against his palm. "Can't let these freaks think they can pull their tricks on decent folks."

"You got that right," Keech said. He accompanied Grogan into the cell.

Sitting on the edge of his bunk, Richard tensed as the guards approached. His memory flashed back to that time in Korea, right before he was abducted, when a bunch of his fellow Air Force pilots had beaten him to a pulp for daring to date a white woman . . . Lily's grandmother, in fact. This whole scene was feeling way too familiar.

He held up open palms. "Look, I don't want any trouble."

"Who cares what you want, you terrorist freak?" Grogan spat venomously. "Ever since you scum came back from God knows where, nobody in the country is safe. You think we've forgotten about fifty/fifty? Nine thousand Americans are dead because of people like you and Jordan Collier!"

Richard considered pointing out that he'd had nothing to do with the disaster, that he had been locked up in this very cell when the outbreak had ravaged Seattle, but figured that would be a waste of breath. Grogan wasn't interested in listening to reason.

Richard braced himself. Was it worth trying to fight back? He was outnumbered and unarmed.

Grogan spotted the family portrait on the wall. "Well, get a load of this." He yanked the photo from its perch and held it up for Keech to see. "Check out Mrs. 4400 here. Gotta hand it to you, Tyler. You may be a good-for-nothing radical, but you've got fine taste in fillies." He leered at Lily's portrait. "I wouldn't mind getting a piece of that."

"You and me both." Keech licked his lips. "Bet she'd like that, too. Both of us," he spelled out, in case anyone missed the painfully obvious innuendo. "At the same time."

Richard glared at the men. Just seeing Lily's photo in Grogan's grubby hands made his blood pressure spike. "Leave that alone."

"Or what?" Grogan dared him. "You gonna tell Jordan Collier on me?" He ripped the precious photo in half and dropped the pieces onto the floor. "Too bad she's six feet under!"

Redneck bastard! Anger took over and he lunged at Grogan. He only got a couple of steps before Keech smacked him in the side of the head with his club. Richard crashed to the floor, his head ringing. His vision blurred momentarily. He tasted blood inside his mouth.

"You saw that!" Grogan crowed. "The crazy skel jumped me." He savagely kicked Richard in the ribs. "You like that, you stupid freak? Have a heaping helping of self-defense!"

Gasping in pain, Richard tried to scramble to his feet,

but Grogan punched him in the face hard enough to loosen teeth. Blood sprayed from his lips. Keech clubbed him in the back, knocking him facedown onto the floor. The room spun around him.

"Hey!" an irate voice shouted from across the corridor. Lifting his head, Richard spied another prisoner standing behind the door of one of the opposite cells. A muscular Hispanic man with a shaved head, he gripped the bars of his cage. "Leave him alone! He doesn't deserve that!"

The protesting inmate was a new addition to the cell block, having just been incarcerated earlier today. What was his name again? Sanchez?

"Mind your own business!" Keech snarled, but the attention seemed to make him uncomfortable. Backing out of the cell, he played lookout in the hall. He fidgeted with his truncheon. "Okay, that's enough fooling around," he hissed at Grogan. "Let's get this over with."

Grogan reacted as though his crony had lost his mind. "You kidding? I'm just getting warmed up."

"Don't push our luck." Keech looked around furtively. He wiped a sweaty palm on his trousers. "Just waste him, all right?"

The guard's ominous words penetrated Richard's dazed and aching skull. Horror merged with pain. This wasn't just a beating, he realized. *They're out to kill me!*

And there was nothing he could do to stop them . . .

"Okay, okay," Grogan said grudgingly. "Don't have a meltdown." He scowled at Richard, clearly unhappy at having his fun cut short. "Time to say good-bye, Tyler." He ground the fragments of the family photo beneath his heel and drew his pistol from its holster. "Give Blondie a kiss for me when you see her in hell."

He cocked the pistol.

Richard wondered if Lily would really be waiting for him on the Other Side. *We already crossed time to find each other . . .*

"That's enough!" Sanchez yelled from his cell. He shook his fist at the guards. "You ignorant *cabrons* asked for this!"

He punched himself in the jaw . . . hard. His bizarre behavior briefly distracted the guards from their mission of murder. "What the hell?" Grogan muttered. "You gone *loco,* Sanchez?"

Ignoring the guard's inquiry, Sanchez stuck his fingers into his mouth and wrenched a loose molar from his gums. He hurled the bloody tooth through the bars of his cell. It clattered against the hallway floor before cracking apart with a peculiar ring that sounded more like broken porcelain than shattered enamel.

That's not a real tooth, Richard realized. *It's an implant.*

The cracked shell split in two to reveal a miniature sphere of energy, about the size of a pea, that shimmered with a strange unearthly radiance. There was something eerie about the glow emanating from the orb, which didn't resemble light as much as a photo negative of light, casting shadows instead of illumination upon the startled faces of the guards. They stared agape at the flickering sphere. Richard blinked in confusion.

I don't understand, he thought. *What's happening?*

Then the orb unfolded like a flower blossoming in

fast motion. The very fabric of reality seemed to twist and contort before Richard's eyes. A blinding flash lit up the corridor, forcing him to look away. He squeezed his eyelids shut against the sudden glare. Grogan swore obscenely. "Holy crap!" Keech exclaimed.

The flash was over in an instant. But when Richard opened his eyes again, he was amazed to see four strangers standing in the hallway where the orb had been only seconds before. All four—two men, a woman, and a young boy—were dressed entirely in black, like cat burglars or commandos. Ski masks concealed their faces. One of the men was panting hard, like he had just run the marathon. The woman stretched her limbs, as though she had been cooped up in a cramped space for far too long. "Thank God!" she exclaimed. "I couldn't take much more of that."

"What?" the tired man quipped. "Too cozy for you?"

"Shut your mouths!" Grogan barked. Overcoming their shock, the guards drew their sidearms on the intruders. "I don't know who you clowns are, or where you came from, but don't move a muscle!"

The second man, an African-American from the look of him, stared at the guns. "Careful with those." He sounded not at all concerned by the weapons pointed at him. "You're playing with fire."

"Wha—?" Grogan squealed. The metal gun turned red-hot in his grip. Flesh sizzled. Yelping in pain, the guards let go of their weapons. The molten guns crashed onto the floor. Grogan clutched his scalded palm. Keech sucked on his burnt fingers. The men whimpered pathetically.

The black guy turned to the woman. "Your turn."

She obliged by cracking her neck loudly. At first Richard thought she was still stretching, but then the guards clutched their own necks in response. Their faces contorted in shock. They dropped limply to the floor. Grogan landed only inches away from Richard. Only his ragged breathing assured Richard that the unconscious guard was still alive.

Sanchez nodded in satisfaction. He spit a mouthful of blood onto the floor of his cell. He glanced at the boy, who appeared to be no more than twelve years old. "Billy?"

"I'm on it," the kid chirped. A pair of horn-rimmed glasses were fitted over his ski mask. He dashed forward and searched Keech's body until he found the guard's keycard. "Bingo!" Hurrying over to unlock Sanchez's cell, he had to stretch to reach the scanner. "Bet you're anxious to get out of there!"

"You have no idea." The prisoner exited the cell. He gave the boy a friendly slap on the back. "And I hope you never do."

Meanwhile, the woman scooted into Richard's cell. Stepping over Grogan's sprawling form, she helped Richard to his feet. "You okay, Mr. Tyler?"

"I—I think so." His battered brain, which had been coming to terms with death only moments ago, struggled to catch up with events. "Who are you people?"

"Your guardian angels," the woman replied. "Sorry for calling it so close. We just got wind of your danger." She extracted a slender carrying-case from a pocket of her vest. The container opened to reveal a syringe of glowing chartreuse fluid.

Promicin.

She uncapped the tip of the syringe and squirted a droplet from the tip.

"Wait a second," Richard said. "What are—?"

Before he could finish, the woman jabbed the needle into his upper arm. The sharp pain jolted Richard out of his daze. He clutched his wounded arm as she withdrew the needle. "What was that for? I'm already p-positive!"

"Just a booster shot," she explained, tossing the empty hypo aside. "To help you overcome the inhibitor."

Was that possible? *Maybe,* he thought, recalling how a similar shot had woken Shawn Farrell from a coma last year. Richard closed his eyes and concentrated. Was it just his imagination or could he already feel a peculiar tingling at the back of his brain, like a sleeping limb waking up after being inactive too long? His bleary eyes spotted the torn halves of the photo on the floor, and he tried to lift them with his mind. Once again, nothing happened, but the prickling sensation grew stronger. Bending over, he rescued the pieces with his fingers.

He was still trying to figure out where his rescuers had come from. "How . . . ? What was that with the tooth?"

Sanchez gestured toward one of the men. "Adams here can fold space in ingenious ways, enough to fit four people into something way too small to hold them. Like a phony tooth maybe." He massaged his bruised jaw. "Think of it as a Trojan molar."

Was that possible? Richard had trouble wrapping his head around the idea that the entire strike team had been hiding inside Sanchez's tooth. Then again, when you thought about it, how more far-fetched was some of the other stuff he had witnessed over the last few years? Like Isabelle growing from a toddler to an adult overnight? Or Jordan Collier returning from the dead?

"Remind me not to do that again," the woman groused. "I'll never complain about my tiny apartment again!"

"That's enough chatter," Sanchez said, taking charge. He dragged Richard out of the cell. "We need to get you out of here, pronto."

By now, the entire cell block was in an uproar. A blaring siren assaulted Richard's ears. All the lights came back on. Roused by the disturbance, the other inmates rushed to the doors of their cells, pleading to be released as well. They reached through the bars, desperate to get the intruders' attention. "Please!" Orson Bailey called out. The middle-aged businessman was one of the first 4400 to be detained against his will. "Take me with you!"

The frantic cries tugged at Richard's heart. "What about them?"

Sanchez shook his head. "Another time. We're just here for you today. You're not safe here . . . obviously."

Richard couldn't dispute that. His throbbing head and ribs attested to the truth of Sanchez's words. Steeling himself against the piteous entreaties of his fellow inmates, he fell in behind the strike team as they sprinted down the corridor. Adrenaline fueled his legs, despite his recent beating. A heavy steel door, with an unbreakable glass window embedded in its frame, blocked their path. Sanchez tried Keech's keycard, but the door didn't budge.

"Damn," he cursed. "The override's kicked in." He

looked at Adams, who appeared to have recovered from his earlier exertions. "You up to this, man?"

"I can give it a go," the other freedom fighter volunteered. He stepped forward and laid his palms against the steel door. A grunt escaped his lips as he focused his ability on the unyielding barrier, which instantly took on that same photo-negative effect. Solid steel seemed to turn inside out, tearing free from its hinges, as the entire door compacted into a luminous black marble, leaving the doorway open before them. Adams scooped up the marble. He was breathing hard. "Open sesame," he gasped.

They weren't out of the woods yet, though. An entire squadron of guards came rushing toward them, clutching automatic rifles. "Freeze!" a uniformed officer commanded. "Get down on the ground with your hands on your head!"

"Don't shoot!" Billy shouted over the alarms. He rushed to the front of the team. "I'm just a kid!"

The guards hesitated, reluctant to fire upon a child, which was all the time Billy needed. His jaws opened wide and a high-pitched shriek issued from his mouth. The guards staggered backward clutching their ears. Rifles slipped from their fingers. The sonic assault drowned out their screams, but Richard could see how the inhuman wail was affecting them. They flailed about in agony. Even standing behind Billy, with the punishing sound waves directed away from him, Richard got a taste of what the guards were enduring; the echoes pounded against his eardrums. He clamped his own palms over his ears.

The other team members joined the attack. What few guards had managed to hang on to their weapons suddenly found them as hot as blazing coals. The woman cricked her neck again and a handful of guards collapsed onto the ground, like marionettes whose strings had been cut. Adams hurled the glowing marble at the flailing guards. Another blinding flash of light preceded the abrupt reappearance of the massive steel door as it crashed down between the escapees and their pursuers. The uprooted door formed an impromptu roadblock in the narrow corridor.

These people are good, Richard realized, impressed by their obvious skills and teamwork. *The guards didn't know what hit them.*

To his ears' relief, Billy's sonic scream trailed off. The boy turned back toward his teammates. His pride and excitement were visible even through his ski mask. "You see that? What I did to them?"

"Way to go, Billy," Sanchez encouraged him. The team leader hadn't displayed any ability of his own yet; no doubt he had been dosed with the inhibitor, too. He pointed to a corridor on the right. "Now move it, everyone!"

They ran through the prison, past the laundry and exercise rooms. Sanchez definitely seemed to know where he was going, which gave Richard hope that this whole escape attempt had been planned out in detail. But even with his new allies' remarkable gifts, he wasn't sure how they were going to get away from the prison. Blaring alarms chased them down the halls. Emergency lights strobed crimson. By now, Richard figured, every guard on the premises had been mobilized, with reinforcements already en route. If they didn't get past the outer walls soon, he'd be back in his cell in no time.

If I don't get gunned down first . . .

To his surprise, they didn't head for the front gates, but toward the rear of the prison. Still groggy from his beating, he lost track of where exactly they were until Adams warped another locked door out of existence. A cold winter breeze chilled his face as they burst out into the prison's sprawling exercise yard. High concrete walls, topped with razor wire, girded the open area. Watchtowers surveyed the scene from above. The rough pavement made him wish that he had thought to snag his shoes before leaving his cell. *What are we doing here?* He knew every inch of the yard by heart. There was nowhere to go but up.

Floodlights targeted the fugitives. Richard threw up his hands to shield his eyes. "Now what?" he asked Sanchez.

"Wait."

The woman did her neck trick again and the sentries on the walls fainted. Exhausted, she steadied herself against the nearest wall. The rest of the strike team was looking fatigued as well. Billy screamed at the watchtowers, but his voice sounded hoarser than before. Richard wondered what their limits were.

"Look!" Sanchez shouted. "Right on schedule!"

A sleek black helicopter descended from the heavens. Richard was surprised by just how silent the copter's rotors and motor were, and by the total absence of any headlights. He had ridden copters back in Korea, but this kind of stealth technology struck him as astounding even by twenty-first-century standards. If not for the evidence of his own eyes, he wouldn't have even known the copter was approaching.

Who are these people? he wondered again. *And what exactly am I getting into?*

The spinning rotors stirred up wind and dust as the copter touched down in the middle of the yard. An automated door slid open, revealing the passenger compartment, which looked just large enough to transport the entire team plus Richard. He understood why liberating the other inmates hadn't been an option. They would have needed an entire fleet of copters to rescue all the prisoners.

"Our flight is boarding!" Sanchez shouted. "Scramble!" He shoved Richard ahead of him. "We're almost out of—"

A gunshot cut him off in midsentence. A crimson fountain erupted between his eyes and he toppled forward onto the pavement. Blood sprayed Richard's face and chest as he spotted the sniper standing in the doorway behind where Sanchez had just stood. The guard swung his rifle toward Richard.

Acting on instinct, Richard flung out his arm like a conductor leading an orchestra. An invisible wave of telekinetic force slammed into the gunman, sweeping him into the door frame with bone-jarring impact. Richard glimpsed more guards heading for the yard from inside the prison. He bowled them over with another burst of psychic energy. All at once, he felt like his old self again. Clearly, that booster shot had done the trick.

But what about Sanchez? Blood pooled around the team leader's head as he lay motionlessly on the ground. Richard moved to check on him, but the woman restrained him. "It's too late," she said as she tugged urgently on his arm. Violet eyes blinked back tears. "He's gone . . ."

She was right, damnit. As much as he hated to leave Sanchez behind, he let the woman drag him toward the waiting copter. Airborne dust and grit stung his eyes as he clambered into the passenger compartment and strapped himself in, while the rest of the team piled in after him. The copter door slammed shut.

"Everybody set?" The pilot glanced back over his shoulder. A sudden frown dragged down his lips. "Where's Sanchez?"

Richard was startled to see that the man's eyes were clouded over with milky white cataracts. The pupils were fixed and unmoving. *Wait a second,* he thought. *The pilot is blind?*

"We lost Sanchez!" the woman shouted. "Take off . . . now!"

Gunfire and racing footsteps outside the copter added emphasis to her plea. Without argument, the pilot turned back to the controls and instrument panel. The engine emitted a gentle hum. Richard's seat lurched backward as the aircraft noiselessly lifted off from the prison yard. It climbed toward the top of the outer wall. He leaned forward anxiously while, a few feet away, the guy with the thermokinetic ability tried to comfort little Billy, who seemed to be taking Sanchez's death hard. Tears leaked from beneath the boy's glasses as he sobbed loudly. A cloudy night sky beckoned to them, offering the promise of freedom.

I don't believe it, Richard thought. *We're going to make it.*

Bullets thudded into the underside of the copter. Glancing out the window, he saw muzzles flare in the upper windows of the prison. The purr of the motor halted abruptly. The copter dipped alarmingly.

"We've lost power!" the pilot shouted. "We're going down."

No! Richard thought. Visualizing the rotors in his mind, he imagined them spinning fast enough to blur in his imagination. Instantly, the copter leveled off and regained altitude. Cheers erupted from the pilot and surviving team members. The woman tugged off her ski mask, revealing the face of a young Goth chick. Kohl lined her dark eyes. Her frizzy black hair was streaked with blue dye. She gave him a thumbs-up.

The rat-a-tat of automatic-weapons fire swiftly faded away as the copter soared above the watchtowers and ascended into the clouds. Settling back into his seat, Richard closed his eyes and concentrated on keeping the ebony aircraft aloft.

He hoped it wouldn't be a long flight.

FIVE

ORDINARILY, EMERALD HARBORS Cemetery was an island of serenity amid the unrest of Promise City. Marble monuments studded grassy slopes. Carved angels watched over manicured lawns. Weeping willows offered shade in the summer. A wrought-iron fence usually kept the rush and tumult of the outside world at bay.

But not today.

A backhoe noisily tore up the earth in front of Danny Farrell's headstone. The granite marker was inscribed simply BELOVED SON AND BROTHER. An earlier headstone, bearing Danny's full name, had been vandalized in days. Too many angry people still blamed poor Danny for the deaths of their loved ones. His mother's marker, adjacent to his own, now bore only her maiden name: Susan Baldwin.

"You don't have to be here for this," Diana said to Tom as they watched the mechanized hoe carve deep gouges in the earth. Loose dirt spilled onto his sister's grave. The sky was gray and overcast. An industrial crane stood by to lift the casket once it was exposed. Diana spoke softly to her partner. "Meghan and I can handle this."

Tom shook his head. "No. If somebody's messed with my nephew's remains, I want to know about it."

"Well, we're here for you, Tom," Meghan Doyle said. The Pacific Northwest director of NTAC stood beside him, keeping his hand warm. Wavy blond hair tumbled past her shoulders. Smoky walnut eyes shone with compassion. "You know that."

"Thanks," he told both women. "I appreciate it."

Besides the NTAC agents, attendance at the exhumation had been kept to a minimum: a coroner, with no known connections to Jordan Collier or his Movement; the cemetery director; and the actual exhumation team. Shawn had offered to attend, but Tom had assured him that wasn't necessary. He hadn't mentioned the disinterment to Kyle at all. Unfortunately, his son was too close to Collier to be trusted with that information. Tom could only hope that someday there wouldn't be any more secrets between them.

Maybe when the future sorted itself out, one way or another.

A privacy screen had been erected to shield the somber proceedings from view. As it was only seven in the morning, Tom had spotted few visitors wandering the grounds when they'd arrived, but the fence struck him as a good idea anyway. He wondered if Simone Tanaka was spying on them from afar.

Probably.

Once the hoe scooped out the bulk of the topsoil, the

grave diggers went to work with shovels. The men carefully cleared away the last of the dirt to uncover the top of Danny's casket. A crushing sense of apprehension came over Tom as the crane lifted the coffin from its vault. Now that the actual moment was nearly upon them, he wasn't sure he could actually go through with it. Memories of Danny as a child and fresh-faced young man flashed through his brain; Danny had been happy and healthy the last time Tom saw him alive. He swallowed hard.

Meghan gave his hand a reassuring squeeze. "This will be over soon."

Tom wished he could believe that. *Was Dennis just jerking my chain, or are we in for a nasty surprise?*

The crane lowered the coffin onto a waiting tarp. Mud streaked the sides of the mahogany casket, which had lost much of its polished sheen after two months underground. A van waited outside the screened-off grave site to transport the remains to the NTAC's private morgue. The coroner stepped forward to inspect the coffin. Stefan Vakos was a retired heart surgeon, who had been serving as medical examiner since before the 4400 returned. "Perhaps," he suggested, "it would be better to conduct the rest of the examination elsewhere?"

"No," Tom insisted. "Let's get this over with."

"As you wish." Vakos rubbed menthol under his nose. "I should warn you that this won't be pleasant. There is bound to be a strong odor."

"We understand," Diana assured him. As NTAC agents, they were all more familiar than they wanted to be with the ugliness of death and its effects. Over the last few years, they had seen human beings electrocuted, burned alive, and devoured by their own house pets. "Please proceed."

Without any further warnings, the coroner unlocked the coffin. Rusty hinges creaked as he pried open the lid. Tattered lining hung like cobwebs from the bottom of the lid. A sickening stench, like cheese gone bad, emanated from the open casket. Tom gagged and placed his hand over his mouth. The cemetery owner and grave diggers backed away from the coffin. One of the men looked like he was on the verge of throwing up. He scrambled away as fast as he could.

Tom barely noticed his hasty exit. He let go of Meghan's hand.

"Let me," Diana volunteered, but Tom pushed past her to look inside the coffin. He gasped out loud.

The body inside the coffin had wasted away to hair and bones. What little flesh remained was waxy and bluish white in color. The lips had peeled back to expose a death's-head grin. Empty sockets stared blankly from a shriveled face. Mold encrusted a fraying dark suit. But it was the grayish beard that immediately caught Tom's attention. His nephew had been a handsome young man when he died.

Whoever the body in the casket was, it was *not* Danny Farrell.

"Hello, Richard," Jordan Collier said. "Welcome back to Seattle."

The self-proclaimed leader of the 4400 stood before

a large picture window offering a scenic view of Lake Washington. A mane of flowing black hair and a neatly trimmed beard and mustache gave him a distinct resemblance to an earlier messiah with the same initials, a look Richard suspected that Collier cultivated on purpose. The charismatic cult leader had been a successful business tycoon before becoming a revolutionary. As Richard knew from experience, Jordan always had an agenda.

Wonder what he wants from me now? Richard thought. He hadn't been too surprised to discover that Collier was responsible for springing him from prison. Who else had the resources, and the audacity, to pull off an operation like that? Richard approached the other man warily. "Don't you mean Promise City?"

"I see you've been keeping up with current events," Jordan said with a smile. Unlike the tailored three-piece suits he had once sported, his clothing now consisted of plain, loose-fitting garments. Wearing a black frock coat over a white cotton tunic, he looked more an ascetic hermit than the de facto ruler of Seattle. "Good." He gestured toward a nearby couch. "Please, make yourself comfortable."

After smuggling Richard back into Seattle, the strike team had delivered him to this luxurious lake house safely within the borders of the city. The stylish furnishings were clean and modern. Stained wooden trim accented the airy lines of the living room. An Impressionistic painting of a sunrise hung upon a wall near the foyer. A white leather couch and love seat surrounded a clear steel-and-glass coffee table. A carafe of fresh ice water rested on the table. A pair of bodyguards lurked silently in the background. They eyed Richard carefully as he took a seat on the couch. A suit of fresh clothes had replaced his blood-spattered prison garb. His face was still bruised from the beating he had received before being rescued. His ribs throbbed painfully.

"I'm sorry about your man, Sanchez," he said.

"Thank you," Jordan replied. A raspy voice conveyed his sorrow. "That was indeed an unfortunate tragedy. Hector was a good man and a loyal soldier. Building a new world requires sacrifice, however. He was not the first to give his life for our cause. Nor, I fear, will he be the last." He sat down opposite Richard. "But all this heartache and turmoil will be worth it when the Movement fulfills its destiny and brings peace and universal prosperity to the Earth."

Right, Richard thought dubiously. He tried to reconcile Jordan's lofty rhetoric with the ruthless businessman he had first met four years ago. The two men had a long and problematic relationship. Although they had worked together on occasion, Collier had frequently interfered with Richard's life, and had even tried to turn Lily against him once. Richard sat stiffly on the edge of the couch, waiting for the other shoe to drop. "What do you want, Jordan?"

"Just to share some information with you." He glanced around the elegant interior of the lake house. "To be honest, I chose this location for a reason." His face assumed a grave expression. "This is where your daughter died."

The revelation hit Richard like a live grenade. He had been informed in prison that Isabelle had died, but, despite frequent pleas, he had never been able to learn the details of his daughter's passing. Apparently, that was "classified" information. Over the last two months, he had spent countless hours wondering and worrying about what had happened to Isabelle in the end. He hadn't even been allowed to attend her funeral!

"How?" he asked hoarsely. "Who?"

Collier poured Richard a cup of water. "Let me tell you about the Marked . . ."

The story he recounted, about time-traveling conspirators hiding in the bodies of modern men and women, would have sounded unbelievable to Richard only four years ago. But after having his own life manipulated by a different faction from the future, and being physically transplanted from the 1950s to the twenty-first century in a glowing ball of light, he took Jordan's fantastic tale at face value, at least for now. But what did this have to do with his daughter?

"The Marked tried to coerce Isabelle into betraying the Movement," Jordan explained. "When she rebelled against them, they killed her." He let out a deep sigh. "She sacrificed her life to save both me and Tom Baldwin. You should be very proud of her."

"That's really what happened?" Richard asked. Conceived in the future, and catapulted into adulthood overnight, Isabelle had grown into a dangerous and volatile young woman with extraordinary abilities. Although he had always loved her, he had struggled to help her resist her darker impulses. Now he wanted desperately to believe what Jordan was telling him, that his beautiful daughter had found redemption in the end. "She did the right thing?"

"Your daughter died a hero," Jordan insisted. "I was there. I saw it with my own eyes."

Richard was overcome with emotion. He wiped the tears from his eyes. "Did she suffer?"

Jordan shook his head. "Not for long. It was over quickly."

They sat in silence for several moments while Richard processed what he had just learned. He mourned his daughter's death all over again, but found some comfort in the knowledge that she had truly turned her life around first. To be honest, he'd feared that Isabelle had gone bad again and been killed by the authorities in some sort of deadly stand-off, but apparently that wasn't the case. He wished he could tell Lily that their daughter had turned out all right, then realized that she probably already knew that. If there was any justice in the cosmos, his wife and daughter were together once more.

A darker thought occurred to him. His eyes dried and his face hardened. He looked up from the floor. "And the Marked . . . ?"

Jordan nodded, as though he'd anticipated Richard's query. He extracted a loose piece of paper from his breast pocket. "Three of the Marked have been eradicated. This list contains the current identities of the seven remaining Marked."

He handed the paper to Richard, who was startled by the names on the list, which included a presidential advisor, a high-ranking Vatican official, a major Hollywood producer, a wealthy Arab sheik, a five-star general, a Chinese bureaucrat, and a world-famous Tibetan lama.

All extremely powerful individuals. *These* were the people responsible for Isabelle's death?

"Where did you get this from?" he asked.

Jordan's answer surprised him. "Tom Baldwin. Given the Marked's political connections and clout, his hands were tied, so he passed the list on to me so that I could 'take care of' the problem for him."

Take care of? Richard put two and two together. "You want me to dispose of the Marked. Using my abilities."

"I'm not asking you to do anything," Jordan declared, carefully maintaining a degree of plausible deniability. "As a friend, I felt compelled to inform you of the circumstances surrounding your daughter's death and provide you with whatever information I had concerning her murderers." He looked Richard squarely in the eyes. Despite his words, there was no mistaking his meaning. "You're an ex-soldier, you have an amazing ability, and every reason to hate the Marked as much as I do. But whatever you do next is up to you. You're your own man. You always have been."

He got up from the couch. "I'll be heading back to my headquarters downtown. Please feel free to stay here at the lake house for as long as necessary."

He left the list behind.

SIX

"ARE YOU CERTAIN it was the wrong body?"

Bernard Grayson, of Grayson & Son Funeral Home, reacted in shock to the news that a stranger had been found in Danny Farrell's coffin. His gaunt face was composed of sharp, angular planes. A widow's peak met above his high forehead. An austere black suit befitted his profession. He sat behind a large walnut desk as Tom and Diana confronted him with their discovery at the cemetery. Bookshelves lined one wall, while another was occupied by photos of Grayson with various civic leaders and celebrities. The pale blue walls were tastefully muted. Organ music played softly over the sound system. Grayson & Son had handled the funerals of both Danny and his mother.

"Positive," Tom confirmed. "Dental records have identified the body as Delbert Ludden, a homeless man who was killed in the rioting last year, about the same time my nephew died." He and Diana had left their NTAC jackets and vests in the car to avoid attracting attention. "There was no trace evidence that Danny's body ever occupied the coffin."

Diana leaned forward in her seat. "But the coffin did match the one Shawn Farrell purchased from your firm two months ago."

"Oh dear." Grayson dabbed at his sweaty brow with a handkerchief. He glanced at the office door to make sure it was shut. "I can't tell you how mortifying this is. I can only assure you that nothing like this has ever happened before. Grayson & Son has enjoyed a spotless reputation ever since my late father founded the business over thirty years ago." He looked sheepishly at Tom. "You and your family have my profound apologies for whatever went wrong."

Diana kept the pressure on. "Do you have any idea what might have happened?"

"I wish I did," Grayson said. "You have to understand, it was a very chaotic time. The outbreak claimed over nine thousand lives in a matter of days. The city's funeral industry was strained to the breaking point. We were overwhelmed with fatalities." He winced at the memory. "I can only assume that, in the confusion of those dark days, some sort of mix-up occurred." He tugged at his collar. "Again, I'm very sorry for this distressing turn of events."

Tom wanted answers, not apologies. "So where is my nephew's body now?"

"To be honest, I have no idea." Grayson called up the relevant files on his laptop. He hastily scanned the display. "All our records seem to be in order. Your nephew *should* be buried alongside his mother."

Diana asked the logical next question. "Well, where is Ludden's body supposed to be?"

"Let me see." Grayson keyed the vagrant's name into his computer. "According to our records, Mr. Ludden's remains were cremated. The unclaimed ashes were eventually picked up by the city to be buried in the planned memorial park. It's possible they're still in storage somewhere."

Tom didn't buy the mortician's explanations. He distinctly remembered viewing Danny's body in the coffin during the memorial service. Or what had *appeared* to be Danny's body. He tried to figure out how they had been fooled. Shape-shifting? A mass illusion? Astral projection? In Promise City, the possibilities were endless.

"Nice office," Diana commented. Getting up from her chair, she strolled over to the wall, where a framed photo of Grayson posing with Jordan Collier was prominently displayed. She nodded at the portrait. "You a fan?"

Grayson stiffened in his chair. "I believe Mr. Collier is a great man." A wary expression dared the agents to contradict him. "Have you read his book? *4400 and Counting*?"

"I have an autographed copy," Tom said dryly. He wasn't surprised by the man's admiration for Collier. Earlier research had already turned up multiple links between the mortician and Collier's Movement. Grayson & Son seemed to be the preferred funeral home for Collier's followers and their families. They had even handled the funeral of Isabelle Tyler. Granted, Grayson might just be trying to cash in on a lucrative new demographic, but the

Collier connection was suspicious. Maybe the disappearance of Danny's body was no accident?

"I'm afraid we're going to have to search the premises," Diana declared.

Grayson's solicitous manner evaporated. "Why?" he said defensively. "Because I support Jordan Collier and his efforts to make the world a better place? That's not a crime, at least not in Seattle."

"No," she agreed, "but the improper disposal of human remains is. We don't want to press charges, but you'd be better off cooperating with us." She glanced at Tom. "Especially if you don't want my partner pressing a civil suit as well."

Grayson blanched at the prospect, but stood his ground. "I'm afraid I value the privacy of my clients too much to compromise on this issue." He rose from his seat and gestured toward the door. "You're free to inspect the public areas, the viewing rooms and chapel and such, but the prep rooms and crematorium are strictly off-limits. It's a matter of principle."

"Is that so?" Tom said dubiously. The mortician's stubborn defiance, even in the face of prosecution and potential bankruptcy, suggested that he definitely had something to hide. Tom produced a folded document from beneath his jacket. "Thing is, our warrant trumps your principles." He handed the court order, quietly obtained from one of the few judges left in Seattle who weren't under Collier's sway, over to Grayson. "Look it over."

"What?" Flustered, Grayson flipped through the document, before throwing it down onto the desktop. His face flushed with anger. "This is unconscionable!" He reached for his phone. "I need to talk to my lawyer."

Or maybe Jordan Collier?

"Go ahead," Tom said, rising from his chair to join Diana. He wondered if the recalcitrant mortician had expected Collier to shield him from any investigation. "In the meantime, we'll be taking a look around, starting with those off-limits areas you mentioned."

"No! You can't," Grayson protested. Forgetting about the phone, he hurried out from behind his desk to detain them. "I don't understand. What do you expect to find? I promise you, Mr. Farrell's body is not here. Why would it be, after all these weeks?"

"You tell me," Tom replied. The man's vehement objections only increased his determination to search the funeral home from top to bottom. He didn't seriously expect to find Danny's body on the premises, but perhaps they could find some clue pointing to what had become of it. And what, if anything, Jordan Collier had to do with it.

"Tell you what?" The distraught undertaker looked like he was on the verge of pulling out what was left of his hair. He wrung his sweaty hands together. Perspiration beaded on his forehead. "I've got nothing to hide!"

Tom tugged open the door. "Then you've got nothing to worry about. But we're going to need to see that for ourselves."

"And we're going to need that laptop," Diana added. Without asking permission, she confiscated the computer from Grayson's desk. "As well as all your records concerning Danny Farrell, Delbert Ludden, and the rest of the fifty/fifty casualties."

Grayson gazed unhappily at his lost laptop. "But we processed hundreds of victims. Hundreds!"

"Then you'd better get started," Tom said.

He and Diana exited the office, with Grayson trailing anxiously behind them. As it happened, there was a memorial service going on in one of the adjacent viewing rooms. Curious eyes turned to look at the agents. Tom felt a twinge of guilt for causing a disturbance, but they could hardly leave and come back later; that would give Grayson a chance to dispose of any incriminating evidence. They would just have to try to be discreet. *All the more reason to begin downstairs,* he decided.

Bypassing the public areas, they headed for the rear of the house. A tasteful EMPLOYEES ONLY marked a staircase leading down to the basement. A locked door greeted them at the bottom of the stairs.

Tom turned to Grayson, who was standing directly behind him on the steps. "The keys?"

"Forget it," the man snarled. He held out his hands, as though offering to be cuffed. "Arrest me if you want to, but I know my rights. You're not going to get away with this."

Was that a threat? Once again, Tom wondered if Grayson was expecting Collier or his proxies to intervene on his behalf. That could happen, he realized, if the mortician was given a chance to contact his glorious leader. *Which is why we need to get past this door now.*

Calling Grayson's bluff, he pulled out his cuffs. "Watch him," he instructed Diana as he shackled the man's wrists behind his back. The middle-aged undertaker appeared to be unarmed and outnumbered, but who knew what strange ability he might possess. Bernard Grayson was not listed among the 4400, but that didn't mean much. Thanks to fifty/fifty, there were plenty of unregistered positives in Seattle these days. For all they knew, he could spit poison from his eyes or set them on fire with a thought.

Instead, he merely glowered as Tom frisked him for the keys. An encouraging jangle gave away their location. Tom claimed the keys and unlocked the door. "All right, let's find out what you're so determined to hide from us. On principle, of course."

Tom had never been behind the scenes at a funeral home before, but he imagined it couldn't be too different from the morgue back at HQ. A quick scan seemed to confirm his expectations. Partitions divided the basement into three or four interconnected chambers. Refrigerated vaults kept the mortuary's customers on ice. A geriatric corpse was laid out on a stainless-steel embalming table. A modesty cloth, draped over the cadaver's groin, helped preserve its dignity. An embalming machine, filled with a translucent pink liquid, chugged in the background. Metal drains were embedded in the tile floor. Trocars, suture guns, loose tubing, and other tools were scattered atop various trays and counters. Glass cabinets held a variety of chemical concoctions. A white porcelain sink rested against the far wall. Overhead lights glowed brightly. Whirring exhaust fans struggled to clear the air, which smelled faintly of formaldehyde and decay. Open doorways led to adjacent chambers. Peering through a door on the right, Tom glimpsed a large steel furnace with adjustable temperature controls. A metal trolley waited to convey bodies into the cremator. Air-conditioning kept the basement several degrees cooler than the offices upstairs.

Everything seemed in order, if somewhat unsettling, so why had Grayson put up such a fuss?

"Tom," Diana said urgently. "Over here."

She peered though an open doorway into what, at first glance, appeared to be a secondary prep room. He hurried across the chamber to join her. "What is it?"

"Look at this equipment," she said, pointing at an array of expensive-looking apparatus. "Centrifuges, test tubes, Petri dishes, electron microscopes, culture incubators, even a state-of-the-art DNA analyzer. Now I'm no expert, but I'm pretty sure this is not standard issue for the funeral trade." She spun around to confront Grayson, who hovered in the doorway at the foot of the stairs. "What's the story, Mr. Grayson? You branching out into germ warfare or something?"

The shackled mortician glared at the two agents. "I'm not saying anything. This is private property."

"Maybe," Tom said, "but this looks like more than a hobby to me." He surveyed the hidden laboratory. Was that a CAT scanner there in the corner? He wasn't a scientist like Diana, but even he could tell that all this high-tech medical gear had nothing to do with preparing bodies for burial. "We need to take pictures of this entire setup, maybe even get Marco down to scope this out."

Marco Pacella was NTAC's resident boy genius, and head of the Northwest Division's brainstorming "Theory Room." If he couldn't figure out what Grayson was up to with all this equipment, no one could.

"Or, if we trust him, Kevin Burkhoff," Diana suggested. A biohazard label was affixed to a metal cabinet. Peeking inside the container, she found enough promicin to carry an automatic life sentence anywhere except Seattle. The greenish glow of the illegal neurotransmitter spilled out into the lab. "Okay, that's definitely not embalming fluid." She shook her head in bewilderment. "But what does this have to do with your nephew?"

"That's what I want to find out," Tom said grimly. Stepping into the freezer room, his gaze fell on the refrigerated cabinets holding the mortuary's nonbreathing clientele. Handwritten labels, affixed to the ends of the vaults, identified most of the occupants by name. One stack of drawers, however, were labeled only by number. On impulse, Tom grabbed on to the handle of the middle cabinet and yanked open the door. A gust of refrigerated air briefly fogged the air-conditioned atmosphere. A pair of bare feet protruded from the sheeted figure lying within the open cavity. A toe tag bore only a code number: *#11.*

"Wait!" Grayson blurted. "Leave that alone."

You wish, Tom thought. Ignoring the undertaker's protests, he pulled out the slab holding the figure. A thin green sheet concealed the corpse's identity, but the size and build of the body gave him a bad feeling. Bracing himself for a shock, he peeled back the sheet.

Danny's face was pale and lifeless.

"You body-snatching bastard!" Wheeling around, Tom grabbed Grayson by his lapels and threw him against the wall. "What do you want with my nephew?"

Grayson smirked at the angry agent. His eyes gleamed with fervor. "The Great Leap Forward is not complete. Danny Farrell still has a part to play in the grand design, despite his unfortunate demise."

"What the hell does that mean?" Tom tried to shake an answer out of his prisoner. "Talk, you goddamn ghoul!"

"Easy, Tom!" Diana counseled him from behind. "I know you're upset, but don't do something you'll regret."

Talk to Bernard here, he thought. *He's the one who made a big mistake here, by messing with my family.* Tom wasn't sure if Diana was playing good-cop/bad-cop here, or if she was genuinely afraid that he might lose control, but either way he wasn't going to let up until the crooked undertaker spilled his guts about just what was going on here. *It's starting to look like Dennis was on the right track.*

But before Grayson could come clean, Tom caught a flurry of motion out of the corner of his eye. To his alarm, a young man in a lab coat lunged from behind the door at the foot of the stairs. Tom mentally kicked himself for not thoroughly clearing the basement before starting their search; he had let his personal connection to the case undermine his discipline. "Diana, watch out!"

His warning came too late. The nameless employee

snatched a stainless-steel tray from a counter and swung it at Diana's head. The improvised weapon connected with a jarring impact. Diana collapsed face-first onto the tile floor. She whimpered in pain.

"Diana!" He couldn't tell if she was unconscious or not. Letting go of Grayson, he spun around to confront her assailant. He drew his sidearm. "Hands up! Don't move a muscle!"

The gangly teenager snickered at Tom's gun, revealing a mouthful of metal braces. Acne scarred his homely face. Greasy blond bangs dangled before his eyes. Blue jeans protruded from beneath his stained white lab coat. Ignoring Tom's order, he ran over to the embalming table and seized a nasty-looking trocar from a set of tools at the head of the table. The shiny steel needle gleamed beneath the overhead lights. He waved it in front of him like a switchblade.

"Drop it," Tom barked. He leveled his gun at the kid's head. "Now."

"Go ahead," Braces taunted him. "Pull the trigger." He looked past Tom at Grayson. "Bernie, get out of here. I'll take care of these fascist storm troopers!"

The undertaker backed away toward the stairs. "What about you?" he called out to his partner in crime.

"You're more important," Braces insisted. "The future needs you. Go!"

Diana groaned weakly on the floor. Despite his gun, Tom felt the situation rapidly slipping out of his control. "Neither of you is going anywhere. Now put that weapon down." He cocked the Glock semiautomatic. "This is my last warning."

"Oh yeah?" The teen brandished the trocar. "How's this for a warning. Let Bernie go or your partner gets stuck like a pig!"

He stepped menacingly toward Diana. Tom pulled the trigger.

Nothing happened.

"What's the matter, big man?" Braces tapped his cranium with his free hand. "Did I mention that I can dampen chemical reactions at will? Pretty useful in the lab, and even more handy in a firefight. Your gunpowder's no good anymore."

Damn, Tom thought. He heard Grayson scurry up the stairs behind him. Within minutes, the guilty funeral director would be long gone, but chasing after him was not an option. No way was he leaving Diana alone with this guy. The violent teen obviously meant business.

Tom didn't bother trying to fire his gun again. Instead he hurled the useless lump of metal at Braces's head. The teen ducked to avoid the missile and Tom took the opportunity to tackle him head-on. He knocked his opponent backward into the embalming table, jarring the defenseless corpse behind them. His fingers clamped around Braces's wrist to keep the business end of the trocar away from him. Years of FBI training kicked in as he twisted Braces's wrist savagely. The razor-sharp surgical instrument flew from the kid's fingers. It skittered across the floor on the other side of the table.

"Give it up!" Tom snarled through clenched teeth. Even if they had lost Grayson, maybe they could still get answers from this creep. He felt like an idiot for not checking for other employees; they should have guessed Grayson wasn't working alone. "You're coming with us!"

"That's what you think!" Braces spit in Tom's face, momentarily blinding him, then butted his head into Tom's forehead. Starbursts exploded inside Tom's skull and he staggered backward. Braces tore himself loose from Tom's grip and scrambled over the embalming table, knocking the elderly corpse onto the floor. Lifeless flesh hit the tiles like the proverbial bag of potatoes. A plastic screw in the cadaver's abdomen popped open. Embalming fluid squirted from the uncapped puncture wound.

Tom wiped the spit from his eyes and vaulted over the table after his opponent. Braces dived for the trocar, but Tom piled into him first. They tumbled through an open doorway into the cremation chamber. The lab worker fought viciously, biting down hard on Tom's ear, as they grappled on the floor, but the seasoned NTAC agent soon got the upper hand. A kidney jab caused Braces to gasp out loud, releasing Tom's ear, and he clambered on top of the thrashing teenager, pinning him to the ground. He drew back his fist to deliver a knockout punch.

"Wait," Braces squealed. He threw up his hands in surrender. "Give me a second!"

"For what?" Tom demanded. He didn't have time to waste on this punk. *I need to check on Diana.*

"To concentrate, you dope!"

The kid grimaced and squeezed his eyes shut. His bruised forehead furrowed in thought . . . and a sudden wave of weakness washed over Tom. All at once, his fist felt as heavy as a bowling ball. His limbs felt like rubber.

Oh crap, Tom thought. *What's he doing to me?*

He tried to follow through with his punch, but the lackluster blow landed with all the impact of a casually lobbed Nerf ball. His knuckles glanced harmlessly off the teen's chin. Tom's head bobbed limply atop his shoulders. He felt groggy, light-headed.

Braces shoved Tom off him and clambered to his feet. Tom knelt unsteadily on the floor. It was all he could do to stay sitting up. He had never felt so exhausted in his entire life. "Wha . . . what's happening to me?"

"Having a little energy crisis?" Braces mocked him. "That's me shutting down your metabolism. The catabolic reactions that power your muscles are slowing to a crawl. Like the world's worst sugar crash." He sneered at the stricken agent. "It takes a bit of focus, but it sure took the wind out of your sails. Let's hear it for high school biology."

Tom tried to come up with a snappy comeback, but his brain refused to cooperate. He could barely string two thoughts together. He propped both arms against the floor to keep from sliding down onto the cold tiles. Bleary eyes watched as Braces fired up the cremator. Propane ignited inside the fireproof retort. The battered embalmer tugged open a top-loading door to reveal the bright orange inferno inside. Refractory bricks lined the interior of the oven. The heat of the blaze hit Tom like a blast furnace.

Braces clicked on the motorized trolley. A spinning conveyor belt waited to propel a load straight into the mouth of the oven.

"No," Tom gasped. Despite the heat, a chill ran down his spine as he guessed what the teenager had in mind. "You can't . . ."

"Sorry, man, but you brought this on yourself." He came up behind Tom and grabbed him beneath the shoulders. The depleted agent was too weak to fight back. Grunting in exertion, Braces hauled Tom up onto his feet and started dragging him toward the whirring trolley. "You should have left well enough alone."

Tom's heels scraped against the floor. Flames crackled above the steady purr of the motor. The heat from the oven grew more intense with every step. "Wait," he panted. "You don't have to do this. Just leave us here."

"No can do," Braces said. "You've seen too much already. I need to relocate all this gear before any other government goons come looking for you." He swung Tom around so that the agent was facing the trolley. The beckoning inferno scorched Tom's face. The edge of the trolley dug into his waist. He dug in his heels with what was left of his energy.

"Please," Tom pleaded. "Don't . . . this is insane . . ."

"You and your cronies are insane if you think you can stop the future." Braces kept on talking, perhaps to distract himself from what he was about to do. "Ordinarily, I'd load you into a cardboard box first, and make sure to remove all your jewelry and personal effects, but I'm afraid this is going to have to be a rush job." He tried to shove

Tom onto the conveyor belt, while talking up a storm. His hands pressed against Tom's back. "Sorry you're going to miss out on Heaven on Earth, dude. But think of this as a preview of Hell . . ."

Tom grabbed limply on to the sides of the trolley. He felt his feet losing traction with the floor. *This is it,* he feared. *Maybe I should have taken that damn shot after all . . .*

Just when he though it was all over for him, however, Braces shrieked in pain. Letting go of Tom, he staggered backward, swearing obscenely. The discarded trocar had been driven deep into his shoulder by Diana, who stood behind Tom's would-be murderer with a determined expression on her face. Intent on avoiding cremation, Tom hadn't even heard her enter the crematorium.

Apparently neither had Braces.

Blood streamed down the lab worker's back. His concentration lapsed and Tom felt his own energy returning. Both relief and adrenaline flooded his veins. His woozy brain started working again. He stumbled away from the trolley and waiting oven. "Diana," he gasped. "That was a close one."

"Tell me about it." She kept her steely gaze fixed on Braces, who found himself backed into a corner by the two agents. He wobbled atop shaky legs. "You okay, Tom?"

"I think so." He was glad to see his partner back in action. "Thanks for the save. You?"

She massaged her battered skull. "Nothing a little

Tylenol can't cure." She fished her cell phone from her pocket and called for backup. "That's right. Get Garrity here—both of them, ASAP, and somebody round up Marco, too." She put away the phone and nodded at Tom. "Help's on the way."

"You hear that, punk." Tom balled up his fists as he blocked the exit. He felt like he could devour a steak in a second flat, but his vigor was definitely coming back as his body worked overtime to recharge his batteries. "If I were you, I'd start talking now."

Braces gulped. His pimply face contorted in pain as he reached around and yanked the trocar from his shoulders. A crimson flood spurted from the open wound. He looked back and forth between the agents as though weighing his chances against the both of them. Blood dripped from the tip of the weapon. His arm shook like a loose car antenna on the highway. The bruise on his forehead was an ugly shade of purple.

"Don't even think about it," Tom warned him. "Look at yourself. You're losing blood fast. No way you're getting past the two of us."

The kid nervously licked his lips. His trembling arm started to dip.

"You just tried to incinerate a federal agent," Diana reminded him. "Not even Jordan Collier can get you out of that."

Wild, bloodshot eyes reminded Tom of a cornered animal. "I'll never betray the Movement," the teen vowed. "You can't make me talk."

"That's what you think," Tom said darkly.

"No, no . . ." The kid's gaze darted toward the cremator. He took a deep breath. An eerie sense of calm came over him. "I won't give you a chance to break me."

Too late Tom realized what the besieged embalmer had in mind. "No!" he shouted, lunging forward, but Braces had already thrown himself facedown onto the trolley. The conveyor belt sped the suicidal youth straight into the open mouth of the cremator. A fresh burst of heat spilled from the oven as flames engulfed the teenager's flailing body. Flesh and clothing blackened and burned. Skin sizzled and popped. His dying screams were mercifully brief.

"Oh my God!" Diana exclaimed. She placed her hand over her mouth in horror. "What kind of fanaticism inspires a sacrifice like that?"

"Ask Jordan Collier," Tom answered bitterly. Gagging on the stench of burning human flesh, he slammed down the door of the oven to spare them from seeing or smelling any more. The teenager's self-inflicted cremation shook him to his core. Would Kyle do the same to protect his beloved Movement? Tom didn't want to think about that.

Turning their backs on the cremator, they wandered numbly back into the prep room. The sight of Danny's body on the slab hit Tom like a blow to the gut. He stepped over the leaking corpse on the floor. The cool air reeked of chemicals and blood. Death seemed to be closing in on him from all sides.

Diana walked over to the vaults. "Well, we found Danny at least."

"A.k.a. Specimen number eleven," Tom said harshly.

Diana gave the other cabinets a quizzical look. "Wonder who the other specimens are." Curious, she opened the vault directly above Danny and pulled out the drawer. Another sheeted body greeted their eyes. "Let's see who we have here."

She drew back the sheet, then jumped backward in surprise. Tom gasped out loud.

The second body was also that of Danny Farrell.

SEVEN

It was said that when Rome fell, the world would end.

Cardinal Emanuel Calabria knew for a fact that this simply wasn't so. In the distant future he hailed from, Rome was naught but a crumbling ruin, and yet civilization had endured, even after the Catastrophe had reduced most of the planet to rubble. Only one great city remained, walled off from the appalling chaos outside. It was his mission in this benighted era to make sure that mankind's last city—*his* city—came to pass.

Despite the infernal meddling of the enemy.

The so-called Eternal City was spread out before him as he dined at an outdoor ristorante on the Vialle Trinita dei Monti, overlooking the famed Spanish Steps. Twilight painted purple shadows atop the rose-colored roofs of the sprawling metropolis below. Jaywalkers darted across the street, deftly dodging scooters and taxis. The cardinal's table occupied a narrow sidewalk in the shadow of a looming sixteenth-century church. The grandest and widest staircase on the Continent, the Spanish Steps were flanked by shuttered mansions and palaces. Terraced gardens and flower pots adorned the steps. Throngs of tourists, dating couples, and would-be artists and photographers crowded the piazza at the top of the steps, enjoying a warm January evening. Palm trees swayed the breeze.

A somber black cassock, with scarlet piping and buttons, denoted the cardinal's elevated rank within the Church. A pectoral cross hung on a chain atop his chest. A scarlet sash girded his rotund torso. A red cap covered silvery tresses. A jowly face, with a pronounced double chin, testified to his healthy appetite.

Calabria washed down a bite of *spaghetti alla pescatore* with a sip of white wine. The Frascati was a good vintage that complemented the pasta divinely. He savored another morsel of sauce-drenched calamari. At moments like this, he was thankful to have been assigned this particular identity. Despite the tiresome burdens imposed on him as a high priest of this primitive religion, there were undeniable advantages to being stationed in Rome. For one thing, it was almost impossible to get a bad meal.

A shame the city was destined to be destroyed many generations from now, but so it went. History demanded its sacrifices, at least if his own future was to be preserved. The cardinal, or rather the time-traveling intelligence that had made itself at home in Calabria's squat, middle-aged form, pined briefly for the shining city he and his fellow Marked had left behind, which they would sadly never see again. Alas, their pilgrimage to the twenty-first century had been a one-way trip. They were stuck in this volatile era for the rest of their natural lives.

But at least the food was good.

"Excuse me, Your Eminence?" A pretty young waitress approached his table. Her nubile charms made him regret that, at least in public, he was constrained by an oath of celibacy. The worried look on her face suggested that she had more on her mind than simply refilling his water glass. "I'm sorry to disturb you, but might I ask you for some spiritual guidance?"

Two tables over, his bodyguards sat up at attention. Members of the Vatican's elite Swiss Guard, they wore civilian garb to better blend into the background. They eyed the impertinent waitress suspiciously. These were dangerous times, and the cardinal was not without enemies. Indeed, as prefect of the Congregation for the Doctrine of the Faith, formerly known as the Holy Office of the Inquisition, Calabria was the Vatican's most outspoken critic of the "false religion" of Jordan Collier. The congregation's recent pronouncement that promicin use could be considered a mortal sin had spawned headlines, and controversy, throughout the entire world. Small wonder his guards were so jumpy. Calabria had received numerous death threats from Collier's outraged acolytes.

Still, he discreetly waved the overeager guardsmen back. He had lived as Cardinal Calabria long enough to recognize a devout Catholic when he saw one; the only threat the girl posed was to his pretense of chastity. He snuck a peek down her generous cleavage. "How may I help you, child?"

"My friends and I have been talking, about the news

from America. The whole world seems to be changing, in a very scary way, and I can't help wondering . . ." She took a deep breath before getting to the heart of the matter. "Do you think that Jordan Collier might be the Antichrist?"

Calabria repressed a smile at the girl's obvious anxiety. Clearly, his labors in the fields of the faithful were bearing fruit. Concealing his glee, he responded to her superstitious query with feigned gravity. "The Holy See has yet to render a final verdict on this vexing issue, but I fear that your suspicions may be well-founded. There is something truly disturbing about this man's rise to power, and his blasphemous promise to personally usher in the Kingdom of God. If not the Beast himself, he is surely a false prophet, and the unnatural gifts of his followers may well have demonic origins."

The girl's face grew pale as she hung on his every word. Watching her trembling grip on the water pitcher, Calabria began to fear for the safety of his spaghetti.

"But do not despair, my child. This evil cannot triumph, not if we strengthen our souls against the godless temptations of promicin. As long as the Church can rely on the prayers and actions of good people like you, this profane movement shall not lure God's children away from salvation."

His words seemed to comfort the waitress. She nodded eagerly, and bent to kiss his ring. "Thank you, Your Eminence. I know I'll sleep better now."

He rose clumsily from his seat and bestowed a blessing upon her. "Now then, perhaps I can see a dessert menu?"

"Yes, Father, of course!"

Covertly admiring the girl's backside as she scurried away, he returned to his meal with a definite sense of accomplishment. His encounter with the credulous waitress encouraged him to think that, despite their recent reverses, he and his fellow operatives still had a chance to turn back the tide and prevent Jordan Collier from changing the future. His elevated position at the Vatican gave him influence over literally millions of gullible twenty-first-century primitives, and he aspired to even greater power. Cardinal Emanuel Calabria had come in third in the last papal election, after all, and the current pontiff would not be around forever. If all went according to plan, Jordan Collier's dangerous ambitions might well disappear in a puff of white smoke . . .

In the meantime, though, best to be on guard. He nodded at his attentive bodyguards, grateful to have them watching over him. Promise City was many thousands of miles away, but he could not afford to get overconfident. Three of his fellow operatives had already been exterminated, and Collier's reach was growing by the day. Glancing around the teeming piazza, he suddenly felt uncomfortably exposed. Perhaps he should not have left the tight security of the Vatican?

His guards had actually argued against this outing, in light of the recent threats, but Calabria had overruled their caution. Sometimes he just had to escape the suffocating sanctimony of Vatican City and breathe a little fresh air. Besides, this particular *ristorante* was one of his favorites.

The enticing aroma of the spaghetti reminded him

of his appetite. Stabbing a fat piece of mussel with his fork, he lifted it to his lips. As he started to bite down on it, however, his eyes widened at the sight of a tall black man emerging from the Metro station across the street. Something about the man's brooding features jogged his memory, but it took him a second to put a name to the face. *I know that man. He's . . .*

Richard Tyler!

His heart skipped a beat. Tyler's daughter, Isabelle, had been intended to be the Marked's ultimate weapon against the 4400, before that operation went badly awry. His contacts in the States had informed Calabria of Tyler's recent escape from prison, but Rome was the last place he had expected the fugitive American to show up. The cardinal realized at once that this could not be a coincidence.

Their eyes met across the busy street. Tyler's face was grim and unforgiving. Calabria opened his mouth to alert the guardsmen, but, before he could get a word out, the greasy mussel leapt from his fork and, like a thing alive, jammed itself into his windpipe. Choking, he coughed and clutched his throat, but his convulsive efforts failed to dislodge the meaty obstruction, which seemed to be held in place by an invisible force. *Tyler's doing this,* the cardinal realized. *He's out to avenge his daughter's death!*

One of the guards, a strapping blond private named Buchs, raced to Calabria's aid. Yanking the thrashing victim off his seat, Buchs applied the Heimlich maneuver to no avail; the murderous mussel refused to budge. His face turning purple, Calabria pointed frantically at Tyler. "It's him!" he managed to gasp. "With his mind . . ."

The other guardsman, Roest, got the message. Drawing a SIG P225 automatic pistol from beneath his jacket, he took aim at Tyler. An unseen force yanked his arm upward and he fired uselessly into the sky. A second later, the gun was ripped from his fingers. It arced over the Spanish Steps before splashing down in the Baroque fountain at the base of the steps. The startled soldier yelped in surprise.

Pandemonium erupted along the street and upon the nearby steps. Terrified diners dived under their tables. Panicked tourists and artists ran for cover. Screams disturbed the tranquil winter evening. Only Richard Tyler remained immobile, standing motionlessly across the street. His dark eyes remained fixed on his suffocating target. His stony expression held no hint of mercy.

It's not fair, Calabria thought. Unfortunately, the process of implanting a mind into another body left the Marked unable to acquire preternatural abilities of their own. Darkness began to encroach on the cardinal's vision. His jowly face took on a bluish tint. *I can't fight back!*

Abandoning his futile efforts to perform the Heimlich, Buchs snatched a knife from Calabria's table setting. The choking cardinal realized in dismay that the desperate bodyguard intended to perform an emergency tracheotomy, minus anesthesia. Calabria braced himself for the pain, but he needn't have bothered; like the other soldier's gun, the knife flew from Buchs's fingers.

The man reached for his gun, only to lose that as well. Gasping for breath, the cardinal couldn't help being impressed by how many objects Tyler was able to manipulate at once. The man had obviously mastered his telekinetic abilities.

"Get him!" Buchs shouted at Roest. Taking the fight directly to the enemy, the unarmed guards charged across the street at Tyler. Horns honked and brakes squealed as the soldiers fearlessly braved the traffic. An artsy-looking student on a green Vespa scooter swerved frantically to avoid the men, and came skidding to a halt only a few meters away from Calabria's table. The youth's eyes bugged out at the chaos in front of him.

Tyler waved his arm and the attacking guards were swept off their feet, as though by a powerful wind. Flailing helplessly, they tumbled down 138 flights of steps before crashing onto the piazza below. Calabria abruptly found himself without defenders.

Or maybe not. Unexpectedly, the pretty waitress from before came dashing from out of nowhere. "Demon!" she hissed as she flung a glass of red wine into Tyler's face. She hurled herself at the startled 4400, kicking and scratching. "Leave the holy father alone!"

The attack broke Tyler's concentration. The stubborn mussel burst from Calabria's lips and he found he could breathe again. Hungrily sucking up huge mouthfuls of air, he lurched away from the table, knocking it over in his haste. China and glassware crashed down onto the sidewalk. Pasta and seafood spilled across the pavement.

The fleeing cardinal couldn't care less about the mess. He needed to get away while he still had a chance!

But time was already running out. Tyler quickly recovered from the girl's assault. Showing admirable restraint, he telekinetically lifted her off her feet and tossed her onto the canvas awning over the restaurant's entrance. A bright red stain soaked the front of his shirt. Scratch marks streaked his face. He wiped the wine from his eyes and looked for Calabria.

The cardinal drew a gun of his own from beneath his cassock. He carried the Beretta with him everywhere, even to Mass. Shaky fingers fumbled too long with the safety. The pistol was painfully wrenched from his hands. It flew straight into Tyler's waiting grip.

Mannaggia! Calabria swore. What he wouldn't give right now for a palm-sized neural disruptor! Just his luck they wouldn't be invented for another hundred years, and had proved impossible to replicate with mere twenty-first-century materials.

Deprived of a weapon, escape was his only recourse.

Unlike the rest of the crowd, who were fleeing the area in droves, the student with the scooter lingered to take in the action. Desperate to get away, Calabria dragged the youth off the Vespa and claimed the scooter for himself. His black cassock tangled about his legs as he hastily climbed onto the seat. White knuckles gripped the handlebars. He hit the gas.

If I can just put enough distance between myself and Tyler, get out of range of his ability . . . !

The scooter's rear wheel spun furiously, but the vehicle

didn't go anywhere. Calabria fumbled with the controls, trying to figure out what he was doing wrong, then realized that the problem wasn't with the Vespa. He glanced back over his shoulder to Tyler glaring at him. The vengeful 4400 held on to the scooter with his mind.

Calabria understood that he wasn't going anywhere.

"No," he pleaded. "You've got the wrong person." He saw his life as Emanuel Calabria coming to a rapid end. He could only hope that his allies from the future would find him a new host after they recovered the nanites containing his personality. "I had nothing to do with your daughter's death . . ."

Richard just stared at the other man. Calabria wondered what he was waiting for.

"You're looking the wrong way," a voice called out, speaking Italian with an American accent. Calabria spun his head around to see another black man step out from beneath the awning of a nearby café. He was younger and stockier than Tyler, but had the same grim expression. He furrowed his brow. His eyes narrowed in concentration. "Say your prayers."

The scooter's handlebars suddenly grew hot to the touch. The temperature gauge on the dashboard flashed red. Steam rose from the engine mounted behind Calabria. He crossed himself out of sheer force of habit.

The Vespa exploded beneath him.

Richard watched the fireball engulf the Marked cardinal and his hijacked vehicle. He threw up his hands to protect his face from the heat and glare while simultaneously enclosing the explosion in an invisible bubble to keep any bystanders from being injured by flying shrapnel. Bright orange flames shifted to white-hot as his partner, Yul Lacey, used his thermokinesis to make sure every last inch of Calabria's body was consumed. It was vital to make sure all the microscopic machines in the cardinal's brain were destroyed; otherwise the Marked could just implant his consciousness in another innocent host.

Or so it had been explained to him.

A twinge of guilt pricked his conscience. Although he had piloted bombers in Korea, he'd never killed anyone in cold blood before.

This was for Isabelle, he reminded himself.

Sirens blared from all directions, growing louder by the second. A police car squealed to a halt a few yards back from the burning scooter. Officers in blue uniforms poured out of the car. Shielding themselves behind their vehicle, they drew their guns on Richard and Yul. *"Fermate!"* a tense-looking cop ordered.

Richard flexed his mental muscles. There had been a time, when he was first discovering his abilities, that he could only lift a few small objects at a time, but that was a long time ago. He effortlessly threw the men backward. They scattered like bowling pins as they went rolling down the street. Up on the awning, the heroic waitress wailed in despair.

Enough, Richard thought. They had done what they had come to do. Now he just wanted to get out of here. *Where's our ride?*

As if on cue, a sleek black Porsche came speeding onto the scene from the opposite direction of the cops. The sports car pulled up to the curb. The passenger side door swung open. The young Goth chick, Evee Borland, called out to the two men. "You guys done here?"

Richard questioned Yul with a look.

"He's toast," the other man said, referring to Calabria.

"And the nanites?" Richard asked.

"Nothing but slag."

That was good enough for Richard. They piled into the Porsche, which drove up onto the sidewalk to execute a tight U-turn before accelerating back toward their safe house in Trastevere. Police cars and fire trucks, their emergency lights flashing, raced past them as they left the cardinal's scorched ashes behind. Richard slumped back into the passenger seat while Nicole and Yul congratulated themselves on the success of their mission. They had been shadowing Calabria for hours, with the help, ironically enough, of a clairvoyant nun who was one of the original 4400, just waiting for their designated target to leave the safety of the Vatican. Tonight all their efforts had paid off.

So why don't I feel more euphoric? Richard wondered. His face stung where the Italian girl had scratched him. Unlike his new comrades, he felt more deflated than elated by tonight's events. Vengeance turned out to have a bitter aftertaste. He couldn't help remembering that the real Emanuel Calabria had perished along with the insidious invader occupying his body. He wished there was some way to free the innocent victims of the

Marked instead of simply killing them, but, according to Collier, that was not the case. The only way to eliminate the threat of the Marked was killing them along with their hosts. Richard sighed at the bloody road ahead of him.

One down. Six more to go.

EIGHT

Marco popped into the morgue—literally.

One minute the tardy genius was nowhere to be seen. The next, he suddenly appeared between Tom and Diana as they waited for him in NTAC's private medical facility. Floppy brown hair needed combing. Intelligent brown eyes peered out from behind a pair of horn-rimmed black glasses. He wore a tweedy jacket over a faded concert T-shirt. "Sorry I'm late."

"Marco!" Diana blurted, startled by his abrupt manifestation. She clutched her chest to quiet the racing of her heart. "You know you're not supposed to do that. Especially not at work."

The endearingly nerdy analyst had gained the ability to teleport after surviving fifty/fifty. Pretty much everyone at NTAC knew what he could do, but public displays of promicin abilities were strongly discouraged. Diana shook her head in disapproval. Marco knew better than to 'port around like that. What if some higher-up from D.C. was visiting?

"I know," he admitted. "But it's just so convenient. And I didn't want to keep you folks waiting." He glanced around the sterile, stainless-steel morgue. "So what did I miss?"

"Just the usual weirdness," Diana said.

In total, they had found four identical copies of Danny Farrell's body at the funeral home. All four specimens were now laid out on autopsy tables in the center of the morgue. Clean white sheets partially covered the bodies. If there was any way to tell the cadavers apart, Diana sure couldn't see it. She could only imagine how disturbing this was for Tom. Suppose these were four identical copies of Maia . . .

"What's the story?" he asked gruffly. "Which one is the real Danny?"

"None of the above," Abigail Hunnicutt replied. The twenty-something blonde had joined Marco's Theory Room team shortly before fifty/fifty. A graduate of MIT, she stood beside one of the bodies, her ungloved fingers splayed across its chest. The outbreak had turned Abby into a human DNA sequencer who could "read" genetic codes without the aid of artificial equipment. She wiped her hands on a blue lab coat as she reported her findings. "These specimens are almost-but-not-quite genetic duplicates of Danny Farrell. About ninety-nine percent identical to the real thing."

"Clones?" Marco speculated.

Abby shook her head. "More like Danny's DNA has been superimposed on someone else's." She struggled to put what she was sensing into words. "There's still an 'echo' of the original DNA left in the cells. My guess is that somebody is trying to turn other people into perfect twins of Danny . . ."

"Before or after they're dead?" Diana wondered.

"Good question." Abby shrugged her shoulders. "I can't tell from the DNA."

A preliminary examination had suggested that all four bodies had died from an overdose of promicin, not unlike the real Danny, who had been suffering from a massive buildup of promicin in his system before his brother euthanized him. Perhaps full autopsies would turn up more info, but Diana had her doubts. They were way beyond conventional forensic science here.

"But why would anybody want to do something like this?" Tom asked. Although he was holding it together, his obvious frustration frayed at his voice. He clenched his fists. "Why couldn't they just let my nephew rest in peace?"

Marco scratched his chin. "You said you found promicin at the mortuary? My guess is that someone is trying to duplicate the process that turned Danny Farrell into the 'Typhoid Mary' of promicin, creating a living biological weapon capable of spreading the fifty/fifty effect everywhere he goes." His eyes widened behind his glasses. "Maybe even an army of carriers . . ."

A hush fell over the morgue as the ghastly implications of what Marco was saying sunk in. One Danny had nearly destroyed Seattle. A legion of Danny clones could cause untold death and devastation.

"Someone like who?" Diana asked, breaking the silence. "Jordan Collier?"

"Let's find out," Tom said.

* * *

The downtown skyscraper that now served as Collier's new headquarters was the old Haspelcorp Building, an irony that surely amused Collier. A huge canvas portrait of the new messiah, many stories high, adorned the outer façade of the structure. Smaller portraits hung inside the palatial lobby.

Talk about a cult of personality, Tom thought. The ubiquitous posters reminded him uncomfortably of Maoist China and other authoritarian regimes. *Wonder when the fifty-foot statues start going up?*

"Can I help you?" a security guard addressed the agents as they entered the lobby. The elderly sentry, who appeared to be in his sixties, was not very physically imposing, but he didn't need to be; as a positive, he no doubt had other ways to repel unwanted visitors. He sat behind a high marble desk. A name badge identified him as HOYT.

More guards were stationed by the elevators, stairwells, and fire exits. Collier was obviously taking no chances with his security. Tom couldn't blame him. Despite all of the Movement's philanthropic efforts, plenty of people still blamed Jordan for fifty/fifty and the deaths of their loved ones. He had already survived several assassination attempts.

Diana flashed her badge. "NTAC. We're here to see Jordan Collier."

The guard looked unimpressed. Tom and Diana were frequent visitors. He peered at the slender brunette accompanying the two agents. Her dark eyes glinted impishly. A tailored Burberry Prorsum jacket testified to a generous clothing allowance. Expensive perfume wafted from the petite young woman, who looked to be in her early thirties. A dollar sign was tattooed upon her wrist.

"What about her?" the guard asked.

April Skouris was Diana's black-sheep younger sister. A former tattoo artist and con woman, April had been one of the first people reckless enough to take a promicin shot when Jordan made them available to the masses. Her newfound ability to compel people to tell the truth had eventually landed her a cushy job working for both NTAC and the FBI. Tom frankly found her a little off-putting, but if she could help them pry some answers out of Collier regarding Danny's remains, he was willing to borrow her for this visit.

"I'm NTAC, too," she boasted, proudly displaying her own ID. After growing up in the shadow of her more accomplished older sister, she seemed eager to point out that they had achieved parity at last. "April Skouris, agent-at-large."

"Uh-huh." Hoyt lethargically keyed her name into his computer. A frown deepened the heavy creases around his mouth. "Sorry. You're on the black list. No access allowed."

"What?" Instant indignation colored her voice. "Who says?"

"I don't know," he confessed automatically. He couldn't have lied if he'd wanted to. "The computer just says so. You've been flagged as a security threat."

"Crap! This is completely unfair!" She looked to Tom

and Diana for support. "Are you going to let them get away with this?"

"I guess so," he admitted. NTAC operated in Seattle only at Collier's sufferance. They were in no position to throw their weight around. "Guess you need to wait in the car."

"Are you serious?" She raised her voice and all but stamped on the floor. "Diana," she whined, sounding more like a bratty kid sister than a government agent. "Do something!"

Her outbursts attracted the attention of the guard by the elevator, who crossed the lobby to investigate. He was a tall, hatchet-faced man with a light brown brush cut. Besides his unknown abilities, the guard was armed with a pistol and stun gun. GALLOWAY, read his name tag. His hand rested ominously on the grip of his sidearm. "Is there a problem?"

"No," Diana insisted. "Just a misunderstanding." She spoke softly to her sister. "I'm sorry, April, but Collier has blocked us here. And we really need to speak with him today." Taking the other woman's arm, she guided her gently toward the exit. "Why don't you head back to headquarters. Maybe we can talk later."

"Fine," April said petulantly. She yanked her arm free and headed for the door. "See if I ever volunteer to help you guys again. Thanks for nothing, sis."

She stormed out of the building. Part of Tom was relieved to see her go. Despite her occasionally useful ability, she was a real loose cannon. Plus, there was something distinctly unsettling about being around someone who could make you tell the truth whether you wanted to or not. He still cringed when he remembered the time April had mischievously forced him to reveal a sexual fantasy about his partner, right in front of Diana, no less!

No wonder so many people wanted nothing to do with the 4400 and their successors.

With April gone, the guards backed off a little. Hoyt called upstairs, then put down the phone. "All right. You can go up now. Jordan is expecting you."

To Tom's slight annoyance, Galloway accompanied them as they took the elevator to the top floor. He would have liked to confer privately with Diana on the way up, but apparently that wasn't going to happen. *Oh well, the elevator's probably bugged anyway.*

They found Collier in Dennis Ryland's old digs. A large executive desk dominated the corner office. Magazine covers bearing Jordan's visage were framed upon the walls, along with the book jacket from his *New York Times* bestselling manifesto. Twenty-foot-high picture windows offered a breathtaking view of Elliott Bay and Harbor Island beyond. Along with a handful of aides and bodyguards, Jordan was busy overseeing holographic 3-D blueprints of Seattle. Shimmering translucent structures rose and fell across the surface of a high-tech conference table, no doubt devised by some nameless technological wizard whose brainpower had been boosted by promicin. He looked up from the laser-generated models as Galloway escorted the agents into the office.

"Ah. Tom. Diana," he said cordially. He stood a head

taller than either of the two agents. "Good to see you again."

Tom was disappointed not to find Kyle present. Then again, perhaps that was just as well. This wasn't a social call.

"Thank you for seeing us," Diana said. "Hope we're not disturbing you."

"Not at all," Collier insisted. A sweeping gesture called their attention to the virtual cityscape before him. "Come see what we're doing here." He beckoned them over. "It's a comprehensive plan for rebuilding Seattle. Structures destroyed during the rioting are to be replaced by cold-fusion power plants, addiction treatment centers, vertical farms and gardens, and other revolutionary civic projects made possible by the singular abilities of the city's promicin-positive population." He smiled proudly. "We're even upgrading the Monorail."

"Looks ambitious," Tom conceded. As much as he hated to admit it, Collier and his Movement had been in the forefront of the recovery efforts over the last few months. He looked more closely at Jordan's vision for the city. "Is that a new courthouse down by Pioneer Square?"

"Good eye." Collier nodded. "State of the art."

"But whose courts?" Diana challenged. "The state's or yours?"

Since taking over Seattle, Collier has established his own shadow judicial system, in which positives who were found guilty of abusing their abilities were stripped of their powers by Jordan himself. Diana's acerbic tone made it clear that she disapproved of Collier running his own private kangaroo courts.

"In time, there will be no difference," Collier stated confidently. "For now, however, the 4400 can hardly expect fair treatment in the regular courts, which means that we have to police ourselves. I assure you, this is a responsibility I take very seriously." The ability to erase other positives' gifts was Collier's own unique talent. "I wish every individual with an ability could be trusted to use it responsibly, and in the best interests of the Movement, but, alas, that's not always the case. Some new converts prove unworthy of their precious gifts."

"Like my sister?" Diana asked.

Collier took a deep breath as he braced himself for the inevitable topic of April. "Ah yes. I heard there was some unpleasantness downstairs. My apologies if that was awkward for you, but I'm afraid that, no offense, your sister's loyalties and associations are suspect. She is indeed banned from the premises." His tone edged toward threatening. "In fact, you should inform her that I will personally rid her of her ability if she gets anywhere near me or otherwise attempts to use her gift to undermine the Movement."

"Why is that?" Tom demanded. "What have you got to hide?"

Collier was unapologetic in his attitude. "Surely you, as a government agent, appreciate the importance of discretion and confidentiality. Loose lips sink ships, and all that. These are dangerous times, and I'm not going to let April Skouris—or anyone else—endanger our security."

Tom wondered how Jordan had learned about April's ability in the first place. That was supposed to be classified information, too. Was there a leak at NTAC or Homeland Security?

Something to think about, he thought.

"Now then," Collier said, changing the subject. "What brings you here today? Official NTAC business, I assume."

"That's right." Tom gave Jordan the bare bones of their investigation, mentioning Danny's missing body, and Grayson & Son's apparent involvement, but leaving out Dennis Ryland's accusations regarding Collier's alleged plans to weaponize promicin. "You know anything about this?"

Collier shook his head. "I wish I could help you. Your nephew is revered as a martyr to the Movement by my people. It's shocking that someone would desecrate his memory in this fashion. I can't imagine anyone here having anything to do with it."

"So you're denying any connection to Bernard Grayson?" Diana asked.

Collier shrugged. "The name sounds vaguely familiar, but the Movement has been growing by leaps and bounds since the Great Leap Forward. I'm afraid that an encyclopedic knowledge of everyone who supports our cause is not among my gifts." He smiled wryly. "More's the pity."

Tom pressed harder. "So you'd have no interest in trying to replicate the airborne version of promicin that Danny emitted?" He let a touch of sarcasm creep into his voice. "Even though that would bring about your glorious new world a little faster?"

Collier appeared unruffled by the accusation. "I don't

deny that I want everyone in the world to take promicin. But I've never forced the shot on anyone . . . as you know from personal experience, Tom."

True enough, he thought. Jordan had certainly had more than one opportunity to inject Tom against his will, but had always refrained from doing so, despite the prophecy claiming that it was vitally important that Tom take the shot at some point. But was Collier's restraint due to his ethical standards, or just out of deference to Kyle's importance to the Movement? Tom was inclined to suspect the latter.

"Fifty/fifty wasn't exactly voluntary," Diana pointed out. "None of those people chose to take promicin."

"But that was not my doing." He washed his hands of any responsibility for the disaster. "That was simply a monumental twist of Fate. An act of God, if you will."

Tom doubted that Heaven had anything to do with killing nine thousand innocent people, and shattering the lives of countless more. "I don't think God stole Danny's body."

"Indeed," Collier said. "And I hope you find whoever is responsible. I give you my sincere promise to look into this matter."

Tom didn't find that terribly reassuring.

Collier glanced at his watch. "Is that all?" he asked impatiently. "At the risk of being rude, I have a very busy schedule today." He tapped a control on the drafting table and the holographic city evaporated. "Transforming the world is a full-time job."

"I'll bet," Diana said dryly.

Jordan scowled. "Give my regards to your daughter." He moved to escort them to the door.

"Not so fast," Tom said. He locked eyes with Collier. "You and I have something else to discuss. Alone."

He rubbed his finger behind his ear.

Collier got the message. "Very well." He turned to his people. "Agent Baldwin and I need the room."

His guards hesitated, clearly reluctant to leave their leader alone with Tom. "Sir?"

"It's all right," Collier assured them. "I have nothing to fear from Agent Baldwin." He eyed Tom warily. "Do I, Tom?"

"I saved your life a while back, didn't I?"

With the help of Isabelle Tyler, Tom had rescued Collier from the Marked during fifty/fifty. If not for the agent, Jordan himself would be one of the Marked now. And sabotaging the very Movement he had devoted his life to.

"So you did." Collier ushered his retinue out into the hall. "Take five, everyone."

Diana shot Tom a puzzled look. He hadn't discussed this with her in advance. "Tom?"

"Just give me a couple of minutes, Diana."

Looking a tad uneasy, she left the office as well. Jordan waited until the door clicked shut behind her before settling down into an executive chair behind Dennis Ryland's old desk. His fingers were steepled before him as he assumed a contemplative pose. "Well? What's on your mind, Tom?"

The cautious agent worried for a moment about hidden cameras or mikes, then decided that Collier wouldn't want any record of this discussion, either. "You know what this is about. The assassination of that cardinal in Rome." His blood pressure rose as he remembered reading on the Internet about Calabria's fiery demise. "Damnit, Jordan. You were supposed to *cure* that man, not kill him!"

It wasn't easy, but it was possible to free the Marked from the invaders who had taken over their minds. Tom was living proof of that. A lethal dose of radioactive polonium, injected directly into his spine, had burned out the nanites infesting his brain. Then Shawn had used his healing ability to ensure that Tom survived the ordeal. The experience had nearly killed Tom, but, when it was over, he had been himself again. The cure had worked.

Just like it had with Collier.

"First off," Jordan began, "you're leaping to the assumption that I had something to do with the late Emanuel Calabria's unfortunate accident." He held up a hand to forestall Tom's indignant rejoinder. "It may well be that Cardinal Calabria was on the wrong scooter at the wrong time."

Tom slammed his fist down on the desktop. A crystal paperweight, in the shape of a glowing ball of light, rattled. "Cut the plausible-deniability bull, Jordan. You and I both know you had the man murdered."

"We know nothing of the sort," Collier insisted calmly. He sounded as though he had been anticipating this conversation for days. "I defy you to find any link between my Movement and the events in Rome. Check my schedule. I haven't left Seattle since the outbreak."

"Screw your alibi," Tom said. "Eyewitnesses placed

Richard Tyler at the scene. It's obvious you got him to do your dirty work."

"Is it?" Collier leaned back into his chair. "Richard and I have rarely seen eye to eye. He's his own man, Tom. You know that." He adjusted the paperweight on his desk. "Can I help it if he chose to rid us of this meddlesome priest?"

The coy literary reference did not amuse Tom. "And what about the innocent man whose mind and body was hijacked by the Marked? Didn't he deserve a chance to get his life back? Like you and I did?"

"In an ideal world, of course." A somber expression came over Collier's face. "But consider the practical realities here. The 'cure' you speak of is difficult, painful, and time-consuming. It requires illegal quantities of highly radioactive materials and the active participation of Shawn Farrell. Given how powerful the Marked are, and how zealously they protect themselves, capturing a Marked for 'treatment' is not always going to be possible. Imagine trying to smuggle a kidnapped cardinal or presidential advisor back into Seattle to be cured. Richard may have simply decided that it's easier just to eliminate them . . . or so I assume. It's tragic, but the threat posed by the Marked is too great to take any unnecessary risks. Hypothetically speaking." He looked Tom squarely in the eyes. "Knowing Richard, I'm sure he'll attempt to cure the Marked—when possible."

Tom refused to let Collier put this all on Tyler. "Are you even going to *try* to save these people?"

"Need I remind you," Jordan said irritably, "who provided me with the names of the Marked in the first place?" His patience for this debate was clearly wearing thin. Tom wondered if his conscience was troubling him. "You asked me to take care of this because you couldn't get to these people. And that's exactly what I'm doing . . . my way."

"That's not good enough," Tom argued.

"I'm afraid that's not your call anymore." He rose and gestured at the door. "Have a nice day, Tom."

NINE

THE LAST TIME all the Marked had met in the flesh had been in Tunis in 2005. Then there had been ten of them. Now there were only six left.

The meeting was not going well.

"Don't you get it? It's over. We lost."

General Julian Roff sat at an oak round table with his fellow conspirators. Five stars glittered on the epaulets of his uniform. Gray hairs infiltrated his temples. An African-American with a deep bass voice, he had a bellicose expression that dared anyone to disagree.

"That's a very defeatist attitude, Julian," Song Yu chided him. A middle-aged Chinese woman with severe features, and the highest-ranking female in the Politburo, she had recently led the campaign to have all Olympic athletes thoroughly screened for promicin. Her lacquered black hair was done up in a bun. She shook her head in disappointment. "What would your colleagues in the Pentagon say?"

She was a long way from Beijing. Located high in the

Hollywood Hills, Wyngate Castle was a misplaced medieval fortress that had been painstakingly transplanted to California by an eccentric silent movie star back in the Roaring Twenties. Heavy oak beams traversed the high ceiling of the grandiose parlor where the surviving Marked had secretly convened. Hand-carved wooden paneling adorned the thick stone walls. A Persian carpet added a touch of color to the floor. A sweeping staircase led to a wooden balcony overlooking the chamber. A roaring fire burned in the imposing stone hearth. A crystal chandelier hung above the round table. A ponderous oak door ensured their privacy. There were no windows.

"Don't get cute with me, Song," the general retorted. By convention, the Marked addressed each other by the names of their current identities. It was simpler that way. "Face facts. Fifty/fifty was a game changer. Jordan Collier is more powerful and influential than ever. The so-called war on promicin is a joke. And we're dropping like flies."

Sheik Nasir al-Ghamdi frowned at the depressing litany. The wealthy Saudi billionaire was the Marked's chief financier now that Drew Imroth was out of the picture. A checkered head cloth framed his handsome Arabic features. The youngest of the Marked, his new body was only twenty-nine years old. Safe from the abstemious eyes of his countrymen, he treated himself to a snifter of expensive cognac. "So what do you propose we do, General?"

"Protect ourselves!" Roff barked. "Look at what happened to Calabria, and Rebecca Parrish, and Matthew Ross. Obviously, our covers have all been blown. We need to discard our present identities and set up shop in new bodies, pronto. Then maybe we can live out the rest of our lives in relative safety and comfort."

Wesley Burke, senior White House advisor, glared scornfully at the general. His silvery mane and ruddy features were familiar to regular viewers of CNN and the Sunday morning talk shows. A flag pin held fast to the lapel of his tailored three-piece suit. "Every Marked for himself, is that what you're saying?"

"Damn right," Roff asserted. "The promicin genie is out of the bottle for good now, and there's no putting it back in. The future we swore to preserve is not going to happen. It's as simple as that."

"Coward," Song Yu accused him. She made no effort to conceal her contempt. "Did you really think we were going to defeat our enemies without any risk to ourselves? I can't believe that you pass yourself off as a military leader. Why not just throw yourself on your sword while you're at it?"

"Hold on," Kenpo Norbo objected. The famed Tibetan lama was believed by his followers to be the twelfth reincarnation of a legendary Buddhist guru. Saffron robes draped his lean, ascetic figure. "Perhaps Julian has a point. I have no desire to end up like our deceased cohorts. And I don't wish to spend every hour of every day looking over my shoulder." He nervously fingered a string of prayer beads. "A new life of wealth and luxury, without any death threats, has its appeal."

Burke snorted in derision. "Admit it, you're just tired of living like a damn monk."

"What if I am?" Kenpo plucked at his robes. "I didn't mind putting up with this ridiculous persona when I thought I was helping our cause. But why bother now?" He threw up his hands. "What's the point?"

Nasir sneered at the lama's self-pity. "We've all made sacrifices. Left our homes and loved ones in order to ensure the existence of the civilization we cherish. What about our friends and families in the future? Are you willing to violate the trust they placed in us?"

"Those people aren't even born yet!" Roff blustered. "And now they probably never will be." Spittle sprayed from his lips. "You're all clinging to a plan that failed. Let it go!"

"Traitor!" Song Yu hissed at him. "You've been corrupted by this decadent era."

"Fanatic," he shot back. He shoved away from the table. "Get yourself killed if you want to, but leave me out of it."

"That goes for me as well." Kenpo flung the prayer beads onto the table. "This *tulku* is ready to be reborn again. Maybe as a fabulously sexy rock star this time."

Song Yu's eyes burned with rage. She looked like she was ready to lunge across the table at both turncoats. She drew a sharpened ivory hairpin from her bun. "You filthy, weak-willed—!"

A deafening gong drowned out her final epithet. All eyes turned to see their host, celebrated film and TV producer George Sterling, standing by the fireplace. He let go of a knotted silk bell cord. His deeply tanned face was Botoxed smooth. Wavy blond hair plugs replaced the unconvincing toupee he had sported since the late nineties. A graying beard carpeted his chin. A pair of tinted designer glasses were perched on his nose. He was dressed casually in a polo shirt and chinos. His new hit show, *Promise City Heat,* about impossibly attractive NTAC agents taking America back from promicin-crazed terrorists, was currently number one in the ratings everywhere but Seattle.

"That's enough, everyone," he said patiently. "Let's chill out a little. Fighting amongst ourselves like this is just what Jordan Collier, and our enemies in the future, want." He rejoined his colleagues at the table, taking his seat between Song Yu and Nasir. He laid a soothing hand on the irate woman's arm. His firm but conciliatory tone was the same one he'd used to talk Russell Crowe out of bolting the *Day of the Triffids* remake. "Look, Julian, Kenpo, I hear what you're saying. Nobody's denying that we've taken some tough knocks lately. The tragic loss of our comrades has affected us all deeply. But I'm sure, if they were with us here today, they wouldn't want us giving up hope."

He used the noble sacrifice of their comrades as an emotional bludgeon to dampen the debate. The way he saw it, their real problem right now wasn't Jordan Collier's death squads; it was the leadership void created when Isabelle Tyler killed Rebecca Parrish. Somebody needed to step up and take charge now that Rebecca was gone. And who better than the Oscar-winning producer of *Beachhead: Seattle*?

"Look, here's the thing," he continued. "I've headed enough summer blockbusters to know that things always look bleakest right before the good guys turn things around. And make no mistake, we *are* the good guys here. If we don't stop Jordan Collier from spoiling the future, who will?"

"But this isn't one of your damn movies," Roff protested. "This is life-or-death for all of us."

"Which makes it all the more important that we stick to our guns, no matter what." Sterling delivered a carefully scripted pep talk. "Trust me, friends. This isn't over. We can still crush Collier's obscene Movement in its infancy. We just need to use our combined influence to get the authorities to do whatever it takes to put humanity back on the right track, even if this means shipping every 4400 to concentration camps, dosing them all with the inhibitor, and nuking 'Promise City' back to the Stone Age."

Nasir and Burke nodded in approval of his vision. And even Kenpo started to look a bit more confident. They were going for his pitch . . .

"Easier said than done," Roff groused. "How exactly do you intend to pull that off?"

"It's all about telling the right story." Sterling had given the matter a lot of thought before calling this summit meeting. "The trick is to provoke the Powers That Be into taking such drastic step. Perhaps by proving that Collier is planning another Great Leap Forward?"

The general grudgingly returned to the table. "That might work."

"We can do this," Sterling insisted. He felt the momentum shifting toward him. "But not if we don't hang together." He focused his efforts on the holdouts. "Without your pull in the Pentagon, General, we don't stand a chance. And you, Kenpo, don't underestimate your influence in the East, not to mention here in Hollywood. We're all essential parts of our grand endeavor."

"But what about Calabria's assassination?" the lama asked fearfully. "Any one of us could be next."

A sly smile lifted the corners of Sterling's lips. "Let me take care of that."

"Pass me another slice," Kyle said.

A large Canadian bacon and pineapple pizza was laid out on the dining room table. "Sorry you have to settle for takeout tonight," his father said in apology. A frosted bottle of Rainier sat on the table in front of him. An open doorway led to the foyer beyond. Soft rock issued from the stereo system in the next room. "But I just didn't have time to prepare a home-cooked meal this week."

"Fine with me, Uncle Tommy," Shawn said. "You forget, I've tasted your cooking before."

The senior Baldwin feigned a wound to the heart. "Ouch, that's a low blow, Farrell."

Kyle grinned as his dad playfully punched Shawn in the shoulder. It was good to spend time with his family again, especially after all they'd gone through recently. These weekly dinners at his dad's house were something they had agreed upon after Danny's and Aunt Susan's funeral, when the three men had vowed to become a real family again, despite everything dividing them. So far the ritual seemed to be working. *This is just what I need right now,* Kyle thought.

Too bad Cassie felt otherwise.

"Pineapple on pizza?" The attractive young redhead made a face. A funky peasant-style purple frock flattered her figure. A turquoise pendant rested atop her cleavage. Hoop earrings peeked out from beneath her straight red hair. Henna-tinted bangs hung above crafty emerald eyes. "Honestly, we came all the way here for that?"

Although there were four people at the table, only Kyle was aware of that fact. A projection of his own unconscious mind, Cassie Dunleavy was both invisible and inaudible to everyone else. But she was more than just his imaginary girlfriend; she was also his ability.

"How much longer are we going to stay here?" she asked impatiently. She polished her nails at the other end of the table, across from Kyle. Cassie strongly disapproved of these dinners, feeling that Kyle should have nothing to do with his dad until Tom Baldwin agreed to take a shot of promicin. "We've got better things to do than hang out with these two."

Kyle declined to respond. His dad and Shawn wouldn't understand if he started arguing with empty air. Although they both knew that he had acquired some sort of precognitive ability after taking promicin, he had never really explained exactly how his ability manifested itself, that all his insights into the future came straight from Cassie. She told him what to do, and so far she had never been wrong.

Except maybe where his family was concerned.

"So how was your day?" Shawn asked. A stringy piece of cheese dangled from his lips.

"Pretty intense," Kyle answered. "We're working overtime just to coordinate all of Jordan's new initiatives."

His dad put down his beer. "Speaking of which, Kyle, I hate to bring this up, but I need to talk to you about something Jordan may be involved in."

"Whoa," Shawn said. "I thought politics was off-limits at these dinners."

Cassie immediately got her hackles up. "Careful, Kyle! I don't like the sound of this."

"I know," his dad said reluctantly. He squirmed uncomfortably in his chair. "But this is a family matter, too." He gave Kyle a serious, somewhat pained look that the young man recognized from awkward father-son talks about sex and drugs. "Did Jordan tell you about Danny's body?"

"Yeah." Kyle lost his appetite. A fresh slice of pizza went cold on his plate. "But Jordan promised me he had nothing to do with that."

Cassie shot him a warning glance. "Don't say anything more! He's trying to trick you into betraying the Movement."

"I wish I could be sure of that," his dad said. "But we have reason to believe that someone is trying to duplicate Danny's ability. Are you certain Jordan, or anybody else in his organization, isn't planning another Great Leap Forward?" He sounded worried. "I could really use your help here, Kyle."

"That's not fair, Dad!" Kyle couldn't believe his dad was putting him on the spot like this. "You know how much the Movement means to me. Don't ask me to spy on my own people." He made sure his dad knew where he stood. "Besides, Jordan would never sanction something like that."

"Are you positive about that?" Shawn challenged him. "Let's be honest here. Jordan can be awfully ruthless when he has to be. Hell, he tried to kidnap Dr. Burkhoff to keep him from perfecting a promicin-compatibility test. And he's deliberately distributing promicin throughout the world, knowing full well that half the people who take it will die horribly." Not even Shawn's healing ability could save someone from a promicin overdose. "I wouldn't put it past him to try something like this."

Kyle bristled defensively. "What, now you're both ganging up on me? I thought this was supposed to be a friendly get-together, not an ambush!"

"I told you," Cassie crowed, rubbing it in. "You can't trust these people. Your father proved that when he refused to take the shot." Getting up from the table, she circled around to come up behind him. She wrapped her arms around his chest. A fragrant perfume made his head spin. Her lips whispered softly in his ear. "They don't understand about the future, not like we do."

"Just think about it," his dad asked. "I'm not asking you to double-cross anybody, or do anything that violates your beliefs. Just poke around a little and see what you can find out about this Bernard Grayson character and his connection to the Movement. Help us track down Danny's remains before it's fifty/fifty all over again. Maybe use your ability."

"Hah!" Cassie snorted. "Like that's going to happen." She tugged on Kyle's arm. "Let's go."

Kyle felt like he was under attack from all directions. He found himself torn between his family, Cassie, and his loyalty to the Movement. *Why does this keep happening to me? I just want to make the world a better place!*

He shoved his plate away and stood up abruptly. "I need to get back to my place."

"Kyle." The stricken look on his dad's face broke Kyle's heart. "Please, I'm sorry. I wouldn't ask this if it wasn't important." He reached out plaintively. "You don't need to go."

"Yes, you do," Cassie said. "Now."

Kyle got his coat. He didn't want to storm off like this, but his father and Shawn hadn't given him any choice. They had broken the rules, not him. A gust of cold air invaded the foyer as he opened the door to the outside. "Thanks for the pizza, Dad," he said bitterly. "This was great."

Cassie took his hand as she led him out the door.

TEN

PROMISE CITY HAD turned out in force to hear its messiah speak. Thousands of people crowded the outdoor plaza in front of City Hall, waiting to hear from Jordan Collier, who had once addressed a similar throng at this very location, in the uncertain days following the Great Leap Forward. A podium, bearing an image of Mount Rainier's snowcapped peak, had been erected at the top of the wide stone steps. A pair of regal stone lions guarded the steps. Towering marble pillars flanked the podium. Banners sporting colossus-sized portraits of Collier hung from the upper stories of the building. Camera crews waited to broadcast Collier's oration to the entire planet. Spotlights kept the fall of night at bay. Peace officers in pine-green uniforms patrolled the plaza. Metal detectors screened new arrivals.

It was a cold, clear evening, but the falling temperature did little to discourage the teeming horde who had gathered for the dedication of a new public sculpture commemorating the epochal return of the 4400. A cloth was draped over the installation, which, according to advance reports, featured a glowing crystalline sphere hovering over a bronze replica of Highland Beach. Newly invented antigravity technology was said to have been employed to keep the orb suspended over the sculpted landscape without any visible means of support. The artist, who had won a citywide competition sponsored by the Collier Foundation, was the daughter of one of the original 4400. Ironically, she appeared two decades older than her beaming mother, who now stood behind the podium, warming up the crowd for Jordan Collier. The expectant throng listened patiently, more or less, to her opening remarks. It was Collier they had really come to see.

Just like April Skouris.

The sheer size of the audience frustrated the petite brunette as she tried to make her way to the front of the crowd. Mirrored shades and a wide-brimmed hat obscured her sly, mischievous features. Cold hands hid within the pockets of her designer trench coat. Milling bodies jostled her as she peered irritably through the packed shoulders of the people in front of her. She had shown up two hours early for this event, but there were still literally dozens of spectators between her and the foot of the steps. How was she supposed to get close to Collier with all these looky-loos in the way?

"Excuse me," she muttered as she stubbornly elbowed her way forward. "Coming through." Worried about attracting the attention of the watchful Peace Officers, she kept her head down. Her pushiness elicited dirty looks and complaints from the other attendees, but who cared what they thought? She was only interested in Collier.

He's going to talk to me whether he wants to or not.

Her blood boiled as she recalled the humiliation she had endured at Collier's headquarters the other day. Getting turned away by his goons was bad enough, but to be dissed like that in front of Diana of all people was just too much. *They didn't throw Di out on her ear. Just me!*

It was the same old story. Diana got all the respect and attention, while she was treated like some sort of embarrassing hanger-on. Diana was the honor student, everyone's pride and joy. April was the screw-up, whose overachieving older sister had to bail her out of trouble time and again. Even now, with an amazing new ability to brag about, April still found herself playing second fiddle to Diana.

Well, not anymore, she vowed. Tonight was the night she proved she was twice the NTAC agent her sister was. She had given her own government-appointed bodyguards, Ralph and Eric, the slip just for a chance to take on Collier one-on-one. She would do more than show everyone she wasn't the immature loser they thought she was. *I'll expose Collier's lies in front of the entire world.*

If she could just make it through this frigging mob scene!

Up at the podium, the artist's mother, one Naomi Snodgrass, was wrapping up her interminable remarks. "And now, without further delay, the man you've all been waiting for . . . the man a wounded planet was crying out for . . . Jordan Collier!"

Collier emerged from City Hall to thunderous cheers and applause. He raised his hand in acknowledgment and the crowd went wild, waving and shouting like he was the Second Coming or something. Cell phones and digital cameras captured his arrival for posterity. It was easy to forget that, less than a year ago, he had been a wanted fugitive. Amazing what a difference one little citywide catastrophe could make. He was like Giuliani after 9/11, but more so. Giuliani had never started his own religion.

Disgusted, April joined in the cheering to avoid standing out like a sore thumb. Granted, she owed her own ability and cushy new lifestyle to Collier's policy of distributing promicin to all and sundry, but she didn't buy into the whole save-the-future ballyhoo. In her experience, lofty rhetoric was usually just a cover for an elaborate scam. *You can't con a con artist,* she thought smugly. Collier was simply working the angles like everyone else.

And she was going to prove it.

Not Tom Baldwin. Not Diana. Me.

She waited impatiently for the clamor to die down. She bounced on her tiptoes in order to see past the annoying rabble blocking her view of the podium. There were still several rows of wide-eyed worshipers between her and Collier, but maybe she was finally close enough for him to hear her anyway? A damning question was poised upon her lips. She had been rehearsing it in her head for hours now.

"Where is Danny Farrell's body?"

Collier accepted the horde's adulation for a moment, then gestured for them to simmer down. The hubbub gradually subsided. A hush fell over the plaza. Rapt faces gazed up at Collier in adoration.

"Thank you, my friends," he addressed the crowd. A microphone and loudspeakers projected his voice across the teeming plaza. "It warms my heart to see you all gathered here, in common purpose, on this auspicious occasion. It is both a privilege and an honor to come before you once more . . ."

April saw her opportunity. She shouted at the top of her lungs.

"Where is Danny Farrell's body?!"

Her brain mentally commanded him to tell the truth, but, to her extreme vexation, he just kept on talking about what a glorious evening it was in Promise City. "A night to celebrate the arts, and for the arts to celebrate the dawn of a new age . . ."

Damnit, she thought. Collier couldn't hear her over his own amplified voice. She was still too far away. Frustration welled up inside her. *I should have brought a bullhorn or something!*

She wasn't about to give up, though. Knowing Collier, he'd be waxing eloquent for a while. There was still time to get to him. Throwing caution to the wind, she started shoving her way aggressively through the crowd. "Out of the way, please! Coming through."

"Hey, watch it!" some idiot objected. He was a homely, frog-faced goober with a stringy brown combover and a bad suit. A double chin bobbed beneath his blubbery lips. He stood protectively behind a shriveled old crone in a wheelchair who was probably his mother. Protruding eyes glowered at April. "Where do you think you're going, sweetheart?"

She tried to squeeze past the moron, but he wouldn't budge from her path. "Don't be a jerk," she said impatiently. "Just let me through."

"Forget it." He deliberately shifted the wheelchair to block her. "You wanted a good spot, you should have got here first."

April's temper flared. A smirk lifted her lips. *Okay, buster. You asked for this.*

"You ever paid for sex?"

"A couple of times," he admitted without hesitation. "When I was really hard up."

Knew it, April gloated maliciously. *This pig's way too gross to get laid on his own.*

A look of utter horror came over the man's face as soon as he realized what he'd said. He clamped a fleshy hand over his mouth. The old crow in the wheelchair looked up at him with a scandalized expression on her wrinkled puss. Bony fingers clutched her chest. "What did you just say, Junior? Did I hear you right?" She squinted suspiciously at April. "Just who is this woman?"

"Never mind, Ma! It's all a misunderstanding!"

He couldn't get away from April fast enough.

That will teach you to mess with me, she thought as he wheeled the appalled old lady out of there. Ma was already giving Junior a piece of her mind. Pleased with herself, April savored her victory over the bug-eyed loudmouth. *He's lucky I didn't ask for every nasty detail.*

She squeezed through the gap left behind by Junior

and his mom. "Excuse me!" Less obnoxious spectators grudgingly let her wriggle past them. Not taking no for an answer, she steadily edged toward the front of the crowd. The crowd ignored her progress, preferring to lavish their attention on Collier instead. They nodded enthusiastically as the great man droned on:

". . . when that shining orb of light first appeared over four years ago, zooming toward the Earth from what was then believed to be the depths of outer space, many people feared it was the end of the world. And, in a sense, it was. The arrival of that celestial sphere, which returned the 4400 to this crucial juncture in history, heralded the end of the troubled world we had all endured for far too long. A world of hunger, poverty, war, fear and ignorance . . ."

Blah, blah, blah, April thought. *Talk about old news. Everybody knows that stuff already.* She couldn't believe how all these deluded suckers were eating this up. *Tell us something we don't know—like what you did with Danny's body.*

Several annoyed looks and irritated shushes later, she made it to almost the front of the audience. The foot of the steps were only a few rows of gullible sheep away. Jordan Collier was so close she could practically make out the individual hairs in his beard. His shrewd blue eyes looked out over the crowd, oblivious to the downfall creeping up on him. April figured she was close enough.

She *had* to be within earshot of him now.

April took a second to compose herself. She eyed the nearby TV cameras impishly. Boy, were they in for a show. Jordan Collier was about to go seriously off message.

Wait until Diana hears about this!

She took off her sunglasses. Her jaws opened wide. "Where is Danny Farrell's body?" she hollered.

Or rather, that's what she intended to yell. What actually came out of her mouth was:

"Yogurt cavorting algorithms?"

Huh? The bizarre phrase echoed inside her head. *What did I just say?* She tried again, even louder this time.

"Meniscus swirling artichoke rhythms?"

The meaningless torrent of words drew baffled looks from the people around her. It was like she was speaking in tongues . . .

"That's enough, Ms. Skouris." A heavy hand fell upon her shoulder.

April's heart skipped a beat. Looking behind her, she discovered two uniformed Peace Officers looming over her. Each guard took her firmly by the arm.

"Please come with us," the guard on the right said. He had six inches and maybe fifty pounds on her.

"Puyallup obliquely!" she protested incoherently, even as the awful truth smacked her in the face. *They've done something to my brain!* No matter what she tried to say, nothing but gibberish spilled from her lips. "Licentious armadillo queues!"

Nearby spectators eyed her dubiously and backed away. April realized that she must sound like she was on drugs. Distraught, she wondered how the guards had identified her. Had they spotted her only minutes ago or had she been under surveillance for days now? Ordinarily, she could just ask them, but not anymore, not with everything she said getting hopelessly garbled on its way to her tongue.

Unable to argue with the officers, she tried to pull free from their grip. A sudden wave of dizziness washed over her, however, leaving her barely able to stand on her own two legs while the world around her seemed to spin like a carnival thrill ride. She realized at once that one of the guards had to be using his ability against her.

"Mermaid toothpicks!"

A second later, the plaza stopped rotating. The dizziness went away.

"Don't make this any harder on yourself," the second guard warned. He was smaller than the other guard, but big enough to push her around. He kept his voice low and menacing. "Let these nice people listen to Jordan's speech."

Getting the message, she offered no further resistance as the officers hauled her away from the steps. No one tried to stop the guards from escorting the crazy lady out. The crowd parted readily to let them through. Up at the podium, Collier kept on speaking as though nothing untoward had transpired. If he was aware of the disturbance, there was no indication of it.

"Thus, it is with great joy and humility, that I unveil this brilliant artistic tribute to a day that changed all our lives for the better." With a dramatic flourish, he whipped the drape off the sculpture. The floating crystal sphere lit up like a star atop a Christmas tree. "Welcome to the beginning of the Promise City renaissance!"

Energetic cheers and applause drowned out April's

forced departure. The guards hustled her out of the plaza and into the back of a waiting green van. Fear gripped her soul. *Where are you taking me?*

"Slippery by catalogs rampant?"

The guard guessed what she was asking. "Trust me, you don't want to know."

Her ability was useless at the moment, but that didn't matter.

She knew in her heart that he was telling the truth.

ELEVEN

THE RAMBLING TWO-STORY farmhouse was hidden away in the Pennsylvania countryside. Harvested corn and tobacco fields, lying dormant for the winter, surrounded the house and outbuildings. An unlit dirt road led to the Lancaster Pike, nearly a half mile away. A wrought-iron rooster perched atop the weather vane. Amish hex signs were painted on the barns and grain silo. Electric lights shone in the windows. The upstairs curtains had been drawn for the night. A fleet of limousines, parked alongside the house, looked distinctly out of place.

Richard took the limos' presence as a good sign. *Looks like we're in the right place,* he thought. He and his team crept through a darkened field toward the rear of the house. A reliable tip had informed them that the surviving Marked were holding a summit at this very location, offering a perfect opportunity to dispose of the entire cabal in one fell swoop. Subsequent research had revealed that the isolated farm was one of several properties owned by Wesley Burke, the president's chief advisor on domestic security. The incongruous limos suggested that they had arrived just in time.

Far from the lights of the city, inky darkness concealed their approach. A thin sliver of a moon gave them barely enough light to navigate. It was a crisp, frosty night. Richard's breath clouded before his lips, as did Evee's. Only Yul appeared unaffected by the cold. Richard envied the other man's thermokinetic gifts. All three operatives—a word Richard preferred to "assassins"—were dressed warmly in black wool clothing, gloves, ski caps, and boots. Despite the frigid temperature, they had worked up a sweat hiking across the rolling farm country to this address. Their stealth helicopter, manned by the same blind pilot who had assisted in the prison break, had dropped them off in a vacant field more than a mile away.

Keeping low, they darted across the frozen field. With Sanchez dead, Richard had assumed command of the assault team. Dried corn husks crunched alarmingly beneath their boots. Richard winced at every treacherous crackle. Taking point, he held his breath until they found shelter behind an old tool shed. He peered around the corner of the shed while he scoped out the terrain ahead.

A spacious backyard stretched between the shed and the rear of the house. Tight security belied the rustic setting. A guard in a fleece-lined parka patrolled a balcony on the second floor. Mounted floodlights illuminated the dry brown lawn. A tire swing hung from the sturdy branch of a denuded oak tree. A large aluminum doghouse worried Richard. He could only hope that any inconvenient watchdogs had been brought inside for the night.

His gaze zeroed in on a pair of painted basement doors. The sloping steel doors were angled against the house's brick foundations. According to their informant, a 4400 whom Richard had met years ago in quarantine, the Marked were meeting in an underground panic room right off the wine cellar.

That's our way in, he decided. Now they just had to get across several yards of well-lit lawn without being detected. *Easier said than done.*

He considered the sentry on the balcony. The nameless guard paced back and forth to keep warm. His gloved hands were cupped around a steaming mug of coffee. Richard almost felt sorry for the poor guy, until he remembered just who the guard was defending. A pair of night-vision binoculars hung around the man's neck. From this distance, Richard couldn't tell if the sentry was armed, but he figured that was a safe bet. Wesley Burke was a powerful man, with a lot of enemies.

Evee crept up behind him. She poked her head around the corner as well. Her kohl-lined eyes followed his gaze up to the balcony. "Want me to take care of him?"

"Save your strength." Richard kept his voice low. "I can handle this."

His dark brow furrowed. His eyes narrow as he focused on the guard—and the flow of blood to the man's brain. It had taken him a while to master this trick, but he had it down now. Slowly, subtly, so as not to alarm his target, he gradually constricted the guard's circulation, putting the man asleep before he even knew what was happening to him. The sentry teetered unsteadily, then slumped over the railing. The coffee mug slipped from his fingers. Richard experienced a moment of panic as the ceramic cup plunged toward the ground. It landed with a muted thump in the flower bed below. Leafy shrubs mercifully cushioned its fall.

"Pretty smooth," Evee whispered, impressed by the ease with which Richard had neutralized the guard. "You ever done that before?"

"Yes," he said tersely. Sorrow stabbed his heart. The last person he had knocked out like this had been Isabelle, back when his rebellious daughter was still alive. He wished now that they had spent less of their precious time together in conflict. If only they could have patched things up between them. But the Marked had stolen that possibility from them.

"What about the lights?" Evee asked.

Richard signaled Yul with a hand gesture. The younger man, who was about a head shorter than Richard, tiptoed over to join them. "Your turn," Richard said.

Yul nodded. He fixed his gaze on the floodlights, which flared up brightly before burning out altogether. Darkness fell across the backyard. Richard wondered how long it would take the people inside to notice.

Just long enough, hopefully.

"Go!" he whispered urgently.

They were halfway across the yard when the dogs attacked. Savage barks and growls preceded the sudden appearance of four slathering Dobermans, who came racing around the side of the house. The dogs' fangs gleamed in the faint moonlight. Drool sprayed from their snapping jaws.

Damn, Richard thought. *I knew that doghouse meant trouble.*

The lead Doberman lunged at him. He instinctively threw up his arm to defend himself, grateful for the thick padding of his insulated jacket and sweater. The dog's powerful jaws clamped onto his arm. Sharp teeth pierced the fabric, breaking his skin. He bit down on his lip to keep from crying out. Pain broke his concentration to bits. There was no chance to use his mind as a weapon. The snarling dog hung on to him like a vise, tearing at his flesh. Its thrashing weight threw him off balance. It was all he could do to keep the vicious canine from his throat . . . until, abruptly, the dog went limp.

Releasing its grip, the Doberman dropped onto the lawn. Richard gasped in relief. He stumbled backward, away from the downed beast. Glancing around, he saw that all four Dobermans were now lying insensate upon the parched grass. They snored and snuffled in their sleep. Their legs twitched randomly.

Evee, he realized.

He looked over at his teammate, who was stretching a crick out of her neck. Apparently her ability worked on dogs as well. "Thanks," he said breathlessly. "Good job."

She shrugged, as though saving them all from a pack of ravenous watchdogs was no big deal. "I've always been more of a cat person."

"How's your arm?" Yul asked anxiously. Blood soaked through Richard's sleeve, looking black as crude oil in the shadows. Shredded fabric barely concealed the bite marks. It hurt like hell.

"I can manage," he said through gritted teeth. He was more worried about the clamor the dogs had raised before Evee silenced them. Agitated voices sounded within the house. A sliding glass door swished open upstairs. Rapid footsteps rushed out onto the balcony. "What the—?" an anonymous voice blurted above them. "You sleeping on the job, Harris?"

A second voice added to the uproar. "What's with the damn dogs?" Irritation warred with alarm. "Hey, when did the lights go out?"

Richard dashed beneath the balcony, out of sight of the newcomers. His partners needed no prompting to join him. He clutched his injured arm as he listened tensely to the men trying to rouse the tranquilized sentry. His heart pounded in his chest. His eyes turned toward the basement doors, only a few feet away. He tried to lift the doors telekinetically, only to find them locked from the inside.

No problem, he thought. He had anticipated as much.

Vince Adams, the space-warping 4400 from the prison break, could have wrenched the solid steel doors from their hinges, but he had begged off on this mission due to moral compunctions. Liberating positives from federal custody was one thing, but Adams had drawn the line at outright assassination. Richard respected the man's position. He might even had agreed with it at one time, before the Marked murdered his daughter.

Now the basement doors stood between him and his revenge. Reaching out with his mind, he located the padlock on the opposite side of the doors. His smarting arm made it hard to concentrate, but he pushed past the pain. Tumblers shifted and the lock clicked open. The freed doors sprung apart. A murky portal beckoned to them.

"Now!" Richard ordered. He sprinted down a short flight of steps, ducking his head to avoid a low-hanging lintel. The toe of his boot kicked the fallen padlock aside. Abandoning stealth for speed, his comrades scampered down the steps after him. A single naked lightbulb, hanging from the ceiling, exposed what appeared to be a well-stocked wine cellar. Dozens of glass bottles were carefully stacked in sturdy iron racks.

Yul whistled in appreciation. "Quite a collection. And all highly flammable."

"Later," Richard said. A convenient blaze might help cover their tracks, but first they had to achieve their objective—without interruption. He glanced back over his shoulder. The cellar doors banged shut. A heavy wine rack scraped across the floor and wedged itself up against the entrance. A second rack fell loudly across a stairway leading up to the ground floor. Dislodged bottles shattered upon the hard concrete floor. A dozen competing bouquets polluted the air.

Evee clucked at the spilled wine. "What a waste."

Richard couldn't care less about the pricy vintages. All that mattered was eliminating their targets while they still had the chance. Seams of light outlined a reinforced steel door directly ahead. Strident voices sounded from behind the barrier. *That's got to be them,* he guessed. *The Marked themselves.*

Or so he hoped.

Unexpectedly, the door wasn't even locked. It opened like magic before them as they charged into the chamber beyond. Richard's eyes quickly assessed the situation. The rumored "panic room" looked more like a furnished basement apartment. Wood-paneled cupboards and pantries were mounted above a small kitchenette at the rear of the room. Shelves were stocked with a library of books and DVDs. A red emergency phone hung next to the door, beside a first-aid cabinet and fire extinguisher. Ventilation grilles ran along the top of the walls, just below the low ceiling. The overhead lights were painfully bright compared to the darkness outside. Classical music played softly over the sound system.

Six startled people stared at the intruders in alarm. An Arab sheik, a Tibetan lama, a Chinese woman, a U.S. general, a bronzed movie producer, and Wesley Burke himself were positioned around a round antique oak table in the center of the room. Richard recognized the Marked from the detailed dossiers they had worked up on all of them. The quorum appeared complete. They were all here, just as promised.

Pay dirt.

Gasps and curses erupted from the Marked's stolen lips. Most of them had already leapt from their seats. Overturned chairs lay on their sides. Burke drew a Glock semiautomatic from beneath his jacket, but Yul was way ahead of him. The blue steel went red-hot in a heartbeat. Burke flung the sizzling handgun away from him.

"No!" the Arab pleaded. "Have mercy."

Evee didn't give Burke's fellow conspirators a chance

to fight back. Her neck cracked audibly. The Marked collapsed like rag dolls.

The steel door slammed shut behind Richard. He didn't want anyone else crashing this party. His somber gaze swept over the fallen men and woman. A nerve twitched beneath his cheek. He wasn't looking forward to this part . . .

"So far, so good," Yul commented. "Guess we didn't need Billy after all."

Over the boy's strenuous objections, Richard had scrubbed the bespectacled twelve-year-old from this operation. Never mind the danger, this was no job for a child. It was bad enough that Isabelle had lost her innocence so horrifically. He wasn't about to let another child get blood on his hands.

Not on my watch.

By now, the Marked's hired thugs were raising hell outside the panic room. Richard heard them struggling with the uprooted wine racks. Frantic voices shouted at each other. Clearly, the team was going to have to fight their way out of here.

"Okay," Evee muttered. She tried to claim Burke's gun, but it was still too hot to touch. She glanced apprehensively at the closed door between themselves and the guards. "Let's waste these fascist body snatchers and make tracks."

"Not yet." Richard approached the sprawled bodies. Before they killed these people in cold blood, and incinerated their corpses, he wanted to make absolutely sure that they had the right people. The helpless targets seemed to match the profiles, but his conscience demanded that he make every effort not to kill the wrong people by mistake. They were talking about human lives here. There could be no margin for error.

Nasir al-Ghamdi was the nearest victim. Richard knelt beside the unconscious sheik. The Arab's prone body was facedown on the carpet, so Richard rolled him over to get a better look. He tugged the man's head cloth away from his face and scrutinized his features. Was he just being paranoid or did the young man's face look slightly different than the one Richard had memorized? He touched the sheik's cheek. Greasepaint came off on his fingers.

A sudden chill ran down Richard's spine. *This isn't Nasir,* he realized. *He's a fake. A decoy.*

He jumped to his feet. "Watch out!" he exclaimed. "We've been set up."

He barely got the words out before the trap was sprung. Flash-bang grenades went off throughout the room, exploding from behind the shelves and cupboards. Blinding flashes went off one after another, disorienting the would-be assassins. Deafening explosions assaulted their ears. Strobe lights flashed overhead, adding to the chaos. The team could barely think, let alone use their abilities. Even if there was anyone to use them on.

Richard heard a hissing sound between detonations. Looking up, he saw thick white fumes pouring into the room through the ventilation grates.

Gas!

Placing his hand over his nose and mouth, Richard raced to the door. He grabbed on to the handle with his free hand, but it refused to budge. A secondary blast door dropped down from the ceiling, nearly slicing off his fingers. They were sealed in tight.

The choking vapors quickly filled the gas chamber. Richard's eyes watered. His throat burned. He tried to fan the fumes away from him, but it was no good. Nonstop strobes and bangs buffeted his senses. His telekinesis was no good against the formless gas. He couldn't get a grip on it with his mind.

Whoever had devised this trap had thought everything out.

Evee was the first to succumb to the gas. She crumpled onto the floor. Yul was next. He toppled over, landing across the supine forms of two of the look-alikes. Within seconds, Richard found himself the last man standing.

The gas invaded his lungs. Dizzy, he grabbed on to the edge of the round table to steady himself. He tried to fight back against the narcotic fumes, but it was a losing battle. His legs buckled and he sank to the floor beside his comrades. His eyelids drooped. He coughed on the caustic fumes. The last thing he wondered, before oblivion claimed him, was what the *real* Marked were up to right now.

His head hit the carpet.

TWELVE

April had made it to Jordan Collier's office at last.

Be careful what you wish for.

She perched anxiously on the edge of a high-backed Queen Anne chair in the middle of the impressive executive office. The two Peace Officers from City Hall stood to either side of her. Neither had offered her any clue as to what lay in store for her, although her fearful imagination had generated no shortage of dreadful scenarios, up to and including her being "disappeared" for good. She had heard unconfirmed rumors about what happened to 4400s who crossed Collier.

The room was uncomfortably warm compared to the outdoor plaza. Her hat, coat, and mirror shades hung on a rack by the door, but she still felt overdressed for indoors. She sweated beneath her fluffy mohair turtleneck and tight leather pants. Her mouth was as dry as Prohibition. She couldn't stand the suspense any longer.

"Tie-dye pigeonhole emeritus?" she blurted.

Roughly translated, *What do you want with me?*

The guards merely snickered in response.

Her maddening inability to speak clearly only made her involuntary confinement here even more excruciating. A frustrated sob burst from her throat. She gnawed nervously at her fingernails. A clock on the wall revealed that she had been held captive for nearly two hours now. She wasn't sure how much longer she could take this.

Just get it over with, won't you?

Finally, just as she felt that she was on the verge of a total meltdown, the office door swung open and Jordan Collier strode into the room. He walked over to face her, while his bodyguards closed the door behind him. A lock clicked shut.

April swallowed hard.

"Hello, Ms. Skouris," Collier addressed her. Speechifying had left his raspy voice even hoarser than usual. He sipped from a plastic water bottle, whose label identified it as having come from the once-polluted Duwamish River delta. Cleansing those toxic waters had been one of the Movement's earliest triumphs—and a demonstration of all that Collier intended for Promise City. "My apologies for keeping you waiting. I understand that you've gone to some effort to see me . . . despite my warnings to the contrary."

His tone was stern and unforgiving. April felt as though she had been called into the principal's office, an experience she was more than familiar with from her school days. She instantly knew what he had in mind for her.

"Sasquatch fax gravy!"

Terrified, she tried to leap from the chair, but the guards clamped on to her shoulders and shoved her back down onto the seat. Another sickening wave of dizziness sent her head spinning. She whimpered and closed her eyes until the sensation passed. Clearly, she wasn't going anywhere. She moaned in defeat. "Fetal seraglio . . ."

Collier laid the water bottle down on a nearby table. He gazed down on her like a judge upon a bench. "It pains me that you chose to disregard my warning, and not only because I sincerely regret seeing any promicin-inspired ability wasted. I have great respect for your sister and her partner."

You and everyone else, she thought bitterly. Apparently even the great Jordan Collier couldn't resist telling her how wonderful Diana was. April's eyes teared up. She pounded her fists against the arms of the chair in anguished disappointment. *It's not fair! I was finally somebody, too!*

"The truth is indeed a thing of infinite value," Collier lectured her, "but not when it can be exploited by those who would thwart destiny in order to preserve a future devoid of hope or justice. I have seen what this world will become if our Movement fails. Lifeless oceans of bone. Endless fires burning on the horizon. The stench of rotting flesh and disease. A sky blackened by smoke and acid rain. The never-ending screams of the dying and the damned."

The frown lines on his face deepened. His eyes turned

cold and hard. He shook his head mournfully. Stepping forward, he laid his palms against her cheeks. His cool hands were surprisingly rough and calloused.

"I cannot allow you to interfere with what must be done."

No! April thought frantically. *Don't do this!* She squirmed helplessly in her seat, held down by the looming Peace Officers. *I've changed my mind! I won't bother you anymore. You'll never see me again, I promise!*

"Crunchy Teflon sublimes!"

But it was too late for words, meaningless or otherwise. Collier's brow furrowed in concentration. A tingling sensation, like static electricity, sparked where he touched her. The buzz spread from her cheeks to deep beneath her forehead. A humming noise, like a swarm of angry bees, filled the inside of her skull. The bees started stinging her brain.

She thrashed convulsively upon the chair. The guards struggled to restrain her, and had to use both hands to hold her still. Her jaws clenched involuntarily. Her eyes rolled in their sockets. Flecks of white foam bubbled at the corner of her mouth. Her heart was going a mile a minute. Veins pulsed at her temples. The fierce humming roared like a hurricane. Jordan held her head fast between his open hands. April felt like her very soul was being blasted to bits.

Then, all at once, it was over.

Jordan released her face. The agonizing pain ceased. The humming died away. He stepped back from the chair, his face drawn and weary. His arms dropped to his sides.

He nodded at the guard on the right. "It's done. There's no need for the aphasia anymore."

"Understood."

The guard let go of April, in more ways than one. She felt something shift at the back of her head. Her tongue untangled.

"What have you done to me?" she sobbed.

Jordan replied without coercion. "Relieved you of a gift you proved extraordinarily unworthy of." He walked away from her and helped himself to another gulp of water. "Let her go," he instructed the officers, without even looking at her. It was like she was beneath his notice. "She's no threat to anyone now . . . except, perhaps, herself."

The truth had never been so hard to hear. Despair gripped her as she realized that her snazzy new life as a prized government asset was over. Collier was right; she was no good to anyone now. Ralph and Eric were going to have to find someone else to shadow, but that was just the beginning. How was she ever going to face Diana after this?

I screwed up again. Big-time.

"You smug bastard!" she shrieked at Collier. "You had no right!"

He turned toward her once more. "Not so. I have every right, and more. I gave the world promicin. Therefore it's my responsibility to see that it is not abused by ungrateful, self-centered people such as yourself." Water in hand, he headed for the door. "Now then, if you don't mind, it's been a long night. Good luck with the rest of your life,

Ms. Skouris. I hope this experience has taught you a valuable lesson."

"Don't walk away from me!" April shouted angrily. "Where is Danny Farrell's body?"

He paused in the doorway. A wry smile hinted at a private joke. "As I told your esteemed sister, I don't have a clue."

She had no idea if he was telling the truth or not.

"Home sweet home," Cassie said. "Finally."

Kyle's new apartment on the twenty-third floor of the Collier Foundation building was definitely a step up from the abandoned bomb shelter they had squatted in when the Movement had first returned to Seattle, shortly before the Great Leap Forward. A black leather sofa and matching love seat faced a state-of-the-art entertainment center, cobbled together from spare parts by Dalton Gibbs, Promise City's most brilliant mechanic. A white shag carpet cushioned the floor. A large leather-bound tome, containing the original "White Light" prophecies, occupied a position of honor on the coffee table. A family photo, taken during happier times, before his mom and dad got divorced, rested on a bookshelf. A photo of Isabelle Tyler sat beside it. A framed photo of Mount Rainier, where the 4400 had first returned to the present, decorated one wall. A potted fern, picked out by Cassie, added a feminine touch.

The ritzy digs did little to lift his spirits, though, after that ugly scene at his dad's place. Flicking on the lights, he angrily tossed his jacket onto the love seat. He couldn't get over the way his dad and Shawn had tried to guilt-trip him over dinner. "Crap, crap, crap," he vented aloud. "Things were going so well between us before. Why did they have to spoil it like that?"

"I tried to warn you," Cassie reminded him. Shucking a knitted shawl, she plopped down onto the couch and kicked off her shoes. She curled her bare legs up beneath her. "It's not a good idea to associate with those people, not until they see the light."

"Yeah, maybe." He joined her on the couch. "But he's my dad, Cassie. And Shawn's more than just a cousin. We used to be best friends."

"I know." Her tone softened as she snuggled up next to him. She rested his head on her shoulder. "The future has asked a lot of you."

Tell me about it, he thought. Although he had been meant to be one of the original 4400, a botched attempt at abducting him had landed him in a coma for three years. Then, after Shawn finally revived him, one of the future people had possessed his body and forced him to shoot Jordan Collier. He'd spent nearly a year in Evergreen State Penitentiary before Jordan had finally managed to spring him from custody. Throw in a stint spent in quarantine right after he'd been possessed and almost five years of his life had been shot down the tubes, while rival factions in the future treated him like a pawn in some kind of time-bending chess game. It wasn't until he'd taken the shot that he'd finally felt like he was taking control of his own destiny.

Maybe.

"It's just one thing after another," he moaned. "I don't know how much more of this I can take."

"It will all be worth it in the end," Cassie promised. Her gentle fingers stroked his hair. "Everything you've gone through, all your trials and hardships, it was all to serve a greater purpose. To bring Heaven to Earth and end mankind's suffering forever."

Kyle wanted to believe that. He *had* to believe that.

"You really think so?"

"Trust me." A cryptic smile lifted her lips. "Have I ever led you wrong?"

I guess not, he thought. Lifting his head from her shoulder, he contemplated the enigmatic woman beside him. Not for the first time, Kyle wondered where exactly his unconscious mind had conjured her up from. Why "Cassie Dunleavy" anyway? Where had that name come from? Some stray memory from his childhood that had been lodged in the back of his brain until the promicin brought it to life? Maybe a character from a storybook or a girl he'd met in kindergarten? According to Jungian psychology, which he'd studied briefly in college before dropping out to join the Movement, everyone had a female side called an *anima.* Was Cassie a psychic manifestation of his anima, or something else altogether?

Look at me, he thought. *I don't even know how my own ability works. How pathetic is that?*

"I don't know." He stared morosely at the floor. "Maybe my dad and Shawn have a point. Who wants another fifty/fifty?" Distraught, he ran his fingers through his hair. He felt like he was at the end of his rope. "I get so confused sometimes."

"Poor baby." Cassie gracefully rose from the couch. She reached down and lifted his chin. Striking green eyes gazed down on him tenderly. "You've had it hard, haven't you? But I know just what you need." She undid a clasp at the back of her dress and the funky purple frock slithered to the floor. To his surprise, she wasn't wearing anything underneath. The turquoise pendant shone brightly against her smooth, pink skin. "It's been a long day. Let's go to bed."

His eyes devoured her undraped form, and he felt his body responding, just like it always did. Part of him realized that there was something wrong, maybe even unhealthy, about this new aspect of their relationship, but he couldn't help himself. He'd felt so alone after Isabelle died, and Cassie had been there to comfort him, night after night.

She's not real, he reminded himself. *She's my own female self.*

But he could see her and smell her and touch her, even if nobody else could.

"Come to me, lover," she whispered huskily. "Let Cassie make it all better."

"I've lost so much," he whimpered.

"But you still have me, Kyle. Forever."

Taking her hand, he let her guide him toward the bedroom.

"You're just making this harder for yourself," Dennis Ryland said.

Richard was a prisoner once more, but his new quarters made his old cell in Virginia seem like a penthouse suite at a luxury hotel. Sickly green paint failed to insulate the drafty stone walls. Instead of a bunk, there was only a hard concrete bench with no sheets or pillows. You'd have to be totally exhausted to sleep on something like that. Not that Ryland and his stooges had given Richard a moment's peace since he'd woken up here, wherever that was. Shackled to a chair in the center of the cell, his wrists handcuffed behind him, Richard had no idea where he was being held. An orange jumpsuit had replaced his commando garb. His bare feet rested against cold cement. A draft chilled him to the bone. He wondered if he would ever feel warm again.

"I'm not telling you anything," he said wearily. Ryland had been interrogating him for hours without a break. He was hungry and thirsty and exhausted. His prison togs were soaked with sweat. His stomach growled. His mouth felt dry as dust. His bandaged arm ached where the dog had bitten it; he'd been given antibiotics and a tetanus shot, but no painkillers. He would have killed for a sip of water.

"What a shame," Ryland said. The man's dapper suit gave him the look of a corporate executive, not a torturer. He took a swig from a bottle of imported spring water. "Your daughter was much more cooperative, at least for a time." Ryland had briefly tricked Isabelle into conspiring against the 4400 a few years back. "We had a good working relationship, before she went berserk."

Richard glared angrily. How dare this witch-hunting

bastard defame his daughter. "Go to hell." If his telekinesis was still working, he would have yanked the water bottle from Ryland's manicured fingers. But he was back on the inhibitor again. "Why should I talk to you, of all people?"

He'd first met Ryland years ago when the man had ordered all the 4400s into quarantine. At the time, the man had seemed like just another paranoid government bureaucrat. Then Ryland had tried to poison all the 4400s with an early version of the inhibitor, mounted an armed assault on a 4400 safe house run by Richard, and corrupted Isabelle. To say there was little love lost between them was an understatement.

"To stop Jordan Collier from killing millions of people?" Ryland's voice was deceptively calm and reasonable. "All we want is for you to confess that Collier is developing an airborne version of promicin."

Richard groaned. "I don't know anything about that," he said for what felt like the hundredth time. "I don't even know if that's true."

"What difference does that make?" Ryland asked cynically. "We just need you to say so, on camera." Surveillance cameras, mounted to record the interview, were currently switched off. "That's all the justification we need to launch a preemptive strike on Promise City."

"Forget it." Richard stared defiantly at the other man. "I'm not giving you a bogus excuse for an invasion."

"Who says it's bogus? Collier?" Ryland shook his head at Richard's apparent naïveté. "Haven't you learned by now that you can't trust a word that man says?" He knelt down in front of the seated prisoner, so they were eye to eye. "Remember that beating in Virginia, those crooked guards that were going to blow your head off?"

Richard could hardly forget that, but said nothing.

"*Collier* set that up," Ryland declared. "It was all a ploy to secure your loyalty, by arranging to save your life."

The accusation caught Richard off guard. "You're lying," he said uncertainly. Doubt sapped his words of conviction. "That's not true."

"Pretty convenient how Collier's freak squad showed up just in time to pull your butt from the fire, don't you think?" Ryland chuckled at the coincidence. "You ever wonder about that?"

"Maia Skouris," Richard insisted. "She warned Collier what was going to happen . . ."

"Is that what he told you?" Ryland shrugged. "Maybe that's so. Or maybe that creepy brat didn't see the whole story." He rose to his feet and looked down sadly. His vulpine face projected a patently insincere facsimile of sympathy. "You don't owe Collier a thing, Richard. Why endure all this misery to protect him?"

Richard refused to be manipulated. "This isn't about Collier. It's about not giving you a pretext to declare war on an American city." He peered past Ryland and his flunkies at the solid steel gate blocking his view of the rest of the prison. There weren't even any bars to see through. "Where are the people who got picked up with me? What have you done with them?"

He hadn't seen Evee or Yul since waking up in captivity.

"They're enjoying similar receptions at the hands of my subordinates." Ryland smirked at Richard. "You should feel privileged that you're getting my personal attention."

Richard doubted that either of his teammates would crack. If anything, they were both more devoted to Collier and his cause than he was. They were true believers. "What makes me so special?"

"Don't underestimate yourself," Ryland answered. "You're much more high-profile than your accomplices. A decorated veteran, a former codirector of The 4400 Center, and father of the infamous Isabelle Tyler . . . Your testimony will carry a lot of weight. I can practically see the headlines now."

So could Richard. He would've spit at Ryland if his mouth wasn't so dry. "Too bad there's not going to be a confession."

"I wouldn't be so sure of that." Ryland turned to one of his associates, an anorexic teenage girl with spiky white hair, pale skin, and a bland, neutral expression. Icy blue eyes regarded Richard with clinical dispassion. A heavy down jacket looked uncomfortably warm even for the drafty cell. Bulky mittens hid her hands. Her breath frosted in the air. Ryland stepped aside to let the girl through. "Astrid, I think you need to apply a little more persuasion."

Fear contorted Richard's face. He had already been on the receiving end of the girl's ability several times before. Ryland sneered in anticipation. Despite his profound antipathy toward the 4400, the former NTAC bigwig wasn't above using the enhanced operatives to carry out his crusade. Richard strained uselessly against his bonds. "No, not again . . ."

Astrid appeared deaf to his pleas. She bent over to look Richard in the face. She took a deep breath, filling her lungs with the stuffy air of the cell. Richard braced himself for an all-too-familiar ordeal, which came upon him with merciless speed.

She blew in Richard's face, her breath like an arctic wind. Frost flowed over Richard's entire body, coating his clothes and skin with an icy white glaze. He shivered uncontrollably, on the verge of hypothermia. His teeth chattered like castanets, no matter how hard he tried to clench his jaw. His lips turned blue. His own breath fogged the air. Frostbite threatened the tip of his nose.

He hadn't felt so cold since the last time she tortured him.

Ryland held up his hand. "That's enough."

Astrid sucked the bitter gale back into her lungs. She wordlessly stepped away from the chair. The frost instantly retreated, evaporating into the air. Within seconds, Richard was no longer frozen, but he kept on trembling. Goose bumps covered his skin. Each session with Astrid left him more chilled than before. It was impossible to get warm again.

Ryland gave him no time to recover. "Now then," he said harshly, abandoning any pretense at sympathy. "Tell me how Jordan Collier intends to weaponize promicin."

* * *

Maia woke up, shivering. Huddling beneath her blankets, she hugged herself to warm up. The awful dream clung to her like a thin layer of frost.

She grabbed her BlackBerry.

Jordan needed to hear about this, right away!

THIRTEEN

KYLE CLOSED AND locked the door to his office.

Feeling guilty, he crept back to his desk and sat down in front of the computer. It was seven in the morning, and most of the Collier Foundation was still asleep, but, just the same, he didn't want anyone walking in on him while he looked up Bernard Grayson, just to lay his worries to rest. Jordan's own office was only two doors down. Kyle had been relieved to see that Jordan wasn't up yet, even though he kept telling himself that he wasn't doing anything wrong.

I just need a little more information, he thought. *Before I can make any sort of decision.*

The Foundation maintained a top-secret database of every positive in the Movement. Teams of enhanced computer geeks protected the in-house network from government hackers and other security threats. Only the upper echelon of the Movement had access to the complete database. Kyle was a member of that elite number. To review the files, all he needed to do was key in his personal password.

SHAMAN, he typed.

The database flashed onto the screen.

"Don't do this, Kyle," Cassie said.

He didn't even jump when she suddenly appeared behind him. By now, he was used to her materializing from nowhere. He sighed in resignation. No locks or doors could keep Cassie away when she had something to say.

"I only want to look into this a little bit," he said. "That doesn't mean I'm planning to inform NTAC or my dad of anything." He kept his gaze on the screen before him. "Chances are, there's nothing to tell anyway. I just need to know that for sure."

She leaned over his shoulder. "I'm your ability, Kyle. I tell you what you need to know."

"Oh yeah?" He spun around in his chair to confront her. "Then tell me all about this Grayson guy. And where Danny's body is."

She shook her head. "That's not how it works. It's about what you *need* to know, to carry out your destiny. Not what you want to know."

"Maybe you don't know everything I need."

She sat down on his lap and wrapped her arms around his neck. "That's not what you thought last night." She wore a blue baby-doll dress over violet leggings. A devilish smile played across her face. "So, the door is locked, right?"

He saw what she was trying to do. "Sorry, that's not going to work this time."

He dumped her off his lap and turned back to the computer. His fingers tapped at the keyboard, plugging

GRAYSON, BERNARD into the database. Sure enough, the fugitive undertaker was listed as a promicin-positive supporter of the Movement, having apparently seen the light right after the Great Leap Forward. His file, however, was surprisingly skimpy, listing only his age, contact info, Social Security number, and a few other inconsequential details. Not even his 4400 ability was listed.

"What the heck?"

"Leave it alone," Cassie insisted. She paced back and forth behind him. "Don't you see your father is using you?"

"Maybe," he answered. "But if we've got nothing to hide, what's the harm in poking around a little?"

Scanning the file more carefully, he noted that Grayson was listed as a "financial benefactor." He clicked on a tab labeled CONTRIBUTIONS and discovered that the missing funeral director had donated over $150,000 to something called the "Global Outreach Committee."

The what? The name meant nothing to him. *I thought I knew about all of Jordan's initiatives.*

He glanced over at Cassie. "You know anything about this?"

She gave him a dirty look. "You care what I think now?" She plopped down onto a sofa in the corner. Crossed arms rested defiantly atop her chest. "Don't expect me to do your dad's dirty work."

Kyle guessed that he wasn't going to hear the end of this for a while. *Hell hath no fury like an* anima *scorned . . .*

"Fine," he said. "I'll handle this myself."

A half hour's search of the Foundation's computer files yielded frustratingly little information on the Global

Outreach Committee. Kyle had never paid much attention to the Movement's finances, but now he found himself scouring budget reports trying to figure out just what Bernard Grayson's extremely generous donation had been used for. *Follow the money,* he told himself, *just like they say in the movies.* He rubbed his eyes as a bewildering blur of debits and credits scrolled across the screen. Jordan liked to say that money would soon be obsolete, that miracles would be the currency of the brave world they were creating, but Kyle was surprised to see how much cash was required to keep Promise City running in the meantime.

Finally, just when he was about to give up, he stumbled onto a payment of nearly a million dollars drawn upon an account identified only as "GOC Operating Fund." GOC as in Global Outreach Committee?

It has to be, he thought.

But when he tried to call up more details on the fund, his computer beeped in protest. An ominous gray message box appeared on the screen:

"ACCESS DENIED."

"You're kidding me!" He was Jordan's right-hand man; he had never been blocked like this before. He impatiently keyed in his password again.

"ACCESS DENIED."

"Crap!" He pounded his fist into his palm. This was getting more frustrating, and worrisome, by the moment. *What's so secret about this damn committee?*

"Having trouble, lover?" Cassie taunted him from across the room. She amused herself by doodling on a sketch pad.

When Kyle had first encountered her, she had posed as a chatty art student before revealing her true nature. "Maybe you should leave well enough alone."

"Like hell." He was going to get to the bottom of this mystery if it killed him, if only to prove that his dad was way off base with his accusations against Jordan. An idea occurred to him. If his computer couldn't be reasoned with, perhaps he needed to try a more human approach?

He picked up his phone and dialed a familiar extension. Alert to his action, Cassie put down her pad and eyed him suspiciously. Her eyes narrowed. "What are you doing, Kyle?"

You're the spirit guide, he thought. *You figure it out.*

"Hi, Irene," he said as the person at the other end of the call picked up. "Kyle here. Got a minute?"

Irene Henkel was one of the original 4400. Once a 1960s flower child, who claimed to have danced for Jim Morrison and Jimi Hendrix, she had returned from the future with a photographic memory for dollars and cents. Irene was now the brains of the Foundation's accounting department. She was *the* person to call if you had a problem getting an expense reimbursed. Kyle hoped that applied to the Global Outreach Committee as well.

"For you, sugah, anytime." A syrupy drawl betrayed her roots below the Mason-Dixon Line. "How can I help you?"

"No big deal. He did his best to keep his tone nice and breezy, while Cassie glowered at him from the couch. "Jordan has me reviewing the books, and I've afraid I've lost track of what one big outlay was for. Maybe you can refresh my memory?"

"You? Looking over the books?" Her incredulous expression was nearly audible. "Lord, what is that man thinking? Doesn't Jordan know you can't even fill out a petty-cash request correctly?"

"I won't tell him if you won't." He wiped his brow, grateful that Irene couldn't see how edgy he was. His fingers drummed nervously upon the desk. "Anyway, about this pay-out . . . ?"

"Go ahead," she encouraged him. "Give me the particulars."

Cassie stalked across the room until she was right at his elbow. Fiery emerald eyes suggested that he would probably be sleeping alone tonight. She looked like she wanted to yank the phone from his fingers and hurl it against the wall, but, not being real, that wasn't exactly an option. "You're making a big mistake, Kyle."

He squinted at the screen in front of him. "Okay, it's a payment for nine hundred and seventy-five thousand dollars, plus change, issued on December tenth." He took a deep breath before pretending that he knew exactly what he was talking about. "It was charged to the Global Outreach Committee."

Irene didn't even need to check her records. "Oh right. That one." To his relief, his mention of the mysterious committee did not seem to set off any red flags in the accounting wizard's head. She seemed to assume that he was already familiar with the operation. "That was a down payment on a storefront downtown. An abandoned plasma center, I think, over by the old Greyhound bus station."

"Right!" he lied. "I remember now." He decided to get off the phone quick before he gave himself away. "Thanks a bunch, Irene. I owe you one."

"You owe me a drink at least, and I mean to collect one of these days. Although I still haven't found anything as good as this dandelion wine I had at Woodstock, right before that big ball of light carried me off." A wistful tone suggested that the displaced abductee still pined for the bygone days of Flower Power and love beads. "Don't be a stranger, hon."

"No way," he promised. As he ended the call, he felt a twinge of guilt for taking advantage of Irene's trust and affability, but at least she had proven more cooperative than his recalcitrant computer. He was finally getting somewhere.

Still, a plasma center? One of those places where winos, and strapped college students, sold their blood for a little extra cash? Kyle remembered seeing such establishments downtown and in the U District, but that was before the Great Leap Forward. Ever since the plague, the FDA had banned Seattle residents from donating blood or plasma for fear of promicin contamination. Promise City was the new Haiti. As far as he knew, all of the city's blood banks and plasma centers had gone out of business. So why would this Global Outreach Committee want to buy up one of those properties? And what, if anything, did Bernard Grayson have to do with it? *Something doesn't smell right here,* he thought. Why work so hard to cover up a routine real estate transaction?

A renegade mortician. A shut-down plasma center. Danny's body . . .

Kyle tried to put the pieces together, but all he got was a jumble. He stared bleakly at the cell phone in his hand. *Should I call Dad? Let him know what I've learned so far?*

He was still kind of pissed off at his dad for putting him on the spot over dinner, but what if this Grayson character really was bad news? And how much did Jordan know about this Global Outreach Committee? Why was it so hard to find out just what it was up to? What was so hush-hush?

And do I really want to know?

He slumped into his chair, his arms dangling toward the floor. The cell phone felt like it weighed a ton.

"Listen to me," Cassie said. She knelt down on the floor beside his chair. Her warm fingers clasped his hand, hiding the phone within their joined grip. "Remember how angry you were at Shawn when he turned against Jordan? You don't want to make the same mistake. NTAC is the enemy. You can't share any of this with them."

"But my dad . . ." Indecision tortured Kyle. "He's a good guy, Cassie. He only wants to do the right thing."

"I'm sure that's true." She adopted a more conciliatory tone. "But he doesn't see the big picture, not like we do. He's still thinking like an NTAC agent, not a visionary. Or a shaman." She squeezed his hand. "Trust me, Kyle. Remember how far we've come together."

She has a point, he admitted. Cassie had never been

wrong before. She had told him how to revive Shawn from a coma, guided him to the White Light prophecies, convinced him to join Jordan's crusade, even brought Isabelle into his life, however briefly. What if she was also right about this?

He had nothing but questions. She held the answers.

"You have to keep your mouth shut, Kyle."

FOURTEEN

Marco's apartment looked much as Meghan had imagined it. Posters for vintage science fiction and monster movies were mounted on the walls of a converted industrial loft. A short flight of stairs led down to a sprawling collage of work spaces and rec rooms. She rolled her eyes at the outlandish titles and lurid colors of the posters. *Plan Nine from Outer Space. The Thing That Would Not Die.* Laser beams shot from the eyes of retro-looking giant robots. Frankenstein's monster wrestled with a dinosaur.

To each their own, she thought. She preferred foreign films herself.

Marco took her coat as she entered the apartment. "All right," she asked impatiently. She had stacks of budget reports and crisis assessment sheets waiting for her back at NTAC headquarters. Usually, she had lunch in her office, but Marco had insisted that she trek out to his place instead. "What's so important that we couldn't discuss it back in the Theory Room or my office?"

"You'll see." His worried tone and expression made it clear that he hadn't summoned her here to play World of Warcraft. "This way," he said as he led her down the stairs to the main floor of the loft. No walls divided the bedroom, home office, and living room. Area rugs were scattered atop the green tile floor. Hanging white globes lit up the apartment. Curtains covered the windows. "The others are already here."

Others?

She was surprised to find Maia Skouris, Tess Doerner, and both Jed Garritys waiting in the lounge. All four visitors looked tense and uncomfortable. Red or blue ties differentiated the two Garritys, who were otherwise completely identical. Once a single individual, Agent Garrity had somehow twinned himself after surviving fifty/fifty. Now two versions of the same dark-haired, thirtyish Caucasian male sat at opposite ends of a black leather couch. Both bore the same habitually dour countenance. Not even NTAC's top scientists and doctors had been able to determine which one was the original and which was the copy.

It was unusual to see both Garritys in the same place at the same time. In general, they tended to avoid each other, working separate shifts in order to share the same apartment and cubicle, which neither had been willing to cede to the other. The telltale ties were a concession to their confused coworkers.

"Hi, boss," Jed Red greeted her glumly.

"Glad you could make it," Jed Blue added.

Even more puzzling was the presence of Tess

Doerner and Maia. Meghan had never met the former before, but she knew of the mind-controlling 4400 by reputation. She tried not to let her anxiety show, but a chill ran down her spine nonetheless. The young brunette lurked ominously in the corner, watching the others with a guarded expression. In theory, she was no longer insane, but her loyalties remained suspect; at various points, she and Kevin Burkhoff had been associated with both The 4400 Center and Collier's Movement. Had Tess compelled Marco to call this off-site meeting?

And what was Maia doing here? Shouldn't she be in school? Meghan stepped protectively between the teenager and Tess. "Does your mom know you're here?"

"Not really," the girl said sheepishly. She sat on the couch between the two Garritys. "You're not going to tell her, are you?"

At least she didn't sound like she was under Tess's control. "That depends." Meghan turned toward their host. "Spill, Marco. Why did you invite us all here?"

"He didn't," a raspy voice intruded on the scene. Jordan Collier entered the lounge through a pair of industrial-looking double doors. "I did."

Meghan's eyes widened. She kicked herself for not carrying a sidearm, even though she was an administrator, not a field agent. She glanced at the Garritys to reassure herself that she had backup if she needed it. Collier's ubiquitous bodyguards were nowhere to be seen, but Meghan doubted they were very far away. Maybe even in the next room?

"Jordan asked me to set up this meeting," Marco explained. "He made a pretty compelling case."

"Did he?" Meghan asked acerbically.

There had been a time, only two months ago, when capturing Collier had been NTAC's number one priority. But that was before he became the de facto ruler of Seattle.

Arresting him was no longer a viable option.

"Please sit down, Ms. Doyle." Collier gestured at a plush easy chair across from the couch. A Darth Vader beach towel was draped over the back of the chair. The floor needed vacuuming. "There's no need to be alarmed. I just want to talk, off the record."

Meghan decided to play this by ear. She took her seat. "About what?"

"Frankly, I need your help." He stood facing the eclectic assemblage of 4400s and NTAC personnel. His austere black frock coat gave him the look of a preacher addressing a wary congregation. "Are you aware that Richard Tyler has been apprehended again?"

What? The unexpected news came as too much of a shock to even try to maintain a poker face. Tyler had been on the top of Interpol's most-wanted list ever since eyewitnesses linked him to the assassination of Cardinal Calabria in Rome. If he had been captured by the authorities, she should have been aware of it.

"No," she admitted. "By whom?"

"Dennis Ryland. Haspelcorp. Possibly in conjunction with the Marked." Contempt dripped from Collier's voice. "I have reason to believe that he is presently being held in a secret prison run by Haspelcorp. No doubt with the tacit approval of the federal government."

"Interesting," Meghan said cautiously. It was no secret that the feds had contracted Haspelcorp to deal with the 4400 situation. NTAC and the company had butted heads before over matters of national security. Dennis Ryland had occupied Meghan's own office before making the move to the private sector. "But even if that's true, why are we here? What's the point of this meeting?"

"It's simple." He smiled wryly. "You need to break him out of prison."

Meghan's jaw dropped. "Come again?" She was taken aback by the man's audacity. Even for a self-styled messiah, this was a bit much. "You must be joking!"

"I'm deadly serious." He walked over to Maia and laid his hand on the girl's shoulder. "A reliable source, who just happens to be our own remarkable Maia Skouris, informs me that Ryland is trying to force Tyler to falsely testify that I'm developing promicin into some sort of biological weapon of mass destruction. That's just the excuse my enemies, including the Marked, need to launch an all-out assault on Promise City." His smile faded as he painted a grim picture of just what that might entail. "An armed invasion, aerial strikes, maybe even the nuclear option. We, of course, would be compelled to retaliate. The potential loss of life would be truly staggering." He swept his gaze over all present. "None of us wants that."

My God, Meghan thought, dismayed by what she had just heard. She wished she could dismiss Collier's prediction as mere alarmist fearmongering, but, sadly, that was hardly the case. As director of NTAC, she was all too aware that similar scenarios were already being gamed out, with varying degrees of enthusiasm, in the corridors of power. Collier had drawn a line in the sand when he first annexed Promise City. Fifty/fifty had escalated matters nearly to the breaking point. If there was tangible evidence—like perhaps a videotaped confession from a known 4400 terrorist—that an even bigger outbreak might be just around the corner, all bets were off.

"Is this true?" she asked Maia.

The girl nodded solemnly. She spoke with a gravity beyond her years. "I saw it, Ms. Doyle. They're going to force him to lie about Jordan."

Meghan knew better than to dismiss Maia's visions. Even still, she wasn't ready to drink Collier's Kool-Aid just yet. "If this is so important, why not rescue Tyler yourself? You broke him out of prison the first time."

"I'm afraid you're laboring under a misconception," he said, deflecting her accusation. "I had nothing to do with any of Richard's recent activities. I'm merely an interested third party in this critical affair."

"Uh-huh, right," the Garritys snorted in unison.

Meghan didn't believe him, either.

Jordan ignored their skepticism. "In any event, it appears that Richard's accomplices are either dead or captured. And I lack the resources to immediately field a rescue mission of my own. In addition, I rather suspect that Ryland's agents are watching me and my people very closely at present, eliminating the element of surprise. Finally, and perhaps most significantly," he admitted, "I have no idea where he is being held."

Guess there are limits to Maia's vision, Meghan thought. "And you think we can find that out for you?"

"I have considerable faith in your resources," Collier replied. "Don't forget that we've successfully worked together before. Such as the time we were all trapped in that illusory game?"

Meghan recalled the incident. P. J. Devine, a p-positive member of Marco's Theory Room team, had tried to mend fences between NTAC and Collier's Movement by snaring key individuals from both factions in a psychic construct that mimicked NTAC HQ. Meghan was unlikely to ever forget the experience, considering that she had actually "died" in that virtual reality. Thank God Collier and Tom had eventually figured out how to snap them all back to the real world!

Speaking of Tom, she noticed belatedly that both he and Diana were missing from this little coffee klatch. As far as she knew, they were out interviewing Bernard Grayson's relatives and associates, but it seemed odd that they hadn't been included. They'd both had more experience with Tyler than anyone else in this room. She gave Marco a quizzical look. "Where are Baldwin and Skouris?"

"Positives only," Collier said, "at my insistence. No offense to your distinguished colleagues, but this is something best handled by those of us whom fate has blessed with abilities." Standing behind the couch, he smiled benignly down at Maia. "And, out of respect for young Maia, I don't wish to endanger her mother's life or career."

"As opposed to the rest of us?" Jed Blue groused.

"You're all positives," Collier said sternly, as though mildly annoyed that they hadn't come over to his side already. "You have as much to lose as anyone if Ryland and the Marked provoke an all-out war between positives and negatives. You should be eager to undertake this vital mission."

"Forgive us if we're underwhelmed at the prospect of committing treason," Meghan responded dryly. She wondered exactly how much Collier knew about their respective abilities, including her own; that was far from public knowledge. Granted, the fact that there were now two Garritys was hard to miss, but she and Marco had hardly advertised their new abilities. *Maybe he has no idea what we actually can do?*

Then again, he had somehow learned about April Skouris's ability. Meghan remembered Tom's concerns that there might be a mole at NTAC. Was it possible that one of the other positives at NTAC might be sharing info with Collier? She didn't want to think that Marco or one of the Garritys could be the leak, but it was possible that becoming p-positive might have changed their outlooks regarding the Movement. As she furtively surveyed her colleagues, it occurred to her that another positive was conspicuously absent. "I don't see Abigail Hunnicutt here."

"That was my call," Marco confessed. "Her ability doesn't exactly lend itself to commando raids, so why get her involved?" He blushed slightly; Meghan suspected that he had a bit of a crush on the blond brainiac. "She's better off not knowing about any of this."

That's probably true, Meghan conceded. The ability to scan a person's DNA was not going to break anyone out of custody. And she couldn't blame Marco for being overly protective of his last surviving team member. He had lost two of his fellow nerds last year. P.J. was currently serving a life sentence for voluntarily taking promicin. Brady Wingate had died during fifty/fifty. . . .

"You actually think we should do this?" she asked Marco dubiously. "Richard Tyler is a suspected terrorist and assassin. He helped kill a man in Rome only days ago."

"Not just any man," Collier corrected her. "A member of the Marked. Don't insult my intelligence by pretending that you were not aware of his true nature. *If* Richard was involved with this alleged assassination, then he was only acting in defense of his people and the future." His dark eyes narrowed as he challenged Meghan. "Or do you condone what the Marked have done, and will continue to do unless they're stopped?"

"Of course not!" Meghan blurted, letting a flash of emotion betray her professional reserve. She was no friend of the Marked, especially after what they had put Tom through. Discovering that her lover had been possessed by a murderous intelligence from the future had been one of the worst moments of her life. Her skin still crawled whenever she recalled how she had unknowingly let the false Tom make love to her. "But that doesn't excuse cold-blooded murder."

"Doesn't it?" Collier asked. "Even when the Marked killed Tyler's only child?" His voice took on a distinctly prosecutorial tone. "Look me in the eyes and tell me that Emanuel Calabria was ever going to pay for his crimes."

Meghan found herself at a loss for a reply. "That's not the point," she said weakly.

"Please, stop arguing!" Maia interrupted. She pleaded on Richard Tyler's behalf. "You have to listen to me. Mr. Tyler is a good man. He saved us all from his daughter years ago. He doesn't deserve what they're going to do to him. Nobody does."

The soulful intensity of the girl's entreaty gave Meghan pause. She had never met Tyler herself; he had already been on the run by the time she took over NTAC's operations in the Northwest. But Tom and Diana had both expressed sympathy for the man at various points, as had Shawn Farrell and many of the people at The 4400 Center. Tyler had lost both his wife and daughter to the future's machinations. Perhaps he truly was more sinned against than sinning?

"They're going to torture him," Maia foretold, "if they haven't already. You have to do something. You *have* to."

Meghan sighed, genuinely conflicted. Liberating Tyler from Haspelcorp was way out of her jurisdiction, but she had never been one to play things by the book. If there was one thing she had learned during her stint at NTAC, it was that matters concerning the 4400 were rarely black-and-white. Shawn had proved that to her when he had cured her father's Huntington's disease. Maybe this was another instance where the greater good demanded that she break the rules?

She looked to Marco and the Garritys for input. "I don't know. What do you guys think?"

"Go for it," Jed Blue said.

"Or not," Jed Red disagreed.

They glared at each other in disgust, canceling out each other's vote as usual. Meghan suspected that the doubles habitually contradicted their twins just to prove that they were still individuals. Both men also stubbornly claimed to be the original Garrity.

"Marco?" she asked in exasperation.

Marco shrugged his shoulders. "To tell you the truth, I'm inclined to trust Maia. If we can stop a war from breaking out, what other choice do we have?"

"You do realize," she pointed out, "that if anyone finds out about this, all of our careers are down the drain. Not to mention our freedom."

The government would not look kindly on NTAC employees who conspired to liberate a wanted terrorist from custody. They'd be lucky not to get locked up for life.

"Maybe not," Tess spoke up. In the heat of the debate, Meghan had almost forgotten that the introverted young woman was present. "If we get caught, you can always claim that I forced you to take part in the mission."

And what if we refuse? Meghan thought. Was there an implied threat in that offer?

"You have to do it," Maia said. The precognitive teen played her trump card. "I saw you."

Meghan wondered if she was telling the truth.

* * *

"Well, that was a waste of time," Tom said.

He and Diana were driving back from Bellingham, two hundred miles north of Seattle, where they had finally managed to track down Grayson's elusive ex-wife, Michelle. Unfortunately, the former Mrs. Grayson, who had left her husband four years before fifty/fifty, seemed to know next to nothing about the mortician's recent activities. She'd neither known nor cared where he might be hiding these days, although she had tried to make the agents a deal on a pair of purebred bulldogs. Thankfully, they had departed without any puppies.

"It was worth a try, I guess." Diana rode shotgun in the passenger seat next to Tom. I-5 stretched before them. Hills of evergreens rose and fell alongside the road. "You think she was telling the truth, that she hasn't been in contact with Grayson since the divorce?"

"Unfortunately, yes." Tom tried to remember the last time he had spoken with his own ex. Their marriage had not survived Kyle's three-year coma. Linda had moved to Spokane a few years back.

Diana did not dispute his assessment of Michelle's veracity. "So where does that leave us?"

"Hell if I know." Since losing Grayson at the mortuary, they had run into nothing but dead ends. Grayson had no children and no known significant other. A thorough search of his residence on the second floor of the funeral home had turned up only plenty of utopian 4400 literature. His address book and home computer yielded only a discouragingly long list of casual acquaintances and business connections. Prior to fifty/fifty, Grayson appeared to have been a serious workaholic who put most of his time and energy into his business. He had no criminal record, and no secondary residences. None of the troopers at the border checkpoints had reported seeing him. His photo had been posted at every known exit from Promise City.

Tom gazed at the highway ahead of them. They had a long drive back to Seattle, and he wasn't looking forward to having to deal with all the checkpoints and barriers again. It would be nearly three by the time they got back to HQ. He wondered if it was even worth checking back into the office. *Maybe we should just call it a day?*

A roadside sign alerted him to a rest stop ahead. An empty stomach reminded him that they hadn't eaten lunch yet. A fresh cup of coffee and a turkey sandwich sounded pretty good right now. "You want to stop for a bite?"

"Might as well," Diana agreed. "It's not like we've got anywhere to get to in a hurry."

Sad but true, Tom thought. He pulled into the exit lane and hit the turn signal. The turnoff was only a mile away when his cell phone rang unexpectedly. Keeping his eye on the road, he fished the phone out of his jacket pocket. He lifted it to his ear. "Hello? Baldwin here."

"Hi, Dad. It's me, Kyle."

Tom's heart leapt at the sound of his son's voice. "Kyle!" He'd left several messages on Kyle's machine, after that blow-up at dinner last night, but this was the first time they'd actually connected since the argument. He hoped this meant that Kyle was still speaking to him. "Thanks for calling back. I mean that."

"Yeah, right." He sounded tense and uncomfortable. "You got a second, Dad?"

This obviously wasn't a social call. "Sure. What's up?"

"It's about that Grayson guy, the one you were asking about . . ."

"Yeah?" Tom asked apprehensively. Was his son still upset about that? "Look, Kyle, I'm not happy about the way we left things last night. You've got to know that I would never want to do anything that might drive us apart."

It felt awkward having this conversation right in front of Diana, but his partner thoughtfully pretended to be reviewing Grayson's dossier instead. She kept her gaze on the folder in her lap. Tom appreciated her discretion.

"I know, Dad." Kyle kept his voice low, almost as though he was afraid of being overheard. "That's the thing. I looked up Grayson for you and I found something weird. It's probably nothing, but . . ." His voice trailed off. He muttered something beneath his breath. "Just leave me alone, will you? I know what I'm doing."

"What's that, Kyle?" Tom wasn't following. *Did I say something to offend him?*

"Nothing, Dad. That wasn't directed at you." He sounded embarrassed by his outburst. "I was just talking to myself, sort of."

Tom got the impression his son wasn't telling him the whole truth. *Is someone with him?*

"Are you alone?" he asked softly. "Can you speak freely?"

That caught Diana's attention. She gave him an inquisitive look.

"More or less," Kyle said vaguely. "Anyway, about Grayson . . ."

"Yes?" Tom tried not to sound too eager, for fear of scaring Kyle off. Judging from his obvious nerves, Kyle was on the verge of hanging up at any minute. "What is it, Kyle?"

Slowly, hesitantly, his son related what he had learned about Bernard Grayson and something called the Global Outreach Committee. The name didn't ring any bells, but Tom's ears perked up when Kyle mentioned that the GOC had recently purchased an abandoned plasma center in downtown Seattle. He instantly thought of the way Grayson had converted the funeral home's facilities into some sort of biological cloning laboratory. His gut told him that Grayson was up to his old tricks.

"Thanks, Kyle. We'll look into it." A troubling thought occurred to him. "Er, you haven't mentioned this to Jordan, have you?"

"Not yet," he said gloomily. Tom guessed that Kyle felt guilty about going behind Collier's back. "Although I've thought about it . . ."

Tom silently cursed Collier's hold over Kyle. "Let's keep this under our hat for the time being," he urged. "At least until we know whether there's anything to it." He hoped he wasn't pushing too hard; he didn't want to drive Kyle away again. "Can you do that, Kyle? As a favor to me?"

There was an agonizing silence on the line before Kyle finally responded. "Okay, I guess." He gave Tom the address of the plasma center. Somebody knocked on a door in the background. "I gotta go, Dad," he said hurriedly. "Let me know what you find out."

"Will do," Tom promised. "And, Kyle, thanks again. I really appreciate this."

"Uh-huh." Kyle sounded like he already regretted spilling the beans. "Talk to you later."

He hung up at the other end.

The exit for the restaurant loomed before him, but Tom kept on driving. He switched off the turn signal. Lunch could wait. A hot lead took priority over a sizzling cup of coffee.

"Change of plans," he informed Diana. "We're due at a blood bank."

He hit the gas.

"The walls are darker, more gray than green," Maia specified. "The bench is lower. There's a cobweb in the right corner of the ceiling. The toilet lid is cracked. The chair is bolted to the floor."

Maia consulted her dream journal as she described Tyler's cell to Marco. He sat at his home computer tweaking an image on the screen to the girl's specifications. He was no sketch artist, but he and Maia had done this routine before. Maia had started them off by drawing a picture of the scene from her vision. Marco had then scanned the illustration into his computer, and was now using his favorite computer-imaging program to fine-tune the picture while Meghan, Collier, Tess, and the Garritys loitered in the background. There wasn't much small talk going on.

No surprise there, Marco thought. *Not a whole lot of trust in the room.*

"How's that look?" he asked Maia.

"Closer." She stood behind him, looking over his shoulder at the computer monitor. She searched her memory for more details. "There was a brown stain on the ceiling, right over there." She pointed at the upper left-hand corner of the screen. "It was blotchy and kind of ragged around the edges. Like a jellyfish."

Marco manipulated his mouse. A few deft keystrokes inserted an irregular brown splotch onto the ceiling. "Like that?"

"Sort of." She scribbled a drawing in her journal and handed the page to Marco. "But darker in the middle and lighter around the fringe."

He adjusted the image accordingly. "Better?"

"Yes." She nodded gravely. "That's the place. That's where they're holding him."

Marco saved the image, then contemplated the virtual prison cell. It looked pretty dismal. He gulped at the prospect of visiting the place firsthand. *Why couldn't Richard be under house arrest in Hawaii or something?*

Meghan stepped forward to inspect the image. "Is that detailed enough for you?"

The way Marco's 4400 ability worked, he needed to visualize a location before he could teleport there. He usually focused on an actual photograph as a mental trigger, but would a CGI facsimile suffice? He suddenly wished he'd spent more time testing the limits of his ability, despite NTAC's policies to the contrary. "Maybe. I hope."

Collier watched the exchange with interest.

Marco checked to make sure his cell phone was charged. The display screen informed him that it was a quarter after two in the afternoon. He realized there was no point in stalling.

"Okay, here goes nothing." He rose from his seat. "Wish me luck."

"Hold on," Meghan said. "If you do get where you're going, you don't want to be recognized."

Good point, Marco thought. They had to assume that Tyler's cell was being monitored. He racked his brain for an appropriate disguise, then rummaged through a foot-locker over by his futon. It took him a moment or two to locate the item in question, but he soon extracted a bumpy rubber Klingon mask, left over from a Halloween party two years ago. (Last year's party had been canceled out of respect for fifty/fifty.) Clutching the mask, as well as a pair of winter gloves, he hurried back to the computer area. *Here's hoping today is not a good day to die.*

Meghan eyed the Klingon mask, with its bristling fake fur and prosthetic ridges, with bemusement. "You do know this is a reconnaissance mission and not a *Star Trek* convention, right?"

Jed Blue cracked a rare smile. Jed Red chucked to himself. Collier sighed.

Tess, a refugee from the 1950s, looked like she didn't know what a Klingon was. "Star Track?"

"Hey, sometimes you've got to make do with what you've got," Marco said. He tugged the disguise over his head and glasses. The interior of the mask smelled of old sweat and rubber. His own breathing echoed in his ears. He slipped on the gloves to avoid leaving any incriminating fingerprints. "Okay, I think I'm ready now."

"Wait!" Maia rushed forward and impulsively gave him a hug. They had been close ever since Marco had dated Diana a few years back. "Please be careful."

He was touched by the girl's reaction. "Don't worry," he promised. "I won't be gone long."

Knock on wood.

Disengaging himself from the girl's embrace, he faced the computer screen. The rest of the world faded away as he concentrated on the bleak-looking prison cell Maia had described. He felt a familiar tingling at the back of his brain. The image rushed toward him like a 3-D movie . . .

In an instant, he found himself someplace else. Plastered concrete walls surrounded him. The temperature dropped dramatically. An ugly brown water stain defaced the ceiling. A cobweb hung in one corner. Richard Tyler lay shivering upon a hard concrete bench.

And here we are, Marco thought. The claustrophobic cell was just as daunting as he'd feared. An imposing steel door trapped him inside the cell with Tyler. Goose bumps broke out across his skin, and not just because of the chilly temperature. This was no place he wanted to be.

But where exactly was he?

He consulted his phone. The high-tech gizmo, which he had blown one's week paycheck on a while back, also contained a built-in GPS unit that, in theory, could pinpoint his location anywhere on Earth. Pushing the controls in the right sequence activated the PlaceFinder, which quickly gave him the exact coordinates in degrees, minutes, and seconds:

39.967814, -75.172595.

He quickly interpreted the digital readout. Pennsylvania, it looked like. Maybe somewhere in the area of Philadelphia?

At least it's not Guantánamo or Syria, he thought.

He could look up the exact location once he got back to Seattle, which couldn't be soon enough. There was no need to linger in the cell now that he had determined its location. It was only a matter of time before his presence here was detected and he had no desire to take up permanent residence in a cell like this one. He took a second, though, to check on the jail's current occupant.

Exhausted from his ordeals, Richard Tyler slept fitfully upon the uncomfortable-looking bench. Uneasy dreams troubled his slumber. He grimaced and thrashed atop the bench. "No," he murmured. "Not again . . ."

Poor guy, Marco thought. He wished he could 'port Tyler away with him, but that was beyond his abilities, at least for the present. So far, he had only been able to transport himself from place to place. Which was going to make getting Tyler out of this hellhole tricky.

A blaring alarm gave him a start. *Sounds like the jig is up,* he realized. Poking the buttons on his phone, he called up a photo of his apartment from the device's memory. "Time to get out of here," he muttered. "ASAP."

The ear-piercing siren roused Tyler, who sat up in alarm. His groggy eyes widened at the sight of the bumpy-headed alien in his cell. He blinked in confusion.

Marco wished he could explain, but who knew who might be listening? Unable to resist a sudden temptation, he threw out his arm in a Klingon salute.

"Qapla'!"

He vanished into the photo on his phone.

His sudden reappearance in his apartment provoked gasps from his fellow conspirators. Tess stepped back warily. Maia sighed in relief. Collier looked suitably impressed.

"You have an extraordinary ability," he observed.

Marco could practically see the wheels turning in Collier's Machiavellian brain. "Well, don't get used to having it at your disposal," he stated, making it clear that he wasn't planning on switching sides. "NTAC pays my salary, not you."

"A pity," Collier replied. "Perhaps you'll reconsider someday."

"Don't count on it," Marco said. Joining a religious cult was nowhere on his agenda.

"Stop trying to poach my people," Meghan warned Jordan, "or I'll come to my senses about helping you." She brushed past Collier to join Marco by his desk. Crossing her arms, she waited for his report. "Well, did you find Tyler?"

"You bet." He hastily entered the coordinates from the GPS system into his computer. Within seconds, it spit out the precise location of the mysterious prison. "Eastern State Penitentiary. Philadelphia."

"Oh," Tess said. She lurked off to one side, avoiding both Collier and the NTAC personnel. "I've heard of that. It's a historic landmark, dating back to the nineteenth century. They turned it into a museum years ago. Al Capone spent time there. It's supposed to be haunted."

Everyone looked at her in surprise.

She shrugged. "Kevin likes the History Channel."

"She's right," Marco confirmed. A quick search on the Internet turned up plenty of sites on the old prison, which was indeed located in downtown Philly, not far from Town Hall and the city's celebrated art museum. "It was closed for renovations right after fifty/fifty. No word on when it's supposed to reopen."

"Renovations my foot," Jed Red grumbled. "Must have been turned over to Haspelcorp for their own private Gitmo."

Jed Blue shook his head in disgust. "Smack-dab in the middle of the City of Brotherly Love."

"Look at the bright side," Marco pointed out. "At least Tyler's still in the U.S."

"Ryland probably had no choice there." Meghan shifted in the easy chair. "Ever since the outbreak, most foreign countries are refusing to allow positives on their soil. Ryland would have a hard time shipping a p-positive prisoner overseas even if he wanted to."

"Which he might not," Collier added. "I doubt that the U.S. government wants a powerful 4400 falling into the hands of a foreign power. Sadly, promicin has added a whole new dimension to the arms race."

And whose fault is that? Marco thought, but held his tongue. To be fair, Ryland and Haspelcorp were exploring the military possibilities of promicin long before Collier offered the shot to the general public.

Meghan was already working out the logistics involved. "In any event, Philly is still at least six hours away by plane. And it's not going to be easy getting out of Seattle without being noticed. The air force is still enforcing a no-fly zone over Promise City."

Collier chuckled. "I may be able to help you out there."

FIFTEEN

THE PACIFIC PLASMA Collection Center had seen better days.

The storefront windows had been boarded up. An out-of-business sign had been posted inside the front entrance. Graffiti had been spray-painted on the walls and windows. "JORDAN COLLIER IS GOD!" read bright orange letters. "PROMICIN = DEATH!" somebody else had rebutted. Cigarette butts and broken glass littered the sidewalk in front of the defunct establishment. A wino dozed on the stoop. If the Global Outreach Committee really owned the property, they didn't seem to have done much with it yet.

"Nice neighborhood," Tom said sarcastically. They had driven straight here from Bellingham. Diana had phoned NTAC on the way to update them on the investigation; unable to reach either Meghan or Marco, she had left a message with Abby instead.

"If you like fixer-uppers," Diana remarked, glancing around. The Skid Row plasma center was located on a street corner in an economically depressed part of town that had not yet benefited from the 4400's ambitious brand of urban renewal. Across the street was the burnt-out husk of a liquor store destroyed during the rioting two months ago. Around the corner was an abandoned Scientology recruiting station; apparently, L. Ron Hubbard had not been able to compete with Jordan Collier in Promise City. An X-rated bookshop, a little farther up the road, seemed to be the only operation still in business. A gray sky threatened to drizzle at any moment.

Welcome to Promise City, Diana thought.

Their voices roused the wino, who looked up at them with bleary, bloodshot eyes. Broken veins defaced his swollen red nose. A shaggy gray beard kept his grizzled features warm. His tattered wool peacoat would have been turned down by Goodwill. A nauseating stench emanated from his presence. He furtively tucked an empty bottle of Thunderbird behind his back before extending a grimy paw. "Spare some change?"

Diana figured it couldn't hurt to slip him a five. Perhaps he'd seen something between his drunken stupors?

"God bless you." He staggered to his feet. His breath reeked of alcohol, but he seemed more or less sober. "City needs more people like you."

"You here often?" Tom asked.

"Used to donate twice a week," the man confessed, "back before everyone got sick." He regarded the agents hopefully. "You know when this place is going to reopen? Damn unfair that I can't sell my own blood anymore. I never took one of those stinking shots . . ."

"What makes you think it's going to reopen?" Diana asked. "You seen any activity lately?"

The wino nodded. "They unloaded lots of crates and equipment the other night. 'Round midnight when I was trying to get a good night's sleep."

And when nobody else was looking, Diana thought. She produced a photo of Bernard Grayson, lifted from his driver's license. "You seen this man around here?"

The wino squinted at the photo. "Yeah, I think so. Looks kind of familiar." He handed the picture back to Diana. "He the new guy in charge?"

"Maybe." Tom passed the guy another five. "Go get yourself something to eat."

The man's eyes lit up at his unexpected windfall. "Talk about my lucky day! You're good people, both of you." Slipping the bills into his pocket, he hurried off in search of sustenance, or so Diana hoped. Chances were, though, the money was going to buy some more Thunderbird and not a Big Mac.

He left the empty bottle behind.

The agents waited until the helpful vagrant was out of earshot before conferring. Diana put her photo of Grayson away. "Well, what do you think?"

"Sounds like probable cause to me," Tom said. He considered the boarded-up storefront. "Front door or back?"

Diana tried to peer through the slats, but all she saw was darkness. There didn't seem to be any lights on inside, let alone anyone moving about. She hoped this wasn't another dead end. "The back. Less conspicuous."

A narrow alley ran behind the building. A loading

dock jutted out from the wall. Greasy puddles filled the potholes. Rats scurried behind a rusty metal Dumpster. Discarded bandages, left behind by the plasma center's former clientele, were still wedged in the pavement. The alley reeked of urine and rotting garbage.

It was a long way from the tasteful decor of Grayson's funeral home.

Ascending to the loading dock, Tom quietly tried the door, which didn't budge. Diana considered knocking first, but decided against it. If Bernard Grayson was hiding out inside, they wanted to catch him by surprise.

Tom got into position to force his way in.

"Wait," Diana said. "Have you taken any U-Pills today?"

He shook his head. "You think I should?"

"Might not be a bad idea." She was immune to promicin, thanks to playing guinea pig for Kevin Burkhoff a few years back, but Tom was not. "If Grayson and company *have* managed to duplicate Danny's ability, and can generate an airborne version of promicin, we could be entering a hot zone."

He didn't argue the point. "Guess it couldn't hurt to play it safe." He extracted an emergency packet of pills from his pocket and gulped them down. "Okay, let's find out what's going on here."

Diana stood by while her brawnier partner applied himself. Grunting, Tom slammed his shoulder against the door, which refused to budge. "That's more solid than it looks," he commented, wincing. He drew his Glock instead. "I think we need a little more firepower."

"If you say so." She covered her ears.

Their sidearms were capable of firing either conventional rounds or tranquilizer darts. There was no question what kind of ammo he was using as he discharged his weapon. A gunshot echoed loudly in the alley, and ten millimeters of lead blew the lock apart.

Diana wondered if anyone would report the gunshot. *In this neighborhood, probably not.*

"Watch yourself," he said as he kicked the door open. Neither of them wanted another close call like they'd had at the funeral home. Diana still had a bump on her head where that crazy morgue technician had coldcocked her. Guns drawn, they cautiously entered the rear of the building.

"NTAC!" she called out. The initials were stenciled on the backs of their heavy blue jackets. "Anyone here, please identify yourselves!"

Nobody responded. Shadows shrouded the interior.

Questing fingers found a light switch to the right of the door. Fluorescent lights hummed to life overhead, revealing what appeared to be some sort of storage area. Wooden crates and cardboard boxes waited to be unloaded. Bags of saline were stacked upon a shelf. A mop and broom were propped up in the corner. A stainless-steel door guarded what looked like a walk-in refrigerator. *Probably where they used to store the collected plasma,* Diana guessed. *Wonder what they're keeping on ice now?*

Danny's body?

We'll have to check that out, she thought, *after we've cleared the scene.*

Holding their firearms in the high-ready position, they

spread out and methodically swept the premises. Just beyond the back rooms, they entered a large area equipped with brown vinyl couches and IV poles. A variety of smaller work spaces surrounded the open floor. "Clear!" Tom shouted out from the reception area up front. Diana poked her head into a series of offices and an employee locker room. A long Plexiglas window divided the donation area from an attached laboratory. Faded posters touted the lifesaving benefits of plasma donation. A flyer on a bulletin board extolled a Thanksgiving Turkey raffle that had probably never happened. Apparently every pint of plasma you donated had earned you another chance at the turkey.

"Clear!" Diana called back from an empty office. They appeared to have the place to themselves.

Bernard Grayson was nowhere to be seen.

The agents converged in the center of the donation area. They holstered their guns. Tom walked across the room and peered through the window at the lab beyond. "You're the scientist," he said to Diana. "This tell you anything?"

"Well, I don't see any plasmapheresis machines on the floor here," she observed, "which suggests that the Global Outreach Committee is not in the business of harvesting plasma from winos." A fully equipped crash cart, complete with shock paddles, implied more serious medical procedures. She took a closer look at the equipment on the other side of the Plexiglas divider. "CAT scans. Centrifuges. A DNA sequencer. At a glance, I've got to say that this looks suspiciously similar to the setup we found at Grayson and Son."

Tom nodded. "That's what I thought, too."

"Which means we're on the right track," she said. The temperature was nicely toasty compared to outside, which meant that somebody had turned the heat back on after the center was shut down. She unzipped her jacket. "We just haven't found our man yet."

"Yeah." He looked back toward the storeroom. "Guess we'd better check out that freezer unit."

Diana could tell that he wasn't looking forward to finding more clones of Danny's body.

"You want me to handle that?" she volunteered.

"Thanks, but that's not necessary." He braced himself for whatever they might discover next. "Let's just get this over with, together."

"Don't bother," a third voice interrupted. "You're not going anywhere."

At first the voice seemed to come from nowhere. Then the air shimmered around them and the agents found themselves surrounded by a trio of gun-wielding newcomers. Bernard Grayson was accompanied by two strangers: a ginger-haired youth wearing a University of Washington sweater and a plump, middle-aged Filipino woman in a white nurse's uniform. The two men pointed semiautomatics at the ambushed agents. The older woman leaned heavily on a cane. She was breathing hard. Perspiration gleamed upon her cherubic features. Diana thought she looked vaguely familiar.

An original recipe 4400, or one of the new "extra-crispies"?

Diana reached instinctively for her sidearm, only to

hear Grayson rack his gun slide. "Don't even think about it," he advised her. A blue lab coat had replaced his somber undertaker's suit. He nodded at the buff young man. "Carl, relieve them of their weapons."

The agents reluctantly surrendered their weapons. The college boy deposited them on an empty couch near the back of the room.

"Hello again, Agent Skouris, Agent Baldwin," Grayson said. "We've been expecting you."

The SSST, short for Silent Supersonic Transport, was an experimental prototype hijacked from Boeing's Phantom Works division by a disgruntled engineer who had joined Collier's Movement after surviving fifty/fifty. The sleek private aircraft was large enough to carry roughly a dozen passengers and fast enough to get them to the East Coast in a matter of hours. State-of-the-art engines muffled the sonic booms associated with the earlier Concorde, allowing them to fly cross-country without rattling crockery across the continent. The stolen plane had launched from a hidden airfield somewhere on the Olympic Peninsula. Meghan and the others had been smuggled out of Seattle blindfolded in order to preserve the security of Collier's illicit air operations.

Seated aboard the SSST, Meghan had a sneaking suspicion she knew how Richard Tyler and his fellow assassins had managed to get to Rome and back undetected. Not that Collier would ever admit that, of course.

She had to wonder what other top-secret resources

Collier had at his disposal. After all, he now had many of the best minds at Boeing, Microsoft, Amazon, and Ubient Software to recruit from, not to mention p-positive geniuses like Dalton Gibbs. In more ways than one, he had the future on his side.

And that was a very scary thought.

She sat across from Marco, while she researched Eastern State Penitentiary on her laptop. A pair of red designer reading glasses perched on her nose. Thankfully, there was no end of information online regarding the historic prison, including a couple of video tours of the ruins. A glance at Marco's own computer revealed that he was busy downloading numerous images of the prison's interior to his cell phone, the better to teleport about the structure if necessary.

Good idea, she thought. *Too bad I can't award him a bonus for this mission.*

Across the aisle, the two Garritys took advantage of the flight to catch up on their sleep. They snored in harmony.

Tess Doerner sat apart from the NTAC agents, keeping to her self. She appeared immersed in a paperback copy of *One Flew Over the Cuckoo's Nest.* Meghan still wasn't entirely comfortable including the former mental patient in this operation, no matter how handy her unique ability might prove. As far as she knew, the girl's only true loyalty was to Kevin Burkhoff. Meghan had to worry about her motives.

If she wanted to take over this mission, how on Earth would I stop her?

Marco looked up from his laptop. His eyes met hers.

"Feels weird not to have Tom and Diana along," he said. "This is more their kind of action than mine."

"Tell me about it." She had already left a message on Tom's home machine, telling him not to expect her for dinner tonight, but she wished she had been able to speak with him directly before embarking on this mission. Despite Collier's bias against agents without abilities, she had been sorely tempted to enlist Tom and Diana anyway. They both had a lot more experience with Richard Tyler than she did.

But, no, she had ultimately decided, Tom and Diana were too urgently needed in Seattle to divert them on this dubious rescue mission. Shutting down the plot to clone Danny Farrell was just as important as liberating Richard Tyler.

Maybe even more so.

"Okay, they're not going anywhere."

Carl finished binding Tom and Diana to adjoining couches. Thick leather straps held their arms and legs down. Tom strained against the restraints, but didn't feel any give. He and Diana were at their captors' mercy.

Grayson lowered his gun. He stood a few feet away, watching the proceedings carefully. The older woman sat on a stool nearby, knitting a sweater.

"Sorry we can't make you more comfortable," the mortician said acidly. Life on the run had clearly taken a toll on him. Stubble dotted his gaunt cheeks and jaw. Purple pouches hung under bloodshot eyes. His voice seethed with resentment. "But this was the best reception we could arrange under such short notice."

Grayson had claimed earlier that he and his accomplices had been expecting them. Tom wondered who had tipped them off. Had Kyle spilled the beans to Collier after all? Tom prayed that his son wasn't to blame for their dire circumstances. *Who else could it be?* he agonized. *We only found out about this place a few hours ago!*

Diana must have been pondering the same question. "Mind telling us how you knew we were coming?"

"That would be my doing," a new voice explained.

Abigail Hunnicutt strolled in from the back, looking just as at home in the refurbished plasma center as she was in the Theory Room. The blond analyst waved at Grayson and the others. "Sorry to be running late. We were shorthanded at NTAC. Everybody seemed to be playing hooky this afternoon . . ."

Tom's jaw dropped. He exchanged a confused look with Diana. "Abby?"

"Hi, Tom, Diana," she greeted them. A wet twill raincoat dripped water onto the floor. She seemed not at all dismayed to see her colleagues trussed up like unruly patients in a psych ward. "Guess you wonder what I'm doing here."

"A little," Tom admitted. Surprise gave way to anger as he realized that Abby had betrayed them. His face flushed brightly. "I'm not used to being sold out by my own people!"

Diana gave her a withering look. "How could you?"

"What can I say?" She shrugged. "The Great Leap

Forward changed everything, including me. It's obvious now that the Movement is the future." There wasn't a hint of guilt in her voice. "I'm not going to apologize for wanting to be on the right side of history."

Diana did not let her off the hook. "No matter how many people perish to build Collier's brave new world?"

"People die every day for no reason at all," Grayson said. "Trust me, nobody knows that better than a mortician. I wasted most of my adult life processing their worthless remains, making no meaningful contribution to the world, until the Great Leap Forward opened my eyes and expanded my perceptions." He raised his eyes heavenward and steepled his hands before his chest. "I'll never forget that day. My brain came alive with new ideas and understanding. I found my purpose for being."

Abby nodded. "Bernie is being too modest. Promicin amplified his IQ to a phenomenal degree, giving him an innate understanding of chemistry and biology. He knows more about DNA and genetic modification than most Nobel Prize winners. He's been a godsend to our project."

"That was no accident," Grayson declared. "All of this was meant to be." He looked at Tom. "When your nephew's body came into my possession, right after I changed, I realized that it was no mere coincidence. I knew at once that I was destined to spread Daniel's gift to all the world." He gestured at Carl, who was keeping a close eye on the prisoners. "With the help of courageous volunteers like Carl here."

The young man brushed away Grayson's accolade. His gun was tucked in his trousers. "It's a privilege and an honor. I only hope I can be the one to bring the rest of mankind into the fold."

"You will be," Abby promised him. Her voice rang with certainty. "We're going to succeed this time. I can feel it."

Tom realized there was no reasoning with these people. They were all true believers, like that fanatic at the mortuary. Even Abby seemed to have embraced Collier's agenda with all her heart. All he could hope from them now were answers.

"But I saw Danny's body at his funeral," Tom said. "I helped load his casket into the hearse."

Grayson indicated the older woman in the corner. "Thank Rosita there. Perhaps you remember her from Danny's service? She projected an illusion of your nephew's body during the ceremony, just as she masked our presence from your senses several minutes ago."

Rosita looked up from her knitting. She beamed proudly.

"But the duplicate bodies?" Diana asked. "How did you manage that?"

Abby raised her hand. "That would be me again. I'm afraid I've been holding out on you guys when it comes to the full extent of my ability. I can do more than just read DNA, I can also manipulate it." She flexed her fingers. "With Bernie's help, I've been attempting to turn willing volunteers into perfect genetic doubles of Danny Farrell."

"I've seen your work," Diana said coldly. "In our morgue."

Abby flinched. "I admit that none of our test subjects have survived the procedure so far," she said defensively. Diana had obviously hit a nerve. "But I'm getting closer every time." She turned to reassure Carl. "We're almost there. I know it!"

"I believe you," the youth said. "I have faith in the future." He scowled at Tom and Diana. "So what are we going to do with these Feds anyway?" He drew his gun and leveled it at the supine agents. "I say we waste them now before they can cause any more trouble."

His bloodthirsty tone reminded Tom of the homicidal morgue assistant. What was it about Collier's message that inspired such blind devotion in young men like Carl and Kyle? A desire to make their mark on the world, no matter the consequences? Carl sounded positively eager to kill in Collier's name.

"Not a good idea," Abby objected. "According to the prophecies, which I believe to be coded instructions from the future, Baldwin has a special destiny to fulfill. Eliminating him would risk everything we've worked for."

"Right," Carl conceded. "I hadn't thought of that." He turned his gun toward Diana instead. "What about her, though?"

Abby vetoed that execution as well. "Skouris is special in her own right. She has a unique immunity to promicin that merits closer study."

"I concur," Grayson said. He eyed Diana with scientific curiosity. "A careful analysis of her blood chemistry could yield valuable insights into the effects of promicin on the human nerve system."

Clearly outnumbered, Carl lowered his gun. Disappointment showed on his face. "So what are we going to do with them?"

"Kill two birds with one stone," Abby said smugly. She had it all worked out. "The prophecies say Baldwin is destined to become one of us, right? And if we can transform you into another Danny Farrell, we're going to need a guinea pig to make sure you can actually infect people with promicin . . ."

Tom realized Abby intended to test Carl's ability on him. "That's not going to work," he warned them. "I dosed myself with U-Pills right before I came in."

Abby shrugged. "Well then, we're just going to have to wait for them to wear off."

SIXTEEN

EASTERN STATE PENITENTIARY loomed before them like something out of the Dark Ages. Nestled in an upscale Philadelphia neighborhood of bookstores, museums, and pricy restaurants, the medieval-looking fortress stood out like an immense stone anachronism, almost as though it had been dropped into place by the same time travelers that had relocated the 4400 in history. Watchtowers and crenellated battlements crowned its gloomy gray façade. Darkened arrow-slit windows looked out over the street below. Moss climbed its weathered thirty-foot walls. The mammoth prison occupied an entire city block. Floodlights, positioned along the base of the gatehouse, illuminated its granite exterior. The building's intimidating appearance was quite deliberate, intended to instill the fear of God, and a profound sense of penitence, in all who were brought unwillingly through its gates. *"Let the doors be of iron,"* one of the prison's nineteenth-century founders had instructed, *"and let the grating, occasioned by opening and shutting them, be increased by an echo that shall deeply pierce the soul."*

Or so Meghan had read. From the looks of the place, Dr. Benjamin Rush had gotten just what he asked for.

Meghan, Marco, Tess, and Jed Blue contemplated the prison from across the street. They loitered casually upon the sidewalk, avoiding the glare of the streetlamps. It was nearly eleven, East Coast time, but there was still plenty of nighttime traffic cruising down Fairmount Avenue. Their own limo, provided by one of Collier's sleeper agents in Philly, was parked a few blocks away on Twenty-fourth Street. Jed Red was currently cooling his heels behind the wheel of the waiting getaway car. The two Garritys had drawn straws to determine which of them got stuck in the car.

"Creepy place," Marco said, stating the obvious. Like the rest of them, he wore dark civilian clothing without any NTAC labels or insignia. They had left their badges and ID on the plane. This mission was strictly off the books. "Who knew Dracula had real estate in the heart of Philly?"

"Actually, this used to be empty farmland, miles away from the city," Tess informed them. She had appointed herself the resident expert on the prison's history. "A cherry orchard to be exact. When they first built the penitentiary, almost two hundred years ago, there was nothing else around. But the city gradually spread out and enveloped it. That's one of the reasons they shut it down in the seventies. People didn't like having a prison full of convicted felons living right next door—even though the prison had been here first."

Meghan wondered what the neighbors would think of

what was going on inside Eastern State these days. If they knew about it, that is.

She turned to Tess. "You ready for this?"

"Not really," the girl admitted. "But what choice do I have?" She seemed to need a moment to talk herself into going forward. "Back in the fifties, before I was abducted, my dad dug a bomb shelter in our backyard, just in case the Reds dropped A-bombs on us. We used to have duck-and-cover drills in school. I had bad dreams about one big war destroying the entire world . . . I can't let those nightmares come true."

Meghan sympathized. Even though Tess's ability still wigged her out, she was relieved to discover that the former mental patient's motivations were understandable enough. Not to mention sane. "We're not going to let that happen."

"I hope not."

Tess crossed the street, leaving the others behind. An electronic bug in her collar allowed Meghan to listen in via a concealed earpiece. She heard Tess gulp and take a deep breath before walking up to the imposing front gate of the prison. A sign on the door declared that the historic site was closed for renovations. Haspelcorp was mentioned nowhere on the sign.

"Here goes," Tess whispered into the mike. She knocked on the iron door, then pressed a button installed in the archway. A buzzer sounded somewhere beyond the gate.

A security camera, mounted above the door, swiveled toward her. A glaring white light illuminated the front steps, exposing her to view. A scratchy voice emerged from an intercom by the gate.

"Yes?" a gruff voice asked irritably. Meghan guessed they didn't get many callers, especially at this hour. "What is it?"

Tess looked straight into the camera lens. "I'm here for the tour."

"There are no tours anymore." Static failed to mask the voice's impatience, nor its pronounced Philadelphia accent. "Can't you read, sister? This place is closed."

Tess disagreed. "I want a tour. Let me in."

The silence that followed made Meghan briefly wonder if Tess's notorious ability had been overhyped somewhat. Then the ponderous steel door creaked open. No dreadful grating sounds pierced Meghan's soul; apparently Haspelcorp kept the hinges oiled. Peering across the street, she caught a glimpse of a uniformed guard standing beyond the doorway. He stepped out of Tess's way.

"That's better," she said. Turning around, she beckoned furtively to Meghan and the others, who dashed across the street to join her. They pulled on ski masks before coming within range of the cameras; Meghan had convinced Marco to leave the Klingon mask back in Seattle.

Although under Tess's spell, the guard still looked alarmed as the masked intruders hustled up the steps toward the open gate. Built like a linebacker, the guard was a beefy young man with a ruddy complexion and greasy black hair. A flattened nose and cauliflower ear hinted that he had spent time in the ring. A name badge identified him as KOZINSKI. He reached for the pistol holstered at his hip.

"No guns," Tess commanded. "My friends are joining us."

His hand came away from the pistol. The consternation on his face made it clear that he was fully aware of what was happening. "You witch! What are you doing to me?"

"Don't be rude," she instructed him. "And keep your voice down. I told you, my friends and I want a tour."

His mouth flapped silently, like a fish out of water, as his tongue fought a losing battle against Tess's influence. "That's not allowed," he finally managed to get out. Meghan could tell he wanted to say something a lot louder and more pungent. "This is a secure facility."

"Sssh!" Tess held a finger before her lips. "Just do as I say."

The guard nodded.

Like he had any choice, Meghan thought.

Kozinski stood by helplessly, his livid face betraying his true feelings, as the team hurried into the gatehouse. Garrity quietly closed the door behind them.

Meghan took stock of their surroundings. The photos she had perused on the flight had depicted a dilapidated ruin deliberately preserved in a state of arrested decay, full of crumbling plaster, fallen rubble, and rusted metal. There were even supposed to be trees growing through some of the roofs.

That was *not* what she saw around them. Haspelcorp had obviously given the interior a serious facelift. Beige industrial paint covered the granite walls. Fluorescent lights dispelled the murky shadows of the past. The guard's security station was equipped with a battery of monitors allowing him to keep an eye on the street outside. Fire extinguishers and smoke alarms brought the facility up to code. A NO SMOKING sign was pinned to a wall.

Meghan didn't see any signs prohibiting torture.

"Take us to Richard Tyler," Tess instructed Kozinski. "Quickly."

The guard's eyes widened at the mention of Tyler. A strangled protest remained trapped behind closed lips. Seething with frustration, he turned and guided them beyond the gatehouse into the prison proper, which was laid out in a hub-and-spoke design, with multiple cell blocks radiating from a central rotunda. A covered walkway, erected to conceal the prison's new guests from aerial surveillance, led them across an open courtyard to another arched entryway, which connected directly to the hub. As nearly as Meghan could tell, based on her research, Kozinski was leading them in the right direction. They jogged after the guard at a brisk clip.

But their invasion had not evaded detection. A high-pitched alarm assaulted their ears. Security cameras tracked their progress. By the time they reached the arched entrance to the rotunda, a trio of armed guards had already fanned out to defend the prison's nerve center. "That's far enough!" one of the guards bellowed. Handguns and rifles targeted the intruders. "Down on the floor with your hands above your head!"

"Quiet!" Tess silenced them. "No fuss, please. You're going to help us now."

The guards lowered their guns. They exchanged baffled looks between themselves. Their lips formed obscenities, but nothing audible emerged. Angry veins bulged beneath their skin. They shuffled restlessly, quivering with useless fury. Clenched fists hung at their sides.

The girl's absolute control over the men both impressed and terrified Meghan. *Thank heaven she's on our side . . . for the time being, at least.*

Tess covered her ears with her palms. "Could somebody please turn off that siren?"

A circular command station, complete with lighted control panels and video monitors, occupied the center of the rotunda. The guards literally raced each other back to the station to carry out Tess's command. Within moments, the nerve-jangling alarms ceased.

Meghan's ears appreciated the relief, but she knew that they had already forfeited the element of surprise. There was no time to lose. Reinforcements were surely on their way. She issued orders rapid-fire. "Garrity, you stay here. Man the controls and keep an eye on the security monitors." She nodded at Tess and Marco. "We'll get Tyler."

"Show us the way," Tess told Kozinski, before providing Garrrity with some unlikely backup. "The rest of you, make sure we're not disturbed."

Against their will, the remaining guards resumed their defensive postures. It was going to be guard against guard. *This could get ugly fast,* Meghan thought. *And bloody.*

She hoped to God they were doing the right thing.

Kozinski escorted them into cell block seven. A thirty-foot-high, barrel-vaulted ceiling gave the lengthy corridor the feel of an unsanctified cathedral. Frosted skylights let in slivers of starlight. Metal catwalks ran along the upper gallery. Closed steel doors, equipped with sliding observation slits, concealed the individual cells from view. A fresh coat of olive paint did little to dispel the oppressive atmosphere. Their brisk footsteps echoed hollowly. Riots, murders, and suicides had been common throughout Eastern State's long history. Small wonder the forbidding structure was said to be haunted . . .

"Boy, am I *not* glad to be back here," Marco commented. His glasses protruded beneath his ski mask. "Give me my Theory Room any day."

Meghan knew exactly where he was coming from. "Hopefully, we won't be sticking around long."

Kozinski halted in front of a reinforced metal door identified only by the number thirty-three. "Here," he admitted through clenched jaws. A muscle twitched beneath his cheek.

Muffled voices escaped Cell 33. It was impossible to make out what was being said, but an agonized yowl was impossible to mistake. Meghan remembered Maia's description of Tyler being tortured. As usual, the girl's prediction had been dead-on.

"Oh hell," Marco said. "It's happening right now."

Galvanized by the obvious suffering going on right behind the door, he rushed forward to the rescue. Meghan grabbed on to his arm. "Wait. We can't just barge right in like the cavalry. We don't know what's waiting for us in there."

She confiscated Kozinki's sidearm and handed it to Marco.

"Surprise them."

The gun felt weird and heavy in Marco's hand. He was an analyst after all, not a field agent. *I should be brainstorming in the Theory Room with Abby,* he lamented, *not storming Philadelphia's homegrown version of the Bastille!*

But Richard Tyler, and quite possibly the world, depended on him getting in touch with his inner James Bond . . . or at least Austin Powers. "Okay, if you don't hear from me in a couple of minutes, send in the troops."

His heart was racing so fast he half expected it to achieve escape velocity. His mouth felt as dry as Arrakis. Swallowing hard, he visualized the cell from his brief visit several hours ago. He had Maia's sketch loaded into a disposable cell phone, along with countless photos of Eastern State cribbed from the Internet, but hopefully the picture was still burned into his brain. Raising the gun, he dived headfirst into his mind's eye.

Geronimo!

A heartbeat later, he teleported into a scene straight out of Maia's nightmare.

Ryland and Astrid were "interrogating" Richard Tyler, who was handcuffed to the chair in the center of the room. Frost coated the prisoner's face and body. He shivered like a leaf while his tormentors looked on implacably. His teeth chattered. His lips were blue. Marco got the chills just looking at him.

"Knock it off!" he ordered, waving the pistol at the

startled interrogators. He had appeared in a corner at the rear of the cell, facing his adversaries. He distorted his voice to avoid being recognized by Ryland. Pulling a gun on his former boss wasn't nearly as fun as it sounded. "Leave him alone!"

Ryland recovered from his shock at the masked man's abrupt entrance. He kept his cool on. "Back again already? You're pushing your luck, but that's fine with me. We've got an empty cell waiting for you."

The skinny teenager glared at Marco. He had already identified her from Maia's description as Astrid Bonner, an "extra-crispy" who had been picked up by NSA several weeks before fifty/fifty. Her file had described her as a teenage runaway with a long list of juvenile offenses, including assault, vandalism, shoplifting, and kidnapping; a court-appointed psychiatrist had diagnosed her as having borderline sociopathic tendencies. A perfect recruit for Haspelcorp, in other words.

"I don't like being interrupted," she said coldly. Frigid puffs of mist punctuated every syllable.

The frost melted off Tyler as she turned her attention to Marco. Before he could stop her, she leaned forward and breathed onto his gun. An icy glaze instantly covered the soldered steel, which turned cold enough to burn Marco's hand. Panicking, he tried to pull the trigger, but it was already frozen solid. Nothing happened.

Frak, Marco thought. *I'm so screwed.*

Refrigerating things wasn't Astrid's only talent. A roundhouse kick revealed mad fighting skills as well. The kick knocked the frozen gun from Marco's grip. It clattered loudly to the floor. Glacial blue eyes stabbed at him like icicles. Thin blue lips turned upward in a mirthless smile.

"You think you've got goose bumps now?" she puffed. "Just wait till we get to absolute zero."

For all his genius, he could think of only one thing left to do.

"HELP!" he shouted at the top of his lungs.

SEVENTEEN

MARCO'S CRY SPURRED Meghan to action. She lunged for the door handle, but now it was Tess's turn to put the brakes on. "Don't," she advised Meghan, who instantly stepped away from the door. The older woman honestly didn't know if she had done so of her own volition or not. Tess looked at Kozinski. "You go first."

The guard gulped. He tugged open the door and marched into the cell. Almost immediately, he was clubbed in the head by someone lurking beside the door. He dropped to the ground, clutching his skull. "What the hell?" a man's voice, which Meghan instantly identified as Dennis Ryland's, blurted in surprise. "I thought—"

Tess and Meghan darted into the cell before he could complete that sentence. "Hands up!" Tess shouted. "No guns!"

Ryland tossed his automatic away. Meghan guessed that was what he had waylaid Kozinski with. The former head of NTAC instantly recognized Tess; he had been in charge when Tom and Diana had first encountered her. "Doerner!"

Astrid Bonner pounced at Tess, but the girl was ready for her.

"Freeze!" she commanded.

Her hasty injunction had an unexpected effect on the hostile teenager. A choking sound caught in Astrid's throat as, with frightening speed, she *froze herself solid.* Her pale, translucent skin crystallized. Her eyes glazed over. Cracking noises escaped her lungs. Spiky white hair turned hard and brittle. In an instant, she looked less like flesh and blood and more like a fragile ice sculpture. Rime-covered boots slipped on the cement floor. She toppled over onto the floor . . . and shattered into pieces.

A horrified hush fell over the cell. Tess freaked out. "No!" she screamed, dropping to her knees in front of the fractured teen. "That's not what I meant!"

"You monster!" Ryland hissed. His hands were still high above his head. "I should have had you lobotomized when I had the chance!"

"Shut up!" Meghan barked. Although as shocked as anyone by what she had just witnessed, she pulled herself together for the sake of the mission. Retrieving Ryland's gun from the floor, she handed it to Marco. "Don't let him go anywhere."

"Er, okay," he said, his voice lower and gruffer than usual. He aimed the gun at Ryland, his discomfort evident even through his ski mask. He sounded like he was doing a bad Jimmy Cagney impression. "You heard the lady. Stay where you are."

Hoping that Marco could keep Ryland in line, at least for a few moments, Meghan checked on Tyler. The brutalized prisoner was cold and shivering. He looked like he was on the verge of hypothermia. His teeth couldn't stop chattering.

"W-w-who?" he stammered. "W-what's happening?"

"We've come to get you out of here," she explained tersely. Inspecting his bonds, she found his wrists handcuffed to the back of the chair. She glanced over at Ryland. "Where's the key?"

He nodded at the freeze-dried remains of Astrid. "You're free to look through the pieces."

Terrific, Meghan thought. She looked briefly at the grisly fragments. Now that Astrid was dead, the frozen body parts were starting to melt into a gory mess. Meghan shook her head. No way was she going to rummage through the grisly debris, not when there was another option available.

She took off her gloves and laid her hands on the cuffs.

Here we go, she thought.

Meghan had first discovered her ability when she had unintentionally transformed a fountain pen into an orchid. Experimenting with paper clips, rulers, and other objects, she had eventually figured out that she could now transmute inorganic materials into organic. Plant life, to be exact, perhaps because of her lifelong love of gardening. She hadn't had the nerve to try to generate animal tissue yet, and wasn't about to start now.

The cuffs were uncomfortably cold to the touch, but her fingers didn't pull away.

Closing her eyes, she visualized slender green vines growing in the sun. The cold steel handcuffs softened beneath her touch, growing warm and vibrant. When she opened her eyes again, the metal bonds had been replaced by leafy green tendrils, which she easily tore apart with her bare hands. “It’s okay now,” she told Tyler. “You’re free.”

She slipped her gloves back on and helped the prisoner to his feet. His orange prison jumpsuit was damp and clammy. He seemed weak and exhausted from his frigid ordeal. “Can you walk?”

“I’m not sure,” he confessed. “Maybe.”

Throwing her arm beneath his shoulder, she helped support his weight, while simultaneously wishing that he had been a somewhat smaller man. “All right, everybody, we’re moving out.”

Unfortunately, Tess was still in meltdown mode. Stricken with guilt, she rocked back and forth upon her knees. A bloody puddle, which smelled like a defrosting meat locker, oozed toward her. “I didn’t mean to,” she keened over and over. “I just said ‘freeze’ to stop her, like on TV, you know? It’s not my fault . . .”

“I know,” Meghan said. She feared for the girl’s hard-won sanity. “Tess, we have to get going. It’s not safe here.”

But Tess seemed lost in her own despair. Tears flooded her cheeks. Her gaze was locked on the thawing remains of Astrid Bonner. “I don’t want to do this anymore. I’m done . . .”

“You can quit later,” Meghan promised. She was tempted to leave the unstable girl behind, but, no, Tess had come through for them when it counted; Meghan wasn’t going to abandon her now. She racked her brain for some way to get through to the girl. “What about Kevin,

Tess? He's waiting for you, remember? You want to see Kevin again, don't you?"

That got her attention. Moist, red-rimmed eyes looked up at her. "Kevin?"

"That's right." Meghan nodded at the door. "We're going to go see Kevin."

"Yes, please." She climbed tremulously to her feet, suddenly eager to leave the dismal cell behind. She forced herself to look away from the shattered corpse. "I need my Kevin."

Ryland shook his head in disgust. "Big mistake," he told Meghan. "She belongs here. With all the other dangerous freaks."

"*Nobody* belongs here," she shot back. "Not with you in charge."

Gunshots sounded outside the cell. The alarms kicked in again, twice as loud as before. Meghan heard what sounded like a full-fledged firefight back the way they'd come. A second wave of guards had obviously arrived on the scene, only to run into Garrity and the brainwashed security force. She wondered how long they could hold off the reinforcements.

"What's taking you guys?" Garrity hollered over the gunfire. "It's feeling like the Alamo out here!"

Ryland chuckled smugly. "You might as well give up. I don't know exactly who you think you are, but you're locked up tight."

"Funny you should say that," Meghan replied. "'Cause you're our ticket out of here."

She traded Tyler to Marco and took custody of Ryland

herself. The nerdy analyst grunted beneath Tyler's weight. She prodded Ryland toward the doorway with the muzzle of her gun. Tess followed numbly behind them, wringing her hands and sobbing quietly to herself. They left Kozinski sprawled upon the floor.

The gunshots sounded even louder out in the corridor. Crouching low, they trotted back toward the rotunda. Meghan led the way, using Ryland as a human shield. "Wait!" Tyler protested weakly, dragging his feet. "My people. Evee. Yul . . ."

Meghan didn't recognize the names, but assumed they were other 4400s imprisoned at Eastern State. "I'm sorry," she called back to him. They were in no position to liberate the prison's entire population, let alone potentially unruly strangers they hadn't been briefed on. They'd be lucky just to get away themselves. "Not on the agenda."

Thankfully, Tyler was in no shape to put up a fight. "I've heard that before," he muttered bitterly.

They reached the entrance to the rotunda. Muzzle flares flashed before their eyes. Garrity and his unwilling allies had taken shelter behind the security station while firing back at a small army of guards trying to retake the command center. Iron bars had been lowered into place, barring the other entrances. Flying ammo ricocheted off the walls and ceiling, producing explosions of powdered stone and mortar. Smoke fogged the circular chamber. The acrid smell of cordite fouled the air. Sparks erupted from bullet-riddled monitors and consoles. None of the defenders appeared to have been hit yet, but Meghan knew their luck couldn't hold out much longer.

She shoved Ryland forward. "Order your people to stand down!"

"The hell I will." He raised his voice to shout to his men. "Don't worry about me! Shoot to kill!"

Bastard! Meghan thought. She couldn't believe this Nazi had ever been in charge of NTAC, let alone a close friend of Tom's. She jabbed the gun into his back. "Not another word!"

A lucky shot nailed one of Tess's recruits in the shoulder. He cried out in pain as the impact spun him around. Bright arterial blood sprayed across Meghan and the others. He dropped to the floor before their feet. He whimpered in pain.

The gory spectacle jolted Tess from her daze. She wiped a stray drop of blood from her cheek, then shuddered from head to toe. Her eyes widened in dismay.

"No more shooting!!"

The guns fell silent, the ringing echoes of the firefight quickly fading away. Lowering his gun, Garrity looked back at them in relief. Perspiration dripped from his brow. "About time," he groused. "I've only got two lives, you know?"

His trademark gloominess was strangely reassuring. "Just take Tyler from Marco," she ordered. Garrity came forward to assist the limping prisoner, freeing Marco up for another vital assignment. "Go get the car," she told him.

"You bet." He pulled out his cell phone and called up a photo of the limo's interior. "We'll be waiting right out front."

He 'ported out of sight.

Now they just needed to make it to the street. Lowered steel bars blocked the exit. Tess walked straight up to the barrier, then looked back at the captivated guards. "Raise the gate. I want to go."

The two guards still standing hurried to the control panel. Moments later, the bars slid upward into the ceiling like the portcullis of a medieval stronghold. The walkway to the gatehouse stretched before them. Meghan started to think they were actually going to make it.

Then the gas started pouring in.

Vents opened in the ceiling. Thick white fumes spilled into the rotunda, mingling with the leftover smoke from the gunfight. Meghan threw her palm over her mouth, but the narcotic mist invaded her lungs nonetheless. Both guards and intruders choked on the gas. Meghan's eyes watered. Her throat burned.

"Stop it!" Tess coughed hoarsely. She wobbled unsteadily. "No gas. No gas!"

The billowing fumes kept on coming. *Some sort of automated system,* Meghan guessed. *Immune to Tess's influence.*

But Tess wasn't the only one with an ability.

A crazy idea flashed across Meghan's groggy brain. Fighting the light-headedness that was turning her legs to jelly, she stretched out her arms to embrace the noxious gas. Closing her eyes, she summoned up a sense memory of fragrant flowers. Attar of roses, to be exact. Vaporous atoms realigned themselves as the caustic fumes took on a much more appealing bouquet. Meghan's head and lungs cleared. She breathed deeply of the redolent perfume. Her eyes opened.

The rotunda smelled like a rose garden. To her relief, her team was still on its feet.

Garrity sniffed the air. He stared at Meghan in wonder. "You do that?"

"What can I say?" she quipped. "I like flowers."

Under Tess's control, the guards in the courtyard stepped aside to let them pass. "Stop them, damnit!" Ryland cursed the men, but Tess's eerie ability trumped his authority. Reaching the gatehouse, she pulled open the front gate. They dashed down the steps onto the sidewalk. Hope surged within Meghan as they finally put the prison behind them.

We're almost clear, she thought.

A jet-black limo pulled up to the curb. Tinted windows rolled down, revealing Jed Blue behind the wheel. "Took you long enough," he griped. "Good thing for you I don't charge by the hour."

The back door swung open. Marco called out to them from the backseat. A ski mask still covered his features. "All aboard."

The waiting limo was a sight for sore eyes. Meghan herded the rest of the team toward the door. "Move it!"

Just when she thought they were safe, a shot rang out overhead. *A sniper,* she realized instantly, *on the ramparts of the castle!*

The shot missed Tyler, striking Jed Red instead. Meghan froze in horror as the Garrity's head exploded like a watermelon.

"Jed!"

In the limo, the other Garrity screamed and clutched his skull.

Tess lifted her chin toward the castle's lofty battlements. Her delicate face turned into a mask of rage. *"Jump!"* she shouted.

The sniper crashed down onto the sidewalk, adding to the carnage. A broken leg jutted at an unnatural angle. He writhed in pain. Meghan rushed forward and kicked his rifle away from him. She had no sympathy for the injured sniper. Frankly, he was lucky to be alive.

Her brain was still reeling from Garrity's brutal demise. *Hold it together, Doyle,* she thought urgently. *At least until you get these people home.*

"Well, that's one less 4400," Ryland said callously.

Meghan's fist took out her frustration on his jaw. Dazed, he dropped to the sidewalk. Punching Ryland didn't bring Jed Red back to life, but damn if it didn't make her feel a little better. *That's for Garrity . . . and all the other positives you've persecuted.*

Leaving her predecessor sprawled on the pavement, she hurried over to Tyler, who had collapsed next to Garrity's body. He stared at the agent's shattered skull. "I didn't even know his name . . ."

"I'll introduce you later," she promised, not bothering to explain. She hurriedly conveyed him into the car, then turned back for Garrity's corpse. They couldn't leave the agent's body behind, not without exposing NTAC's involvement in the breakout. Her stomach turned as she and Tess loaded the body into the back of the limo with the rest of the passengers. Blood and brains ended up smeared all over her gloves and jacket.

She'd have to burn them the first chance she got.

Tess climbed into the back with Marco, Tyler, and the

corpse, while Meghan checked on the surviving Garrity. Jed Blue was pale and trembling but appeared physically unharmed. Had he somehow experienced his counterpart's death? *Shades of the Corsican Brothers,* she thought. Looking back over his shoulder, he gazed in shock at his own gruesome remains. "Look at me," he croaked. "They blew my head off . . ."

Clearly, he was in no shape to drive. Meghan yanked open the driver's-side door.

"Scoot over . . . now."

She shoved him into the passenger seat and slid in behind the wheel. Tinted windows slid back into place, hiding the fugitives from view. She peeled off her ski mask. Eschewing her seat belt, she pulled away from the curb. Indignant horns honked behind her as she forced her way into traffic.

And none too soon. Sirens howled in the night. She heard police cars converging on the prison. Had someone reported gunshots, or was the manhunt already under way? Either way, this neighborhood was going to be crawling with cops, FBI, and Homeland Security soon.

She hit the gas.

Flashing lights appeared in the rearview mirror. A shrieking police car came squealing around the corner. "Marco!" she called back to him. "Call Collier's people. Now's the time for that distraction he promised us."

"I'm on it!" Nimble thumbs texted the message. "Done!"

Collier's sleeper agents didn't waste time. Seconds later, the lights went out all along the avenue as a citywide blackout threw Philadelphia into darkness. Cars collided as traffic lights blinked out. The limo wove through a confused intersection, barely missing an oncoming semi. More honks added to the clamor. She didn't slow down.

That should keep the authorities busy for a while, she thought. *Long enough for us to make it to the airfield at least.* Peeking in the rearview mirror, she saw that they seemed to have shaken that police car. Maybe it had stopped in front of the prison to attend to that sniper?

Richard shivered in the backseat. "W-where are we going?"

"Someplace safe," she promised. Collier's agents were waiting in Seattle to escort him to a Movement safe house. She turned up the heat to help him get warm again. A vital question occurred to her. "Did you talk? Did Ryland get what he wanted?"

He shook his head. "You got me just in time, though. I'm not sure how much longer I could have held out."

Thank you, Maia Skouris, Meghan thought. She was glad that Jed Red had not died in vain. *Mission accomplished.*

Retrieving her own cell phone from her pocket, she contacted the plane. "We're on our way."

"Affirmative. We'll keep the engines running."

It took her a second to recognize the voice at the other end of the call. She couldn't believe her ears.

"Garrity?"

Marco and Tess reacted in the backseat. Jed Blue nearly jumped out of his seat.

"Who else?" the voice replied. "Everything okay? You sound kind of funny."

Meghan glanced back over her seat at the dead Garrity on the floor behind her. His blood was still leaking onto the limo's carpeted interior. Her gaze swung back to the phone. There was a *new* Garrity now? To replace the one who died?

True to form, Marco was already churning out a theory. "Maybe it's an automatic backup system, generating a safe copy every time one Garrity gets offed." Excitement filled his voice as he warmed to the idea. "It's like the ultimate insurance policy."

"What's that?" the new Jed asked. "I didn't catch that."

"Never mind," Meghan said. She had too much on her hands right now to deal with any more weirdness. "We'll explain later."

If that was even possible.

EIGHTEEN

THE EXPERIMENT WAS under way.

Carl was strapped to a couch across from Tom and Diana, nude except for a pair of dark boxer shorts. A tattoo of Jordan Collier embellished his right bicep. Danny's body—the real thing, apparently—was stretched out on a gurney beside him. Abby stood between the dead boy and the live one, facing the captive agents. A gray cashmere sweater dress confirmed that she had much better fashion sense than the usual Theory Room geek. She flexed her fingers.

Electrodes were attached to Carl's temple and chest. An IV ran into his arm. A battery of sophisticated medical equipment monitored his vital signs. Grayson attended to the apparatus, carefully charting the readings. Rosita manned the crash cart, just in case of an emergency.

Still bound to their own couches, Tom and Diana could only watch as Abby and her cohorts completed their preparations.

"This is your last chance," Abby told Carl. "Nobody will blame you if you want to back out."

"No way," the young man said passionately. "I've waited my entire life for this moment. It's my big chance to make a difference."

Tom imagined suicide bombers felt the same way. He was horrified at how eager Carl was to throw his life away, all for a chance to obtain the same horrible ability that had ruined Danny's life. Didn't he realize that Danny had died in torment, with thousands of deaths on his conscience?

"Your commitment to the cause is an inspiration to us all," Grayson said in a professionally soothing tone he had surely used to console countless grieving loved ones. He injected several cc's of a dark yellow chemical into Carl's IV line. "This new compound should ease the transformation and overcome your body's natural resistance factor. I also included an anesthetic to help with the pain."

Tom wondered how many earlier compounds Grayson had tried in the past. They knew of at least four fatalities.

"I'm not afraid of the pain," Carl insisted, not entirely convincingly. Despite his bravado, he looked a little pale. His fingers drummed nervously against the couch beneath him. "Let's do this."

"All right," Abby said. A quaver in her own voice suggested that she wasn't nearly as confident as she was pretending to be. She took a deep breath, then laid her hands upon the bodies on opposite sides of her, forming a circuit between the living and the dead. Her fingers were splayed atop the chests of both men. She closed her eyes.

"Abby, wait!" Diana called out. "This is insane. You're going to kill that boy!"

"Shut up!" Rosita barked. She lifted a syringe from the crash cart. "Don't make me knock you out."

Tom didn't want to know what was in the syringe.

Ignoring Diana's desperate plea, Abby kept her eyes tightly shut. A look of intense concentration came over her face. Her nails dug into the boys' chests. Tom felt sick to his stomach at the sight of his nephew's body being desecrated like this. *Leave him alone, you backstabbing nutcase!*

Danny's lifeless form remained inert. Carl was not so lucky. Convulsions rocked his body. He thrashed violently against his restraints. His back arched as though he were being electrocuted. His eyes rolled back until only the whites were visible. Swollen veins throbbed beneath his skin. An agonized moan tore itself from his throat. Clumps of ginger hair fell from his scalp. He foamed at the mouth.

His vital signs spiked alarmingly. Tom was no MD, but he'd spent enough time in hospital wards during Kyle's coma to tell that Carl's blood pressure, heartbeat, brain activity, and other metabolic functions were going through the roof. Warning beeps sounded from the expensive monitors. Jagged graphs shot upward. Tom guessed that Carl was only moments away from total cardiac arrest.

"Damnit!" Grayson cursed. He injected more of his experimental compound into the IV. "We're losing him . . . just like the others!"

Rosita fired up the defibrillator paddles.

"No!" Abby exclaimed. Her smooth brow furrowed in

concentration. Her entire body seemed to vibrate. Sweat dripped down her face. "It's working. I can feel it!"

Something was definitely happening to Carl. His flesh bubbled and melted, flowing into new configurations across his writhing frame. His features blurred. Sandy blond hair—the color of Danny's—sprouted across his scalp, replacing the loose tufts of hair upon the floor. His tattoo disappeared beneath a wave of fresh pink skin. A new face gelled atop his skull.

Danny's face.

Oh God, Tom thought. If he didn't know better, he would have sworn it was his dead nephew suffering before his eyes. Danny/Carl screamed in agony. Tom looked away in revulsion. He felt like he was going to throw up.

"It's not him, Tom," Diana called out to him. "It's not Danny."

I know, Tom thought, *but still . . .*

It was like Danny was dying all over again.

The heartrending moans gradually quieted. Tom forced himself to keep on watching as Carl's convulsions ebbed away. His vital signs stabilized. Gasping, he sagged against the vinyl cushions of the couch. His chest heaved as his lungs sucked in air. Trembling flesh was drenched in sweat. His eyes rolled back down. They were brown now, the same color as Danny's. A chill ran down Tom's spine as his nephew's eyes looked back at him.

"Did it work?" he asked weakly. Even his voice was Danny's. "Did we do it?"

Abby withdrew her hands from Carl and Danny. She looked exhausted, but exuberant. "Absolutely!"

Grayson undid Carl's restraints. He produced a hand mirror from a tray of medical instruments. "See for yourself."

"Holy crap!" Carl stared at his new face in wonder. His fingers explored the unfamiliar contours. He looked over at Abby. "And I'm not going to die?"

"Doesn't look like it." She let out a sigh of relief, clearly glad not to have more blood on her hands. "Congratulations. You're the first person to ever survive a total DNA transplant."

Grayson looked like he wanted to break out a bottle of champagne. He enthusiastically shook Carl's hand while Rosita looked on beatifically. "Now we just need to inject him with promicin and see if he develops Danny's ability."

"He will," Abby said confidently. "He's a perfect match now." Her face glowed with pride at her accomplishment. "And this is just the beginning. Now that we've perfected the procedure, we can create hundreds of Danny clones to spread the gift of promicin. Just think of it," she rhapsodized, "a veritable army of carriers dispatched throughout the world, creating all-new outbreaks everywhere they go. It will be the Great Leap Forward all over again, but on a global scale."

More like another fifty/fifty, Tom thought, *killing off half the world's population.* He couldn't imagine a greater tragedy. *And all because these fiends wouldn't let Danny rest in peace.*

"Not so fast," Diana said. "Don't forget. The authorities know about ubiquinone now. They can use it to combat any outbreaks, just like they did in Seattle."

"They can try," Abby said, unconcerned. "And maybe, if they're really on the ball, they can spare a few key population centers for a time. But what about the Third World and such? Once the epidemic starts raging worldwide, I doubt that any government has the resources to keep it from spreading out of control. Nobody has *that* many U-Pills stockpiled. The Movement has seen to that."

Diana had no ready response. *That's because,* Tom realized, *we both know she's right.*

"If you'd like to leave a message, press one."

Kyle swore in frustration. He stabbed the keypad on his cell phone. "Dad, this is me again. Kyle. Give me a call as soon as you can, okay? I'm going nuts here."

His father's voice mail beeped back at him.

"Crap!" Kyle angrily threw the phone across his office. It smacked down between the cushions of the couch on the opposite side of the room. He paced restlessly, pulling on his hair in frustration. It had been hours since he'd squealed to his dad about the GOC and that closed plasma center, and he hadn't heard anything since. He'd tried his dad's home phone, his work phone, his cell phone, even his email address, but just couldn't get hold of his father. Diana wasn't returning his urgent calls either. Hell, he'd even tried calling his dad's new girlfriend, Meghan Doyle, without any luck. *Why isn't anyone getting back to me? Are they deliberately cutting me out of the loop?*

"Better hope nobody checks your phone records," Cassie scolded him. She sat behind his desk, paging through a photocopy of the White Light prophecies. "Might have a hard time explaining to the folks around here why you kept calling the director of NTAC."

Kyle was in no mood for her lectures. "Is that the best advice you can offer right now? In that case, maybe you should just leave me alone."

A knock at the door interrupted. The door opened a crack and Susan Meldar, Kyle's personal assistant, poked her head into the office. "Kyle?" Concerned eyes looked him over. "Is everything okay in here?"

To his embarrassment, he realized that his outburst a few moments ago had been audible even through the door. "We're fine—I mean, I'm fine," he corrected himself. "Sorry about the noise." A casual shrug dismissed the incident. "A little too much stress, you know?"

"Anything I can help you with?" Susan volunteered. She still looked a bit worried about Kyle's state of mind. "Maybe a cup of herbal tea?"

He shook his head. "No thanks," he said, mustering a weak smile. "Seriously, I'm fine. Just got some family stuff to deal with, that's all." He tried to laugh it off. "You know how crazy parents can be."

"Yeah, I guess," she said before retreating back into the hall. The door clicked into place behind her. Muffled footsteps headed back to her desk.

Kyle breathed a sigh of relief. *Great,* he thought sarcastically. *Now I'm starting to lose it in front of the staff. Some shaman I am.*

"That was smooth," Cassie teased him. It seemed like she was always with him now, never giving him a chance to think by himself. "You need to watch your temper, Kyle. People look up to you here. You need to set an example."

"Thanks for the tip," he said irritably. Crossing the room, he retrieved his phone from the seat cushions. Irrationally, he checked his messages again, even though only a few minutes had passed since the last time he'd checked them.

Nothing.

He resisted an urge to hurl the phone again. *That's it,* he thought. *I can't stay cooped up here any longer. I need to know what's going on.*

The copy of the prophecies mocked him. For all their wisdom, they didn't contain the info he needed right at this very moment. They were no help at all.

Just like Cassie.

There was only one place left to turn.

Jordan, he thought. *Maybe Jordan knows something.*

He'd promised his dad not to mention any of this to Jordan, but that was before he and Diana had dropped off the face of the earth. *I don't have to tell Jordan the whole story,* he rationalized, *but maybe I can pry some information out of him without tipping my hand. It's worth a try.*

Anything was better than suffering in suspense one more minute.

His mind made up, he exited his office and walked briskly down the hall. To his surprise, Cassie didn't try to stop him. Perhaps she knew better than to try and talk him out of it? The carpeted hallway was bustling with activity as his fellow positives went about their business, attending to the rebuilding of Seattle and, by extension, the entire world. The hubbub of numerous phone calls and conversations testified to the vitality of the Movement. A framed portrait of Jordan hung upon a wall. Muzak, performed by the Promise City Boys' Choir, played softly in the background. The preternaturally gifted singers hit notes that even castrati would have balked at.

Kyle felt strangely self-conscious. How many people had heard him erupt before? Was he just being paranoid, or could he really feel dozens of eyes targeting him as he strolled past the various cubicles outside his office? Susan Meldar watched him warily from behind her computer. Her hands were nowhere near the keyboard; she searched the Web just by waving her fingers at the screen. A group of chatting coworkers, socializing around the water cooler, fell strangely silent as he walked by them. He stumbled over a bump in the carpet. For all he knew, someone was reading his thoughts at this very moment.

It took all his effort just to act like he had nothing on his mind.

Jordan had the corner office at the end of the hall. As usual, two bodyguards were posted outside. Galloway could induce blinding headaches and seizures just by looking at someone. Quinn could smell gunpowder and other explosives from hundreds of feet away. Neither man moved out of the way as Kyle approached.

Kyle played it cool. "I need to see Jordan."

"He asked not to be disturbed," Galloway said without too much attitude. Kyle had first met the man in Evanston a year ago. He had been with Collier since the beginning.

"Even by me?" Smiling broadly, he pulled rank a little. "C'mon, dudes. I'm Mister Prophecy, remember? Jordan always has time for me."

The guards looked at each other, then stepped out of the way. They were used to Kyle coming and going pretty freely. "Okay," Quinn relented. "But make it snappy."

Kyle found Jordan at his desk, conversing via a headset. Rain pelted the picture windows behind him. A flat-screen television set, mounted to one wall, cast a phosphorescent glow. The TV was set on mute. Jordan used a remote to flick through various cable news channels as he spoke on the phone.

"Good, good. Glad to hear that our friend has been recovered. Just remember, we need to hang on to our asset now that he's out of the box again. Under no circumstances should our present allies be allowed to retain possession of the individual in question . . ."

Jordan noticed Kyle's entrance. A flicker of annoyance flashed across his bearded features. "Excuse me," he said to whomever he was talking to. He looked up at his visitor. "Now is not a good time, Kyle."

He glanced again at the TV screen. Kyle saw that the closed-captioned broadcast was reporting on a citywide blackout in Philadelphia. He gave Jordan a time-out signal. "Anything I should know about?"

"Not at all," Jordan replied. "I'm merely negotiating the release of a political prisoner on the East Coast. But I really don't have time to chat now."

Kyle didn't care. "Just a quick question," he said apologetically. "What do you know about something called the Global Outreach Committee?"

"Is that all?" The name did not seem to put Jordan on guard. "It's a minor publicity initiative. To promote promicin-positive coverage overseas." He gave Kyle a puzzled look. "Why so interested?"

"No real reason," he lied. "Just saw the name on some paperwork. Wondered what it was all about."

Jordan sighed impatiently. "I'm sure somebody on the tenth floor can fill in all the details for you, but, honestly, you should not be wasting your time and energy on such minutiae. We have plenty of talented PR people disseminating our message to the masses. You need to focus on the big picture instead. That's your true purpose." His gaze darted back to the TV screen. "Now then, I really need to get back to this call."

Kyle wasn't done yet. "One more thing. I don't suppose you've heard from my dad this afternoon? Or Diana Skouris?"

"Believe it or not, Kyle," he said with a trace of irritation in his voice, "I don't spend every waking hour obsessing over what your father and his partner are up to. If you're having problems with Tom for some reason, I suggest you work that out with him, not me."

Kyle felt like he was getting the bum's rush. "You brushing me off, Jordan?"

"Not at all." Jordan sighed again, more wearily this time. "But, alas, my gifts do not include stopping time in its tracks." He adopted a more conciliatory tone. "Perhaps we can discuss this later?"

"Yeah, sure," Kyle said sourly. He realized he wasn't going to be getting any more out of Jordan. He turned his back on his mentor and walked away. "Later."

Jordan let him leave. "Please shut the door behind you."

Fuming, Kyle marched back to his own office. He slammed the door shut, not caring anymore who might hear. His dad was missing, maybe even in trouble, and he was the only person who seemed to give a damn.

Cassie was waiting on the couch. "Calm down, Kyle. Just let it go."

"Easy for you to say," he snapped. "You don't have a father. You never did."

"Ouch," she said, looking hurt. "That was unkind."

He instantly regretted his words. "I'm sorry. I shouldn't take this out on you. This is just tearing me up inside." Guilt added to his anxiety. "I *gave* Dad that address, Cassie. What if that was a big mistake, like you said? Suppose he's in danger because of me?"

She got up and took his arm. "You shouldn't be so hard on yourself. You've done everything you can."

"Not yet I haven't." A sudden decision gripped him. Pulling free of Cassie's grip, he snatched his winter coat from a rack by the door. He pulled it on in a hurry, then rummaged through his desk until he found the address of the plasma center. "I'm going down there myself."

Cassie reacted with alarm. "That's not a good idea!"

"Oh yeah?" he challenged her. "Why not?"

She got between him and the door. "It's not safe."

That wasn't good enough. "How come?"

"You don't need to know that," she said stubbornly. "Just believe me, you shouldn't go there. It's too dangerous."

"Then maybe you ought to help me out a little more!" The bitterness in his voice surprised him and he took a second to calm down. He didn't want to argue, especially when he really needed her on his side right now. He took her gently by the shoulders and looked into her eyes. "Please, Cassie!" he begged hoarsely. "Don't you understand? I'm all on my own here. Until I find out what's going on, I can't trust anyone at NTAC or in the Movement. You're all I've got left. I'm counting on you, please!" His eyes desperately searched her face. "Do you love me or not?"

"That's not fair, Kyle," she protested. "This isn't about us. It's about what's best for you—and for the future." She cradled his face between her hands. "You're too important to the Movement. I can't let you put yourself in jeopardy for your father's sake."

"Tough. 'Cause I'm going anyway." He swung her out of the way, then stepped past her toward the door. "Which means you can either stay here and sulk, or you can help me stay alive."

She glared at his back. "You wouldn't!"

"Try me."

Quaking with frustration, her fists clenched at her sides, she watched impotently as he took hold of the doorknob. He opened the door and left her behind.

"All right," she said petulantly. "You win!" She hurried after him. "But you owe me one!"

NINETEEN

THE PLASMA CENTER was in a bad part of town. Kyle glanced around nervously as Cassie grudgingly led him down a dingy alley behind the derelict building. A cold rain drizzled down his neck. Dark clouds obscured the fading sunlight. Greasy puddles spilled over onto the pavement.

"For the record, I'm doing this under protest," Cassie reminded him. A vintage fur coat and mittens protected her from the cold, or at least presented the illusion of doing so. Her entire wardrobe was just as fictitious as the rest of her. Kyle sometimes wondered what part of his unconscious mind picked out her clothes and accessories whenever she appeared to him; they always seemed to suit the occasion.

At the moment, though, he had more pressing questions on his mind. "My dad is here? And Diana?"

"Yes, but we're going to have to be sneaky about this." She slunk up a short flight of steps to a loading dock at the back of the building. She kept her voice low, even though nobody else could hear her. "There are four dangerous people inside, and they're not going to be happy to see you."

Kyle joined her at the back door. He wished he had thought to bring a weapon of some sort, although he had no idea where he would have found one. Jordan frowned on guns in Promise City; he preferred positives to rely on their abilities instead. *Fat lot of good that does me now.*

"The lock is broken," Cassie revealed. "Your dad's handiwork, as it happens. But you can't just barge in. You need to wait until the right moment, when the people inside are distracted and looking the other way."

Kyle shivered upon the loading dock. He hugged himself to stay warm. "And how am I going to know when that is?"

"That's what I'm here for, silly." Cassie lowered her voice to a conspiratorial whisper. "Now listen carefully. Here's what you need to do. . . ."

"We have promicin!" Grayson declared triumphantly. He waved a metallic wand under Carl's arms, like an airport security employee scanning a potential passenger with a metal detector. A thin electronic cable connected the wand to a handheld air quality monitor. Grayson stared at the monitor's illuminated display. "Carl is definitely exuding promicin from his pores. I'm detecting roughly three hundred sixty parts per million."

Abby clapped her hands. "We did it! Finally!"

"I knew it would work!" Carl sat atop the vinyl couch, his legs dangling over the side. A terrycloth bathrobe hung open, exposing his bare chest. The IV and electrodes had been detached from his body. He rubbed his arm where Rosita had injected him with promicin earlier. His uncanny resemblance to Danny continued to unnerve Tom. Now that, mercifully, the real Danny's body had been wheeled back into the freezer, it was easy to forget that the young patient was an imposter and not really his nephew. Danny seemed to have risen from the dead, just like Jordan Collier.

This is a nightmare, Tom thought. *And it's just getting worse.*

Carl looked at Tom, who was still strapped to a couch beside Diana. He frowned impatiently. "How come he's not reacting yet?"

"The effect is seldom instantaneous," Abby observed. "I didn't develop my own ability until days after I was infected. Plus, it's possible he still has too much ubiquinone in his system."

Tom prayed that was the case. *Am I infected already,* he fretted, *or are the U-Pills protecting me?* According to Kyle, he was doomed to become positive. Was today the day that prophecy finally came true?

"Easy enough to find out," Grayson commented. He put down the sensor wand. "A simple blood test will measure his ubiquinone levels and tell us if he's positive or not." He nodded at Rosita. "Would you do the honors?"

"Of course, Bernard." The Filipino woman rolled a metal cart over to Tom's couch. She extracted an empty hypodermic needle from a drawer beneath the cart, along with gauze and other supplies, and laid them down on a sterile silver tray. She rolled up Tom's sleeve and tied a rubber tourniquet around his upper arm. A pudgy finger palpated the vein at the crook of his arm until it plumped up. She swabbed it with antiseptic. "You have good veins."

"Thanks," Tom said wryly. He strained once more against the restraints binding his wrists and ankles, but with no luck. "I hope you know what you're doing."

"Don't worry," Abby assured him. "Rosita used to work as a phlebotomist here, before it went out of business. That's how we found out about this place." She strolled over to observe the procedure. "You're in good hands."

That's debatable, Tom thought. Before he could say as much, however, he was startled to see Kyle creep into the room from the rear, the same way he and Diana had. Confusion and hope both bounced around inside his brain. *What's he doing here?*

Raising a finger to his lips, Kyle edged along the back of the donation floor toward one of the unoccupied couches. Tom grasped that his son was going for the guns Carl had carelessly deposited there earlier. Unfortunately, the weapons were all the way across the floor. Could Kyle make it there without being spotted by Abby and the others?

Tom's face froze as he struggled not to betray his son's arrival. With luck, his momentary flash of surprise would be taken as anxiety over his impending bloodletting. He resisted a temptation to look at Diana, who had surely spotted Kyle as well. At the moment, all eyes were upon Tom, so that his captors had their backs to Kyle. *I've got to keep it that way,* he realized. *Long enough for Kyle to get to those guns.*

Rosita's hypo was poised above his elbow. "You'll just feel a pinch."

The needle penetrated his skin. As promised, it only stung a little, but Tom screamed bloody murder anyway. "Ow! What the hell are you doing to me?" He grimaced in mock pain. "You call yourself a phlebotomist!"

"Don't be a baby," Rosita scolded him, sounding mildly offended. The Vacutainer tube filled up with blood. "That was a perfect stick."

"What a wimp!" Carl sneered.

Grayson headed over to collect the blood sample.

"This is monstrous!" Diana added to the uproar. No doubt she realized what he was up to. "You're like Nazis, performing obscene medical experiments on human subjects. You should be locked up for good!"

"Jesus, Diana," Abby exclaimed. "It's just a stupid blood test. Don't be such a drama queen."

Rosita withdrew the needle from Tom's arm. She pressed a cotton ball down on the puncture site. "There! You see, that wasn't so bad."

"Oh yeah?" Tom snarled. "Tell that to my damn arm!" Peering past her shoulder, he saw that Kyle was still a few paces away from the guns. His son looked horrified at what was being done to him. *Don't worry about me,* he thought. *Just get those guns!*

"What did you do?" Tom accused Rosita. "Spear right through the vein? Or did you hit the bone, too?"

"I've never done that in my life!" the woman said indignantly. She removed the Vacutainer from its plastic holder before handing it over to Grayson. "I'm a professional!"

"A professional sadist maybe!"

Keep looking at me, he entreated them silently. *Don't turn around!*

"What's next?" Diana ranted, doing her part. "Are you going to dissect us for parts?"

The guns were right where Cassie said they would be. Kyle held his breath as he crept along the back of the room, even as the bad guys tortured his dad. Despite Cassie's warning, it had come as a shock to see both his dad and Diana at the mercy of Grayson and his accomplices. His father's angry cries scraped at his nerves. *What are those slimeballs doing to him?*

"Don't get distracted," Cassie whispered. She tiptoed after him. "Stick to the plan!"

Easier said than done, he thought. It wasn't her father being experimented on only a few yards away. Still, at least he knew now that he had done the right thing coming here this evening. From the looks of things, he had arrived just in time. Maybe.

He inched across the room, wincing at every minor creak and tread. Thank God he hadn't stepped in any puddles on the way here; he could just imagine his sneakers squishing loudly with every step. *Too bad I'm not invisible like Cassie.* The room was uncomfortably warm compared to outside. Perspiration glued his shirt to his back. It felt like hours before he finally reached the unattended weapons.

He spotted his father's modified Glock. His sweaty palms grabbed on to the grip of the gun. Suddenly, he was very grateful for the firing lessons his dad had given him when he was growing up. He bit back a gasp of relief.

Made it!

"Good job," Cassie said. She pointed at the nurse bending over his dad. "That's Rosita. You need to shoot her first, before she can use her ability."

In the back? Kyle didn't want to shoot anyone, let alone an unsuspecting woman. He clumsily released the safety on the gun. *Is Cassie serious?*

She frowned at his hesitancy. "This is no time to be squeamish, Kyle. You wanted to be the hero. Now do what you have to."

Kyle's arm trembled as he raised the gun. He didn't think he could go through with this. He had never shot someone before—if you didn't count the time a disembodied intelligence from the future had taken over his body to assassinate Jordan. This time was different, though. He was in charge now. The blood would be on his hands . . .

"Do it!" Cassie ordered. "Pull the trigger!"

Kyle listened to his dad and Diana shouting. He wanted to save them, but . . .

"I can't!"

He didn't even realize that he'd spoken out loud until the bad guys spun around in surprise. Kyle recognized Grayson from his file, but it was the young man in the bathrobe who really shocked him. Kyle's jaw dropped. His heart missed a beat.

"Danny?"

His dead cousin was standing only a few yards away.

"It's not Danny!" Cassie yelled. "He's fake." She shouted in his ear. "Shoot the old lady!"

But he was already too late. The nurse scrunched up her face. Her solid-looking frame shimmered like a mirage before vanishing completely. She disappeared right before his eyes.

"Huh?" Kyle stammered in confusion, his gun aimed at empty air. Now what was he supposed to do?

Cassie took charge as usual. Grabbing on to his gun arm, she swung it to the right. "Over there! Now!"

He squeezed the trigger.

The deafening report of the gun pounded his eardrums. The recoil jolted his arm from Cassie's grip. At first it looked like he'd fired at nothing, but then Rosita shimmered back into existence, clutching her side. Blood seeped through her fingers. Moaning, she crumpled to the floor.

Oh my God, Kyle thought. Cassie had known right where the invisible woman was. *I just shot someone. For real.*

"Rosita!" Grayson started to rush to the injured woman's side, then remembered the smoking gun in Kyle's hand. He halted halfway to Rosita. "Please, you've got to let me help her!"

"Careful, Kyle!" his dad shouted from the couch. "He's armed, too. Don't let him do anything until you get his gun!"

"Fine!" Grayson said, before Kyle could even follow his

dad's advice. He drew a small handgun from beneath his lab coat and slid it across the floor toward Kyle. He looked anxiously at Rosita, who was whimpering in pain upon the floor. "Is that good enough for you?"

A crimson pool formed beneath the fallen nurse. Kyle swallowed hard. He swung the gun back toward the fake "Danny" and an attractive blond woman who looked only a few years older than he was. He struggled to keep an eye on all the players. "Go for it."

That was all the agitated mortician needed to hear. He grabbed a first-aid kit from a cart and rushed over to the writhing victim. "Somebody call 911!"

"No!" Diana shouted. Still tied to a couch beside her partner, she raised her voice to get Kyle's attention. "That clone has Danny's ability. You can't let anyone else in here. This whole place needs to be quarantined!"

"Don't listen to her, Kyle," the blonde said. She was a stranger to Kyle, but she clearly knew who he was. "You don't want to stop us. We're only trying to spread the blessing of promicin to the entire world, just like Jordan Collier wants."

Cassie regarded the blonde speculatively. "You know, Kyle, she's got a point there."

"She's crazy, Kyle," his dad warned. "She's killed four people already. And wants to kill billions more."

"A single generation of sacrifice to ensure paradise for all who follow," the blonde insisted. "That's what Jordan always says, isn't it?" Holding up her hands, she took a step toward Kyle. "I know you share our ideals, Kyle. We're on the same side."

"Back off!" Kyle ordered. "I don't know you, lady, but your argument would be a lot more convincing if you weren't holding my dad hostage!"

"We weren't going to hurt him," she insisted. "We were only—"

"Shut up!" Kyle wasn't going to listen to any more of this, not while his dad and Diana were still trussed up like lab animals. He waved his gun at the captives. "You two," he ordered the blonde and Danny's twin, "untie them now."

The blonde snickered at Kyle. "Is that your idea or Cassie's?" She glanced around the lab. "Is she here with us?"

"Cassie?" his dad echoed, puzzled. "Who is Cassie?"

His redheaded muse was amused by the exchange. "You know, you're really going to have to tell him about me one of these days."

Kyle's face flushed in anger and embarrassment. He aimed the gun right at the blonde. "How do you know about her?"

"Jordan told me." She chuckled mirthlessly. "We share a lot of things. I've been feeding him classified info ever since I joined the Movement."

"April!" Diana suddenly realized. "You're the mole. You're the one who told him about my sister."

The blonde smirked at Diana. "Just figured that out, did you? Kind of slow on the uptake, Diana." She shook her head. "Got to wonder what Marco ever saw in you."

"You'll have to ask him," Diana shot back. "When he visits you in prison."

"Dress it up any way you like, Abby," Tom accused the blonde. "You're still a traitor and a murderer."

Kyle put the pieces together. He looked to his dad for confirmation. "She works for NTAC?"

"I belong to the Movement," Abby declared. "Just like you do." Despite his orders, she made no move to unbind the prisoners. "Think about Jordan, Kyle. You think he'd approve of what you're doing now? Or would he want you to step aside and let us complete his work?"

"Jordan never forced anyone to take promicin!" He clung to that belief as tightly as he gripped the gun in his fist. "Never!"

"Which is why he needs people like us," Abby asserted. "To do the things that have to be done."

She sounded eerily like Cassie.

"Just untie them!" Kyle shouted. There were too many people telling him what to do. He felt like he was on the verge of a nervous breakdown. "I'm not going to debate this with—"

An anguished scream yanked his attention back to Rosita and Grayson. The mortician was crouched over the injured nurse as he applied pressure to her wound. Agony contorted the woman's face, which was pale and clammy. Trembling fingers clutched Grayson's gore-streaked lab coat. There was blood everywhere.

"Oh crap." Kyle's heart sank. "Is she going to live . . . ?"

His momentary distraction was just the opening Abby had been waiting for. "Kyle, watch out!" Cassie shouted as the blonde snatched up a metal tray from the cart by the couch and hurled it at Kyle. Alerted by Cassie's cry, he threw up his arm just in time to deflect the flying tray. It clattered to the floor along with scattering medical tools and bandages. A test tube of blood shattered into pieces. Red stains splattered the room.

Abby yelled at the Danny clone. "Run, Carl! Get out of here now!"

She lunged at Kyle, who instinctively raised the gun to defend himself. It went off before he even knew what was happening. A crimson flower blossomed above her heart. For a single endless moment, she stared back at him in shock before she toppled backward onto the floor.

She was dead before she even hit the tiles.

No! Kyle thought. *I didn't want to do that!*

The sight of her lifeless body transfixed him.

"Kyle!" his dad shouted urgently. "Carl! The clone! You've got to stop him!" The urgency in his voice cut through his shell-shocked daze. "He's just like Danny!"

Diana yelled at him, too. "He'll infect the whole city!"

What? Kyle looked up to see the imposter making a break for it. Diana's warning reminded him how much was at stake. Leaping over Abby's bleeding corpse, he took off after Carl, who got as far as the reception area before Kyle caught up with him. Wearing only a bathrobe, Danny's twin fumbled with the lock at the door. It clicked open.

"Hold it!" Kyle hollered. Both hands held on tightly to his gun as he swung it toward the fleeing clone. "That's far enough."

The false Danny froze at the doorway, his hand resting on the doorknob. Only a slim wooden door stood between him and thousands of vulnerable people. Kyle remembered all the funerals he'd attended after the Great Leap Forward. Including his cousin's and his aunt's.

Not again, he thought. *There has to be another way to bring Heaven to Earth.*

Wasn't there?

The clone looked back at him. "C'mon, Kyle. Get real. You're not going to shoot me." Danny's face smiled slyly. "We're flesh and blood."

"You're not my cousin!"

"I am now." He looked and sounded exactly like Danny. "You're the shaman and I'm the carrier. We're two parts of the same prophecy."

"Stop him, Kyle!" his dad shouted frantically from farther within the plasma center. The couch rattled against the floor as he tried furiously to escape from his bonds. "If he gets away from here, it will be fifty/fifty all over again!"

Cassie appeared behind Kyle. "He says that like it's a bad thing."

"But if I let it happen, it will be my fault this time." Kyle shook his head. He kept the gun aimed squarely at the imposter's head. He had already hurt too many people tonight. "I'm sorry, but I just can't live with that."

"Hypocrite!" A livid expression rendered Danny's face almost unrecognizable; Kyle didn't remember his cousin ever looking so furious. "You're happy to preach the gospel of Jordan Collier to anyone who will listen, convince people to take promicin even though you know it will kill half of them, but you're too weak to get your hands dirty when it matters most." He snorted derisively. "What exactly do you think you've been doing since Collier came back?"

He turned his back on Kyle and twisted the doorknob. A cold breeze entered the building. It was dark outside.

"Don't do it, man." The gun shook in Kyle's hand. "I don't want to hurt anyone else."

"Then you don't know what you're doing," the imposter said. "And who you really are."

He stepped over the threshold.

Kyle fired.

Danny died all over again.

Numb with horror, Kyle dragged the body back into the building and slammed the door shut. A tear trickled down his face as he slumped against the door, exhausted and drained of feeling. The gun slipped from his fingers. He barely heard his dad and Diana shouting to him from the donor area. He'd untie them in a moment, but right now all he could do was stare at the dead man on the floor.

What's happening to me? What have I become?

Cassie stepped over the body. She snuggled against him, resting her head upon his chest.

"It will be all right, Kyle. You'll get over this. *We'll* get over this."

He wasn't so sure. "I've killed two people, Cassie. Maybe three."

"There's a first time for everything." She smiled knowingly. "Think of this as a learning experience."

For the first time, he was truly scared of her.

And himself.

* * *

Kyle left before the paramedics and hazmat team arrived. Tom had seen that his son was deeply shaken by what he'd been forced to do, but Kyle had brushed off his dad's attempts to comfort him. He had staggered out of the center like a zombie, barely saying a word.

I'll have to talk to him later, Tom promised himself, *make sure he gets through this.* He knew from experience just how hard it was to live with killing someone, even in defense of others. Especially the first time.

Selfishly, he hoped that Kyle wouldn't turn to Jordan Collier instead.

Diana took charge of the cleanup operation. Per her instructions, only positives who had already survived exposure to promicin were allowed on the site. Grayson and Rosita were both dosed with the inhibitor before being shipped off to quarantine. Thankfully, it appeared that the injured phlebotomist was going to survive.

Unlike Abby and Carl.

Their bodies were destined for immediate cremation.

Along with Danny's, Tom guessed. *Shawn will understand, I'm sure.*

"This entire place is going to have to be sterilized," Diana stated. She sighed wearily as she contemplated the bloody aftermath of tonight's horrors. "But at least we recovered Danny's remains and shut down Abby's insane project. Thanks to Kyle, of course."

"Yeah," Tom agreed. "That's something, I suppose."

He just hoped their victory hadn't cost his son his soul.

"How are you doing?" Diana asked him. "You feeling any different?"

"Not really." His arm still stung where Rosita had poked him, but that was all. "No abilities that I've noticed yet."

"Well, we'll have to get you tested when we get back to HQ, but I'm guessing that those U-Pills staved off any infection." She offered him a comforting smile. "Prophecy or not, chances are you're still the same Tom Baldwin."

For now, Tom thought.

TWENTY

THERE WERE ONLY five Marked left.

Or four, depending on how you counted.

Wesley Burke had died three days ago. Killed in a "freak accident" while honeymooning in Niagara Falls with his latest trophy wife. A suspicious "gust of wind" had hurled him over a railing overlooking the Falls. His body had been smashed to pieces on the rocks below, his precious bodily fluids washed away in the churning froth. Curiously enough, no one nearby, not even his horrified bride, had felt more than a breeze.

That this tragedy had occurred only forty-eight hours after Richard Tyler's escape from custody implied an alternative explanation for Burke's demise.

The Marked were being hunted once more.

Sheik Nasir al-Ghamdi had not waited for Tyler to track him down. The dashing Arab was slumped facedown on the round oak table in the parlor of Wyngate Castle. A smoking pistol still rested in his hand. A bullet hole marred the checkered head cloth covering the back of his skull. A crimson stain spread across the fabric.

Clear plastic sheets, draped over the walls and furnishings, protected the parlor's elegant decor from ugly blood spatters. Frankly, George Sterling would have preferred to use another location for today's unpleasantness, but security concerns had trumped convenience. Wyngate was the most secure location available on such short notice. Or at least the only one the surviving Marked could all agree on. *Besides,* he reminded himself, *what does it matter if we make a mess? It's not like I'm going to be living here much longer . . .*

He pried the Glock from the sheik's lifeless fingers. He handed it to Song Yu, who, along with General Roff and Kenpo Norbo, was seated around the plastic-shrouded table. "Your turn."

She accepted the handgun without hesitation. "For the cause." She smiled grimly. "We will meet again, my friend."

He admired her courage and commitment. "Absolutely."

Calmly, her face displaying nary a flicker of trepidation, she placed the muzzle of the Glock between her lips and pulled the trigger. A single explosive report splattered her brains across the walls behind her. Her body lurched against the back of her chair before bouncing back toward the table. Her face hit the tabletop, exposing the gory wound at the back of her skull.

"Christ almighty!" Julian Roff reacted. The decorated military leader was proving to have little stomach for this kind of wet work. "I don't think I'll ever get used to that!"

Kenpo averted his eyes from Song's remains. He looked distinctly green around the gills. "Are you quite sure we can't simply take a cyanide pill instead?"

"This is faster and more painless," Sterling stated firmly, as though they hadn't already hashed this out ad nauseam. "And any foreign substances in the bloodstream might interfere with the transference process." He was disappointed by the two men's squeamishness; they clearly hadn't produced as many splatter films as he had. "Our comrades are to be commended for their steady nerves and resolve at this crucial juncture."

Unlike certain other Marked I could name, he thought acidly. *Had these two always been so weak or had the sentimental morality of this mawkish era gotten to them?* He wondered if they would be able to do what was necessary when their own turns came, or if he would have to pull the trigger himself. *I'd bet the gross receipts on my last two blockbusters that one of them wimps out at the last minute.*

First, though, he had another vital task to perform. Retrieving a gleaming metallic syringe from a tray on the table, he came up behind Song Yu's slumped body. Her glossy black hair was done up in a bun, providing easy access to the nape of her neck. As he bent over her, the empty syringe in hand, he glimpsed the Mark behind her left ear. As far as he was concerned, it was a badge of honor. He intended to do right by her—and ensure her imminent return.

He jabbed the needle into the base of her skull, right where it met the spinal cord. A clear plastic capsule was lodged behind the needle. He tapped a keypad along the side of the syringe and drew back the plunger, filling the syringe with a shimmering silver elixir. Molecular filters in the stylet excluded mere cerebrospinal fluid, which was clear and colorless, so that all that was harvested was a concentrated solution of nanites. The microscopic machines were individually encoded with Song Yu's personality and memories, just waiting to be implanted in the brain of a new identity.

He already had the perfect host picked out for her: an obscure blond actress who had played a bit part in *Don Incubus, Demon P.I.* Alas, that particular picture, the final "masterpiece" in the dubious oeuvre of the late Curtis Peck, had gone straight to DVD, but Sterling had a much bigger role in store for the aspiring starlet. She had eagerly agreed to a private audition later this weekend, where he intended to make the casting final.

And the best part is, her acting can only improve once Song Yu takes over.

The capsule filled up quickly. Sterling withdrew the needle from the corpse and expertly extracted the vial from its metal casing. He placed it gently onto the tray, next to an identical capsule bearing nanites harvested from Nasir. They were intended for an unlucky African-American stuntman in prime physical condition. The handsome Arab playboy had been reluctant to give up his current physique. Sterling hoped he would find the stuntman an adequate replacement.

Both hosts were total nobodies, completely off Collier's radar.

At least that was the plan . . .

Colored labels precluded any mix-ups down the road. Sterling loaded a new capsule into the syringe. "All right. Who's next?"

"Me," Kenpo volunteered, raising his hand like an eager schoolchild. His saffron robes rustled about him. "I feel like there's a target painted on this worthless body. I want out of it now!"

"Of course," Sterling said. "Just as we agreed." After opposing the notion earlier, he had reluctantly come around to the idea that new bodies were a necessity for all of them. With Tyler on the loose again, and their covers thoroughly blown, there was no choice but to change faces one more time. *A shame I'll have to miss the Oscars,* he lamented. *That* Fahrenheit 4400 *has a real shot at Best Documentary.*

But there were more important contests to be waged in the future.

"Let's be clear about one thing," he added emphatically. "This is merely a strategic maneuver, not a surrender. We're not doing this just to hide from enemies. The war continues, albeit in new guises." He addressed both the lama and the general sternly. "Can I count on you to continue the fight—and avenge our martyred comrades?"

"Yes, yes," Kenpo muttered. "For the cause and all that." Grimacing in distaste, he reached across the table and liberated the gun from Song Yu's cooling fingers. "Let's just get this over with."

"Go ahead," Sterling said. He intended to kill himself later, after he had successfully transferred the essences of the others to their new hosts. This left him exposed and vulnerable longer, but he didn't trust anyone else to carry out the final stage of the transfer. Not even Song Yu or Nasir. "We're none of us getting any younger."

Unlike Song Yu, the celebrated lama looked positively ill at the prospect of blowing his own brains out. Trembling hands lifted the Glock to his lips. He closed his eyes and braced himself for the fatal shot. Sweat glistened upon his hairless pate.

A minute passed.

And another.

"Well?" Sterling asked, disgusted by Kenpo's obvious cowardice. The man was a disgrace to the glorious city that had birthed him. Sterling wondered if it was even worth implanting his feeble spirit in a new identity. "Is there a problem?"

The distraught lama extracted the Glock from his mouth. "Allow me a moment, will you? This isn't easy."

Roff snorted in contempt. "What's the matter, monk? Don't you believe in reincarnation?" He reached for the gun. "Gimme that. I'll shoot you myself!"

"Don't you dare!" Kenpo yanked the weapon away from the general's grabby fingers. "I have the right to terminate my own host! And I won't be badgered into doing it before I'm good and ready!"

I knew this was going to happen, Sterling thought, annoyed at having his worst expectations realized. *Why couldn't Burke have survived instead?* Sighing, he was about to intervene when, unexpectedly, a sudden tremor rocked the parlor. The crystal chandelier swung wildly above the table. Dust rained down from the ceiling. A brace of Oscars and Emmys tumbled off the mantel over the fireplace, crashing down onto the floor. The bodies of Song Yu and Nasir slipped off their chairs to land with a thud beside the table legs. A priceless Ming vase toppled over, shattering into dozens of porcelain shards. Plastic tarps came loose from the walls. A Dolby-level grinding noise drowned out the startled yelps of the Marked. Roff grabbed on to the table for support, while Kenpo dived beneath it. Sterling lunged for the vials, rescuing them right before they bounced off the tray. He looked about in confusion as he fought to keep his balance.

I don't understand, he thought. *History didn't record any major earthquakes on this date. The Big One is still years away . . .*

Booming cracks of thunder penetrated the quaking walls of the parlor, adding to his bewilderment. An earthquake and a thunderstorm at the same time? The truth hit him with the force of a head-on collision.

This isn't a natural phenomenon, he realized. *This is enemy action!*

Wyngate Castle was under siege.

Gunshots and shouts from outside the parlor confirmed his assessment. "Damn it all!" Roff hollered over the tumult. "We're under attack!"

"Your military acumen never ceases to amaze me, General," Sterling sniped. Moving quickly, he placed the precious vials into the padded interior of a leather valise and snapped the valise shut. He stumbled across the room to the wall by the door. A hand-carved wooden panel slid aside to reveal an intercom and miniature television monitor. He stabbed the controls with his free hand. "Sterling here! What in blazes is happening out there?"

The screen lit up, displaying the disheveled features of Conrad Yerkes, his head of security. He was a grizzled ex-Marine with a glass eye. His blocky head and shoulders filled the screen, blocking Sterling's view of the high-tech command center behind him. The control room was located in the castle's belfry four stories above the parlor. Yerkes looked crazed, overwhelmed by the chaos.

"Things are going crazy, sir!" the man blurted. "We've got lightning, earthquakes, even a friggin' tornado tearing the place up. And intruders spotted on the perimeter. The men are doing the best they can, but it's like Mother Nature is fighting against us!"

More like the 4400, Sterling thought. *Collier's throwing everything he's got at us.*

A roaring wind could be heard over the intercom. "Oh my God!" Yerkes shouted, glancing back over his shoulder. Static and electronic snow wreaked havoc with the transmission, but Sterling glimpsed the shingled roof of the tower flying away behind Yerkes. A furious gale whipped the man's gray hair around like waves on a stormy sea. White knuckles grabbed on to the console in front of him for dear life. Stone and mortar came apart as the very walls were dismantled by what looked like a rampaging tornado. Another man was yanked away into the spinning vortex. "We're losing it!" Yerkes shrieked over the wind. "We don't stand a chance . . ."

Sterling was unconcerned with the guards' safety. From the vantage point of his own time, the teeming people of this era had already been dead for millennia. They were walking fossils. "Stand by your post!" he ordered harshly. "Hold off the intruders as long as you can!"

"But sir!" Yerkes began. "The tornado! It's tearing us apart!"

So? Sterling thought. *I just need you to buy me a little time.*

"You heard me, Yerkes!"

Before the agitated security chief could raise another objection, a fountain of sparks erupted from the console. Static garbled his scream as a powerful jolt of electricity seared his body. Unable to tear his hands away from the sparking equipment, he convulsed violently. Smoke rose from his scalp. His mouth opened wide. Bright blue flashes arced between his fillings.

The screen went black.

So much for Yerkes, Sterling thought coldly. Stepping away from the intercom, he glanced over at the fireplace. *Time to go.*

Kenpo Norbo poked his head out from beneath the table. His famously serene visage was now completely ashen. He brandished the Glock above his head. His hand was shaking so hard Sterling feared death by friendly fire. He breathed a sigh of relief as Roff grabbed on to the gun and wrested it from the lama's grip. "Give that thing to somebody who knows how to use it!"

Kenpo didn't try to get the gun back. He fidgeted with his prayer beads instead. "This is your fault," he yelled shrilly at Sterling. "We should have abandoned these bodies a week ago, right after Calabria was murdered! But you said we'd be safe!" He ripped the beads from his neck and flung them across the room. "I wish I'd never set foot in this wretched era! We should have stayed safe in the City!"

"Which won't even exist if you don't pull yourself together!" Sterling snapped. Holding on tightly to the valise containing his comrades' personalities, he briskly made his way across the debris-strewn floor toward the immense stone fireplace on the other side of the room. Fallen awards and bodies waited to trip him, but he somehow managed to keep his balance nonetheless. "This way!" he shouted to the others. "We need to make a judicious exit."

Roff gave him a befuddled look. "Where? Up the chimney?"

With his free hand, Sterling tore away the plastic sheets draped over the fireplace. A chiseled rosette adorned the edge of the mantel. Taking hold of the ornament, he twisted it clockwise.

A low rumbling emanated from the fireplace as concealed gears ground against one another. Dormant machinery awoke from slumber and the sooty brickwork at the rear of the hearth swung away to expose the mouth of a murky tunnel. A cold draft blew in from somewhere outside the castle.

"Well, I'll be damned," Roff exclaimed.

The secret passage was a legacy of Edmund Wyngate, the whimsical silent film star who had overseen the castle's rebuilding eighty years ago. Legend had it he had used the passageway to smuggle moonshine and mistresses in and out of his domicile back in the twenties. Sterling had always suspected that this architectural novelty would come in handy someday. The tunnel led to an underground garage, nestled at the foot of the Hollywood Hills, where a fully fueled Jaguar waited to carry them to safety . . . if only they moved swiftly enough.

Kenpo gasped in relief. He looked as though he had just found Nirvana. "I'm sorry, Sterling. I should have never doubted—"

The door to the upper balcony blew off its hinges. Richard Tyler, clad entirely in black commando gear, burst through the open doorway onto the landing. He glared down at them like an avenging angel, looking none the worse for his recent captivity. Clearly, Ryland had been too easy on him . . .

We should have taken care of him ourselves, Sterling thought spitefully. *Not outsourced the job to Haspelcorp.*

"You!" Roff blustered. He swung the gun up toward the balcony, only to have it wrenched from his hand by an invisible force. Finger bones snapped audibly. He swore profanely.

The heavy oak table flipped onto its side and slammed into the general like a battering ram, crushing him against the wall behind him. The chandelier tore itself from the ceiling and rocketed into Roff like a crystal meteor. Blood splattered the hanging plastic sheets.

Another seismic tremor shook the castle, throwing Richard off balance. He seized the railing to keep from falling off the balcony.

It's now or never, Sterling realized.

Clutching the valise, he dived through the gap at the

back of the hearth. He scrambled to his feet in the tunnel beyond and tugged on a lever behind the fireplace. The heavy brick door began to swing back into place.

"No!" Kenpo shouted as he realized the door was closing. He sprang for the vanishing exit, grabbing on to the side of the door with his bare hands. "Wait! You can't leave me here! He'll kill me!"

No great loss, Sterling thought. To his mind, the weak-willed monk was infinitely more expendable than either Song Yu or Nasir. He kicked at Kenpo's face and hands. "Let go of the door, you idiot!"

A iron poker rose behind the frantic lama. It leaped forward like a thing alive, skewering Kenpo through the back. The scarlet point of the poker burst from his chest. Blood gurgled in his throat. A bloody froth spewed from his lips. Limp fingers lost their grip on the door. A final kick knocked his body out of the way.

The door swung shut at last.

Thank God for that poker! Sterling thought. The hysterical monk had nearly gotten them both killed. He bolted the secret door securely in place, then sprinted down the dimly lit tunnel. He didn't know how long it would take Tyler's telekinesis to reopen the passage, but he sure as hell wasn't going to stick around to find out. It was time to bid farewell to show biz forever.

Abandoning Wyngate Castle to the enemy, he scurried down a long spiral staircase to the garage below. This far below the castle, he could barely hear the tempestuous battle raging above. He was the last Marked standing, but not for long. He held on tightly to the grip of the valise. One way or another, Nasir and Song Yu would live again.

This isn't finished, he vowed. Tyler and his 4400 allies may be riding high at the moment, but if Hollywood had taught him one thing, it was that the best stories didn't end so easily.

There's always a sequel . . .

TWENTY-ONE

"I'M DONE," RICHARD told Jordan.

Sunlight shone through the lake house's large picture windows. The temperature was turned up to seventy-five degrees, but Richard didn't even think of taking off his sweater. Days had passed since he'd been rescued from that hellish prison in Philadelphia, but he was only just starting to feel warm again.

"I'm sorry to hear that," Jordan said. He leaned back against the couch, while Richard stood facing him. Steaming cups of peppermint tea rested on the coffee table between them. Jordan's guards were posted outside the room. This conversation was strictly between the two men. "As I understand it, one of the Marked is still on the loose. The film producer, George Sterling."

This was true. By the time Richard had telekinetically pried open the doorway to the secret passage, Sterling had been long gone. His mysterious disappearance, following the "terrorist attack" on Wyngate Castle, had been all over the news for days now. No one, including the paparazzi, had laid eyes on him since.

"Someone else will have to find him for you," Richard stated. "I've done my part."

The massacre at the castle, on top of the bloodbath at the prison, had been the last straw. He didn't like what his life had become. He didn't like what *he* was becoming. *This isn't what Lily would have wanted,* he realized now. *She saw something better in me.*

"What about Isabelle?" Jordan reminded him. "Have you forgotten who killed your daughter?"

"No," he answered, "but killing more people isn't going to bring her back. Too many people have paid the price for my vengeance. Sanchez, Evee, Yul, Garrity, that girl at the prison . . ." He shook his head. "The cost is too high."

"What about the cost of leaving a Marked on the loose?" Collier persisted. He was not the sort of man who readily took no for an answer. "We need to eliminate them once and for all."

"Do we?" Richard challenged him. "That's another thing. That woman from NTAC, Meghan Doyle, she told me it was possible to cure the Marked instead of killing them." He had not been happy to learn that. "You forgot to mention that to me before."

Jordan scowled. "I had my reasons."

"I'm sure you did. But I doubt that they're good enough for me."

Jordan sighed. "I see there's no dissuading you. I suppose I shouldn't be too surprised. You always were a man of conscience." He rose from the sofa. "Before you go, however, I have a gift for you."

A gift? Richard felt a flicker of apprehension. Even at his most beneficent, Jordan usually had an ulterior motive. His blessings always had strings attached. "What kind of gift?"

"You'll see." Jordan strolled across the room and opened the door to an attached hall. "Please send Willard in."

Richard braced himself for a double-cross. He hadn't forgotten Ryland's claim that Collier had secretly arranged for that beating in Virginia. He had considered asking Jordan about Ryland's accusation up front, but what was the point? He had no way of knowing which man had told the truth. Both were far too ruthless to be trusted entirely.

He tested his telekinesis, summoning a teacup from the table. Ryland's inhibitor had worn off quickly, as the Marked had discovered to their chagrin. *At least I can defend myself if I have to.*

"Who is Willard?"

A scrawny, hippyish-looking man entered the living room. A graying ponytail hung down his back. A pair of granny glasses rested on his nose. He wore a loose macrame poncho over a long-sleeved T-shirt and jeans. His sandals padded against the hardwood floor.

"Meet Willard Trice," Jordan said. "Willard is a talented forensic sculptor, formerly employed by the Seattle Police Department to reconstruct the faces of murder victims. Back in the eighties, he helped identify many of the victims of the Green River Killer. He used to work in wax and clay, but, since the Great Leap Forward, he's found an even more rewarding medium."

Richard waited for Jordan to get to the point. "That's very interesting, but what's it got to do with me?"

"It's very simple," Jordan said. "Willard is going to give you a new face."

"What?" Richard wasn't sure he'd heard Jordan right. "A new face?"

"For a brand-new life, safe from the most-wanted lists." Jordan seemed amused by Richard's startled reaction. "I'm quite serious. Willard can sculpt flesh and bone as easily as he once molded clay. He can readily give you a whole new identity if you're interested."

"Better than plastic surgery," the sculptor boasted. "And much more painless."

"I confess," Jordan divulged, "that I had intended to use Willard's gift to help you carry out your vendetta incognito, but I suppose it can serve as a parting gift as well." He laid a hand on Richard's shoulder. "You've suffered much, Richard, sometimes because of me. Allow me to make amends before we go our separate ways."

Richard thought about it. He had to admit that he was hardly looking forward to spending the rest of his life on the run. And thanks to his exploits in Rome, he was now an international fugitive as well.

He regarded Willard's hands warily. "Does it hurt?"

"Not at all," the artist promised. "The process deadens the nerves while the tissue is being reshaped." He stepped forward and raised his hands toward Richard's face. "Think of it as psychic Botox."

Richard flinched as the man's warm fingers touched his

cheeks. He started to back away, then thought better of it. As long as he had this face, he would always be looking over his shoulder for Ryland and Sterling and people like them. Maybe Jordan was right, and this was his best chance for a fresh start. "Go ahead."

"Good man," Willard said approvingly. "This won't take long."

Calloused fingers, strong from wrestling with clay for decades, began by massaging Richard's face. At first he seemed to be simply exploring the planes and contours of Richard's lean countenance, but then, rather disturbingly, the bone and tissue started to shift and slide beneath his touch. A moist, syrupy sound put Richard's nerves on edge as Willard poked and prodded his face, which suddenly seemed to have the consistency of Play-Doh. It was all too easy to imagine the gooey flesh falling away onto the floor. Or what if Willard moved things around too much? *I could end up looking like the Elephant Man . . . or worse.*

"Would you like a mirror?" Jordan asked.

"No!" Richard blurted. The sounds and sensations were bad enough. He didn't need to see his face being turned into some sort of distorted work-in-progress. It was too late to back out now. He had to let the artist finish, or else spend the rest of his life looking like a melted wax sculpture.

Willard whistled while he worked. He clearly enjoyed his craft. It took Richard a second to place the tune.

"Funny Face."

The process seemed to go on forever. Just when Richard thought he couldn't take any more, however, Willard stepped back to admire his work. "Excellent," he declared immodestly. "My best yet!"

Richard's hand probed his face. It felt solid enough, thank heavens. The mouth, nose, and eyes all seemed to be in the right place, more or less, but everything felt subtly different. *Is that really my chin?*

Jordan proffered a hand mirror. "Take a look, Richard. You have nothing to fear."

Easy for you to say, Richard thought. He nervously accepted the mirror, then braced himself for what he might see. His mouth went dry. He took a deep breath and looked in the mirror.

A stranger's face looked back at him.

The reflection belonged to a decent-looking man, whose features were somewhat broader and flatter than Richard's. Care lines had been erased, giving him a slightly more youthful appearance. His ears were smaller and set more closely against the sides of his head. A square jaw bore a distinctive cleft. Even his eyes seemed slightly farther apart.

Not even Lily would have recognized him.

"I'll have new ID and travel papers prepared in a matter of days," Jordan stated. "You'll have to be careful about leaving fingerprints and DNA behind, but with a new face that's unlikely to be an issue."

Richard figured he could keep enough of a low profile to avoid any complications. "Thank you," he said to both Jordan and Willard. "I appreciate this."

Curiosity showed in Collier's eyes. "What will you do now, Richard?"

"Start over, I guess. Just to find a little peace and quiet somewhere."

Preferably somewhere warm. Hawaii maybe, or Jamaica.

"I wish you luck, Richard. I really do." Jordan smiled ruefully. "You may find, though, that such an idyllic retreat may not be possible."

Richard frowned. That was not what he wanted to hear. "What do you mean by that?"

"Just that these are volatile times. An epic conflict is brewing, one that will determine the very destiny of this planet." Jordan claimed to have witnessed that struggle firsthand, during a temporary sojourn through time. "The future chose you to play a part in this struggle, along with the rest of the 4400. Frankly, and forgive me for saying this, I doubt that you will be able to retire from the fray forever."

Richard prayed that, for once, Jordan Collier was wrong.

"Give me that BlackBerry," Diana told her daughter. "And, by the way, you're grounded for the rest of the month."

Maia looked up from the smartphone in dismay. She was sitting at the kitchen island at home, texting her friends while simultaneously killing off a microwaved bowl of macaroni and cheese. Buttery yellow walls gave the kitchen a cheery feel. Magnets pinned school bulletins to the refrigerator.

She clutched the phone. "How come?"

"I don't know," Diana answered sarcastically. She braced herself for the battle to come, which she had been putting off for several days now. "Maybe because you went straight to Jordan Collier with your last vision. And I'm guessing that wasn't the first time."

A flicker of guilt passed over Maia's face, followed almost immediately by a sullen pout. "Who told on me? Meghan? Marco?"

Diana didn't want Maia blaming anyone but her. "They're just worried about you, honey. Because they care." She sat down at the other end of the kitchen island. "This is dangerous stuff you're getting mixed up with. That message you sent Jordan? People got hurt, even killed, because of it."

"But I saved the world, didn't I?" Maia protested. "I stopped a war." She stabbed the macaroni with her fork. "The future picked me for a reason. Jordan understands that. Why won't you let me be part of everything that's happening?"

Because I don't want you to end up like Kyle Baldwin, Diana thought. She had seen how Collier's Movement had come between Tom and his son. And how totally devastated Kyle had been by what he had been forced to do at the plasma center the other night. He had looked like a lost soul when he'd staggered out into the rain after killing those people, rejecting Tom's love and support. She guessed that his part in the bloodshed, on top of everything else he'd done in Collier's service, was going to scar his soul for the rest of his life. His life was being ruined by his obsession with the Movement, not to mention his relationship with his father.

I'm not going to let that happen to Maia, she vowed. *Even if it means she thinks I'm the worst mother in the history of the world.*

"Because I'm your mother and I say so." She reached over and confiscated the BlackBerry. "One month. No exceptions."

"Whatever!" Brimming over with adolescent attitude, Maia hopped off her stool and stalked toward her room. She paused in the doorway to get in one last shot. "You can't stop me, you know. I'm going to do what I'm meant to do."

Diana stood her ground. She placed her hands against her hips. "Is that a vision, or a threat?"

"Wait and see," Maia said.

She slammed the bedroom door behind her.

Kyle lay awake staring at the ceiling. The display on his alarm clock read 4:20 A.M. He had been tossing and turning for hours now, unable to catch a moment's sleep. Sweaty blankets were tangled about his body. Fatigue weighed him down, and he felt more dead than alive, yet sleep remained tantalizingly, frustratingly elusive. He had never felt so tired.

"Another bad night, lover?"

Cassie materialized in the bed beside him. She rolled toward him under the covers. The warmth of her body did little to dispel his misery.

"I just can't get to sleep," he moaned. "No matter how hard I try."

This was rapidly becoming a nightly ordeal. He

hadn't had a decent night's sleep since that ghastly nightmare at the plasma center. Every time he closed his eyes, he saw himself gunning down Abby and "Danny." Their agonized expressions and glazed, lifeless eyes haunted him. Their violent deaths were seared into his synapses. Even when sheer exhaustion overcame him, and he finally managed to snag a few hours of uneasy slumber, he relived the entire hellish experience in his dreams, over and over again. The sharp pop of the gun echoed endlessly in his ears. The harsh smell of the gunpowder scorched his lungs. Hot blood washed over him like a ceaseless tide.

Sobbing, he threw his arm over his eyes in a futile attempt to block out the awful images. Guilt twisted his stomach into knots.

"You have to accept what happened." Cassie rested her head upon his pillow. "Don't push it away. Embrace it. Let it make you stronger, harder. More like the warrior you need to become."

Who says I want to be a warrior? He rolled over, so that their faces were only inches apart. "But I killed two people, Cassie. How am I supposed to live with that? Don't you understand? I ended their lives!"

That didn't seem to bother her. "Creation and destruction are two sides of the same coin. As a shaman, you should understand that. We're changing the world, Kyle, but we can't succeed until you truly face the difficult sacrifices required."

A single generation of sacrifice, in exchange for Paradise. That was what Abby had said, quoting Jordan, right before he killed her. It seemed like a fair bargain, and yet . . .

"I don't want to hurt anyone else."

She gently stroked his face. Wise green eyes offered him absolution. "That's not the way it works, my love. The sooner you accept that, the better you'll sleep."

Deep down inside, he knew she was right.

TWENTY-TWO

"So you still claim you knew nothing about what Grayson and Abigail were up to?"

Tom and Diana confronted Collier in his office downtown. It had taken over a week to arrange this appointment. Tom wondered if that was because Collier had needed time to dispose of any evidence linking him to the operation. A good cover-up required plenty of attention.

"Emphatically," Jordan stated. Along with Kyle, he was once more engaged in redesigning Seattle via his holographic blueprints. A new skyscraper was apparently destined to rise above the razed and sterilized earth formerly occupied by the Pacific Plasma Collection Center. "Mind you, I confess that the late Ms. Hunnicutt provided me with useful intelligence on NTAC's operations. I would have been a fool not to take advantage of such a well-placed source. But this horrid business with your nephew's body . . . I had no part in that."

"You see, Dad," Kyle said. Heavy circles under his eyes suggested that he hadn't been sleeping well. He had been ducking Tom's calls for days. "I told you Jordan was clean."

His son might have been inclined to give Collier the benefit of the doubt, but Tom was less convinced of the man's innocence. "And this so-called Global Outreach Committee? That was part of your Foundation, wasn't it?"

"Our organization has grown exponentially since the Great Leap Forward," Collier stated with irritating self-assurance. "Alas, I'm afraid that rapid growth has outstripped my ability to stay on top of every new program and initiative. Grayson and Abigail were misguided devotees who grossly exceeded their authority. Clearly, more effective oversight is required. You have my word that this will be a top priority."

Diana got in Jordan's face. Barely controlled anger colored her voice. "That's all you have to say, after what you did to my sister?"

NTAC had informed them that April Skouris was no longer employed by the federal government—and why. So far she had refused to answer Diana's calls and emails. They weren't even entirely sure where she was living these days.

Jordan was not surprised by Diana's outburst. No doubt he had been anticipating such a response. "I make no apologies for that regrettable incident. Your sister forced my hand." He turned his attention back to the holographic skyline. "And, just to be absolutely clear, I had nothing to do with that genocidal conspiracy you so effectively thwarted. I'd offer you both a medal if I thought you'd accept them. Forcing promicin is antithetical to everything I've always espoused."

The truth or yet more plausible deniability? Unfortunately, there was no way to know for certain. Both Grayson and Rosita had refused to implicate Collier. April Skouris might have been able to pry the truth from them, but, for better or for worse, Collier had taken that option off the table. *And what if we did manage to pin this on Collier?* Tom mused unhappily. *That would just give Dennis the excuse he needs to declare war on Seattle.*

It was a lose-lose situation.

"That's right," Diana said acidly. "You don't believe in playing God, except when it suits your purposes."

Tom admired his partner's restraint. *If Collier pulled his vampire act on Meghan or Kyle, I'd probably take a swing at him. Guards or no guards.*

"Believe me, Tom, Diana," Collier asserted. "I would never unleash an airborne version of promicin on the world—except, perhaps, in retaliation for a military attack on Promise City."

Was that a confession? Or a warning?

Tom couldn't shake a sense that Collier was playing a very dangerous game.

At least I'm still promicin-negative, he thought. A blood test had confirmed that the U-Pills had protected him from infection. *If that damn prophecy is right, Collier can't win until I take the shot.*

And that wasn't happening anytime soon.

Later, after dropping Tom off at headquarters to brief Meghan on their inconclusive meeting with Collier, Diana took care of another loose end. She shoved open the door to Kevin Burkhoff's laboratory at The 4400 Center. There was still the matter of those stolen blood samples to be dealt with.

"Kevin? Dr. Burkhoff?"

To her surprise, she found the lab stripped bare. All of his equipment and files were missing, aside from a solitary laptop sitting open atop an acid-scarred counter. There was no sign of either Burkhoff or Tess.

What in the world? She had called in advance to set up this appointment. Kevin should have been here. For a second, she feared that Collier had abducted Burkhoff again, just as he had several months ago, in hopes of stopping Kevin from perfecting his promicin-compatibility test. Shawn and Tess had rescued Kevin from Collier's clutches then, but perhaps the master of Promise City had tried again?

But why leave that laptop behind?

Diana gave the computer a closer look. A screen saver featuring aerial views of the Space Needle occupied the monitor. A Post-it note was stuck to the keyboard. "*Play Me,*" it read in Kevin's distinctly cramped handwriting. Stray sunflower seeds had infiltrated the keys.

Diana hit ENTER.

Streaming video replaced the Space Needle. Kevin Burkhoff appeared upon the screen. He looked tired and at the end of his rope. His voice issued from the speakers.

"Hello, Diana. I'm sorry I can't be here to meet you as planned, but Tess and I are going away for good. There's a war brewing and we don't want any part of it. What happened at the prison was the last straw. Tess has already suffered too much. I can't let anything else happen to her.

"On this computer are all my notes on the compatibility test to date. You and Shawn are the only people I trust with my findings. Please thank him for all his hospitality. I wish we didn't have to sneak away like this, but we couldn't take the chance of you or Shawn or NTAC or Collier trying to stop us from leaving. The rest of you will have to work things out without us. We're through. Goodbye and be well."

Tess stuck her head into the frame. "Don't try and find us."

The video clip ended.

How about that, Diana thought. Kevin and Tess had gone AWOL again. Granted, she couldn't blame them for wanting to opt out of the never-ending conflicts surrounding the 4400 and Collier's glorious crusade. Heck, Diana had once tried to do the same, running off to Spain with Maia and a shiny new fiancé, only to be sucked back to Seattle. The fiancé was history now. She wished Tess and Kevin luck. *Hope your escape lasts longer than mine.*

She couldn't help worrying about those missing blood samples, though. Was there another hidden lab out there, looking for yet another way to re-create Danny Farrell's terrible gift?

Only the future knew—and they weren't telling.

ACKNOWLEDGMENTS

Like every other 4400 fan, I was disappointed by the TV show's premature cancellation, so I was thrilled to get the opportunity to continue the saga in this novel. I want to thank my editor, Margaret Clark, for enlisting me once more—and for waiting graciously for this book while I wrapped up another project. I also want to thank Paula Block at CBS for approving the book, and my agents, Russell Galen and Ann Behar, for handling the contractual details. In addition, I need to acknowledge the input of Dave Mack, whose upcoming novel, *Promises Broken,* will pick up where my book left off. Dave and Margaret and I worked closely together to make sure our stories meshed and that we shared a common vision of the future of Promise City.

Meanwhile, I remain impressed and encouraged by all the devoted 4400 fans who have written me, from all around the world, to express their enthusiasm for the series and its characters. I can only hope this book lives up to their expectations!

I also feel obliged to point out that the *real* Eastern State Penitentiary, unlike the version in this book, remains open to tourists and is definitely worth visiting if you're in the Philadelphia area. For more info on this historic site, check out www.easternstate.org.

Fort Casey in Washington State is also a real place, and worth checking out. Bring a kite!

And "Wyngate Castle" is loosely based on the real-life Gillette Castle in East Haddam, Connecticut, which, thankfully, has yet to be attacked by superpowered terrorists.

Finally, I wouldn't have been able to write this book without the support and encouragement of my girlfriend, Karen Palinko, and our four-legged family: Alex, Churchill, Henry, Sophie, and Lyla. They don't need promicin to be extraordinary.

ABOUT THE AUTHOR

Greg Cox's previous 4400 novel, *The Vesuvius Prophecy,* was published a year ago. He has also written the official movie novelizations of *Daredevil, Ghost Rider, Death Defying Acts,* and all three *Underworld* movies, as well as books and stories based on such popular series as *Alias, Batman, Buffy the Vampire Slayer, Countdown, C.S.I.: Crime Scene Investigation, Fantastic Four, Farscape, 52, Infinite Crisis, Iron Man, Roswell, Spider-Man, Star Trek, Underworld, Xena, X-Men,* and *Zorro.* He lives in Oxford, Pennsylvania.

His official website is www.gregcox-author.com.

Made in the USA
San Bernardino, CA
25 June 2016